OF KINGDOMS AND CROWNS

USA TODAY BESTSELLING AUTHOR

CAMEO RENAE

OF KINGDOMS AND CROWNS

4

HEIR OF BLOOD AND FIRE

USA TODAY BESTSELLING AUTHOR

CAMEO RENAE

MORE BY CAMEO RENAE

TALBRINTH

To Incendia →

CRIMSON COVE

Isle of Aria

SANGERIAN SEA

CARPATHIA

Merchant Port

Nicolae's Island

To those who are broken and standing in the shadows.
There is hope.
You are worthy.
Rise and burn bright.

CHAPTER ONE

WHISPER WOODS

THE WORLD PAUSED.

The warmth of Trystan's kiss lingered on my lips, but it was his words. Those three beautiful and powerful words he had declared that resounded through my entire being.

My breath stalled as I gazed deep into those brilliant azure eyes. Eyes that not long ago were laden with so much affliction and pain, eyes that had looked at me with so much confusion, hate, and contempt.

I remember everything. Those words had altered my world. Our world.

Time stood still as I gazed deep into those eyes, now bright and clear, emitting a myriad of emotion. Hot tears swelled in my eyes and streamed down my cheeks.

Leora was right. What I had been frightened of before, to seal the blood bond with Trystan, a bond that would bind our souls together forever, was what it took to break free from the curse. A curse Roehl thought was unbreakable. A curse he vowed would end us.

But fate had known from the beginning that Trystan and I were destined for each other. Roehl had underestimated the bond we shared. A bond even we couldn't explain. A bond that had Trystan travel across the continent, from his castle in Carpathia, to seek me out in Sartha. And on that pivotal and momentous night he strode into my world — into my life—and those beautiful eyes found mine, my world transformed and has never been the same.

"Trystan," I breathed. My heart wanted to explode with excitement.

His warm lips pressed against mine. So soft, so gentle was that kiss that it stole my breath away.

We had broken the curse, and *my* Trystan was back.

He smiled against my lips, then pulled away. Tilting his head to the side, a dimpled grin rose on his lips. "Come with me." Rising to his feet, he held out his hand, and I took it without hesitation.

Pulling me up, I noticed that the cave behind us had fallen eerily silent. Peering behind him, every eye was fixed on our location, carefully watching us.

With tears streaming down my face, I smiled brightly at them, letting them know that everything was okay. It would be, now that we had broken the curse and Trystan was at my side.

Sabine smiled and bowed her head, her eyes also brimming with tears.

Trystan never turned back to look at the others but held tightly to my hand and led me directly out of the cave. With him, I had no fear of what lay outside because I had seen what he could do. I had seen that raw and terrible power that exuded from him, and I knew that while I was with him, I was safe.

The sky was still dark when he led me into the forest, far enough from the cave that we had privacy. He suddenly stopped and faced me.

Taking a step closer, his body was inches away, and those sinful lips were so deadly close.

"Calla," Trystan spoke softly, a tinge of pain present in his voice and embedded in his eyes. "I am truly sorry for what you've endured. Especially for the pain I've caused you."

"Trystan." I shook my head, placing a finger to his lips. "I am indebted to you for all you've done. For what you risked saving my father." I looked deep into those eyes, swirling with so much emotion. "Roehl killed my father, but if he killed you too, I—I—" The thought of it caused pain to radiate in my chest.

Trystan grabbed my waist and pulled me against him. His strong arms enclosing around me, and his scent—that wonderful scent—filled me as I breathed in.

"My love," Trystan spoke, his voice soft and sweet. "I am yours now. Body and soul." Those eyes, glimmering like a million diamonds, smiled. And then . . . he dropped to a knee.

"Trystan," I breathed, shaking my head, reaching down to pull him up. I didn't feel worthy. Especially after all he'd endured. After all he'd done for me. I should be the one kneeling in front of him.

Trystan smiled and then bowed his head, placing a fist over his chest. "Calla Caldwell, my mate. My flame. From this day forward, I vow to love you without bounds or limits, and will protect you at all costs." His head raised and those beautiful eyes pierced straight through my soul.

"What about your engagement to Princess Ivy?"

A snide grin pulled on his lips, his hands capturing both of mine. "The moment I claimed you, the engagement was broken. And when you bit me, you sealed our bond. You are mine now, Calla. And I am yours, until death. There is no turning back now."

"I would never think about it," I exhaled. Tears spilled down my face, my heart nearly bursting.

Trystan stood, grabbing my waist, pulling me back against his solid frame. "When I was cursed and woke up on that bed in Nicolae's home . . . the moment I laid my eyes on you, on your beautiful face and those shimmering golden eyes, I knew there was something special about you. Every time you cried, especially by my doing, it broke me inside.

"But the curse was strong and unrelenting, and every single time I felt any concern for you, it made me pay a dear price."

I shook my head, pain radiating through my chest. "You suffered because of me."

"No, my love." Trystan's thumb gently swept across my cheek, wiping my tears. "I suffered because I knew that despite what the curse told me, you were different. You weren't the person the curse fed me lies about, trying to convince me you were my enemy and would destroy me. After spending those few moments with you near the shore at Nicolae's, I knew the voices in my head were wrong. I saw your heart. I felt it, like there was a connection between us. I just couldn't place it. My innermost being sensed you were someone I cared about, just as my men had said."

Trembling from his words, I fell to my knees and buried my face in my hands, my heart fracturing. "I'm so sorry, Trystan. I'm sorry for what you endured. The pain and suffering caused because of me."

Trystan kneeled in front of me and wrapped me in his arms. "It wasn't your fault."

I shook my head. "You went to Aquaris to save *my* father and were captured and tortured because of it." Tears were streaming down my face. "The sounds of the whip against your flesh, and the pain in your eyes, will forever be embedded in my mind.

"Time and time again, you've risked your life to save me. And even if given a lifetime, I would never be able to repay that debt."

Trystan sighed, his hand gently stroking my hair. "There is no debt to be repaid, my love. Not between us."

More tears fell from my already swollen eyes. "In Aquaria, when you came to me, I wanted to run away with you, but I feared the repercussions. Your father dislikes me. And now, so do the royals of Northfall."

Trystan let out a breathy chuckle. "Now that I am in my right mind, there is no way in hell I would have agreed to be engaged to Princess Ivy. In fact, she would be the one to destroy me and my kingdom."

My mind was a whirlwind. We already had so much to deal with. "Northfall will not take lightly to you breaking off the engagement."

Trystan gave me a warm smile. "We have much more pressing matters to deal with at the moment. Ivy and Northfall are the least of my concerns."

I nodded in agreement, knowing what was coming and what had to be done.

"Trystan, I cannot run much longer. I have to go to Morbeth, no matter what the consequences. I cannot sit back when so many lives—the lives of those who served my great-grandfather—are depending on me."

Trystan placed his hands on either side of my face. "Calla, your burdens are no longer yours to bear alone. I am here now and will stand beside you, from this moment until the next realm welcomes me."

I let out another deep sob. Trystan had been there for me from the start, assuring my safety and the safety of my family. He was gone for a moment, lost to the curse, and for that brief time, I had never felt more lost and alone. This man, even under the Lethe curse, had brought me so much strength and hope. Even cursed, his loyalty was unwavering.

"We have seventeen days to respond to Roehl," I sighed, knowing the dark days that lay ahead. "We all know whoever crosses the Red Wall of Morbeth will be walking straight into Roehl's trap. I won't—I can't ask anyone to come with me. But I can't stand by and let him execute those who served under King Romulus. They were his people . . . and they are my people, too."

Trystan leaned forward and pressed a kiss against my forehead. "Yes, they are. And your heart—that beautiful, fiery heart—proves you will be a great queen one day. We will find a way to save them." He pulled me into his arms, and then . . . his lips met mine. The intensity of that kiss made my world tilt. I felt it in every cell, every fiber of my being. The overwhelming need to be near him. To touch him. Kiss him. To consummate our bond. It was growing more powerful the longer we were together. I know he felt it, too.

Trystan was now mine, and I was his. Our lives were forever intertwined. I was no longer alone. I had my mate by my side. A mate that was powerful and had proved that he would do anything—give anything—for me. And I would do the same for him.

Now that he was back, I would make sure he knew how much I appreciated and truly loved him. Even now, more than ever.

We stood in the middle of Whisper Woods, and for the first time in a long time, an overwhelming serenity swept over me. Something only Trystan could offer me at a time like this.

My head dropped back as his lips caressed my neck. His tongue and teeth dragged across my delicate skin, causing a moan of pleasure to escape my lips.

Trystan let out a soft growl, then pulled away, resting his forehead against mine. "You have no idea how much I want to claim you and seal the mating bond right now. But I won't take you here. Not in a place like this." He paused, his eyes darkened, his arms tightening around me. "But know this, my flame. You will be fully satisfied on the day I unravel you. And before the end, I will savor the sound of my name on your lips."

I could scarcely breathe. His words nearly caused me to combust.

I'd gotten a glimpse of this side of Trystan at my birthday party. In Brynna's spare bedroom, when I'd first asked him who he was. He'd replied, *"A dark knight come to protect you. A knight who can pleasure you beyond anything you've ever imagined."* That was before I knew who he was and what his intentions were.

He'd given me a taste of his pleasure in Aquaria. Now, the need to have him, to feel his bare skin against mine, claiming me fully and sealing our mating bond was growing, becoming more and more intense.

I slid my arms around his shoulders as he kissed me, his tongue delving into my mouth, caressing mine. His kiss became dominant, filled with want and need. Filled with passion and desire. But then he pulled away, leaving my mind spinning and my body weak and trembling.

"We need to get back to the others," he breathed, resting his forehead against mine.

"Why?" My voice was just above a whisper.

"Because our blood bond is new and powerful, and I don't know if I will be able to stop myself if I remain too close to you."

I could feel the intense pull, but I also knew this wasn't the time or place to consummate that bond. Not while there were lives dangling on a tenuous thread. Lives that were depending on mine and Nicolae's next move.

Trystan leaned forward and kissed me again. "I only wanted to have you alone, just for a moment. But we must return. I need to speak with my men."

"Will you have to leave and return to Carpathia?"

"I am not certain. But if I must, it will not be for long."

"What will happen when your father finds out about us?"

Trystan shrugged and trailed his fingers down my cheek. "My father will not take lightly to what happened, but he has no choice. *You* are the one I have chosen. *You* are my mate and have willingly sealed the blood bond with me. No one can deny that. Not my father. Not Roehl. They have no idea how fiercely I will fight to protect and defend what is mine. You are my priority now, Calla. You are my life and my future."

He'd stolen my breath again. Because of the Lethe curse, I never thought I'd be hearing those words from Trystan so soon. I could feel the power behind them, piercing my soul, wrapping around and mending my fractured heart.

Trystan's lips caressed mine, the heated kiss expelling all the air from my lungs.

When he pulled away, I heard a branch snap nearby.

An arrow whizzed past our heads and lodged into the tree directly behind me—inches from my right ear.

Trystan blinked, his eyes turned black as night, incisors elongated. A growl ripped from his chest as he pulled the arrow from the tree.

"Stay here," he urged, turning away from me.

CHAPTER TWO

AT LEAST TEN HOODED men stepped from the shadows, circling us with arrows nocked at our heads and chests. Behind the men were deep growls of something I'd never heard before. A sound that raised the hairs across my body.

As my vampire eyes focused, I saw them. Dozens of red eyes glowing behind the men with arrows. Wicked immortal beasts that were solely meant to live within the pages of my books. Creatures that looked as if they'd crawled from the underworld itself.

"Move, and we will kill you both," one of the men spoke, his voice deep and rash.

"You can threaten me," Trystan roared, "but NEVER threaten my mate."

I could feel his rage vibrating through the air. Felt the raw power radiating from him. I felt it in my own palms, tingling in my veins, and in my core. Now that we were blood bonded, it was intensified. And seductive.

An arrow released, and before I could blink, Trystan caught it with his bare hand. In one fluid movement, he created an air bow, nocked, and shot the arrow right back at the man who had sent it. With a loud thump, the arrow plunged deep into the middle of the man's forehead. His eyes rolled back, and his lifeless body dropped to the ground.

"Stay here. Protect yourself," Trystan spoke through our bond, his eyes on the enemy.

I called to my power, and my palms heated.

The men fired their arrows, but Trystan moved like the wind, dodging them all. Thrusting my palms upward, a dome of fire surrounded me. The arrows that touched my shield immediately turned to ash.

Trystan charged forward, his movements blinding. One of his fists punched through a man's rib cage, ripping his heart out, while his other hand gripped another's neck, snapping it in two.

We were outnumbered. He couldn't do this alone. Especially with the beasts out there.

I had to fight. I had to protect him.

Dropping to my knees, I dug my fingers into the frozen ground, the heat from my palms thawing it. Knowing we were enveloped by trees, I called to the earth. And it answered.

Energy pulsed through my fiery palms and vibrated through my fingers. It rushed out from my fingertips through soil and rock, through the roots and trees surrounding us.

I was linked to the earth. And it to me. Ready to answer my bidding.

"Save him," I spoke.

Roots exploded from the ground, shooting skyward like harpoons. Two men were instantly impaled, while roots and branches from adjacent trees wrapped around three others. Excruciating cries reverberated as those roots coiled tightly around them, crushing their bones.

I could feel it all, as if my own hands were killing these men, and it made me falter.

They were here to murder us, I had to remind myself. If I didn't continue, we would die.

I held the power, and when the screams stopped, I stood, my entire body engulfed in flame.

Trystan.

He was ahead of me, his air gift acting as a shield and weapon. He was so fast I could barely see him move as he slaughtered man after man, ripping hearts from their chests, and beheading them with his blade.

But with his attention on the surrounding men, he failed to notice the others deeper in the woods, hidden in the shadows. I watched as the men released the tethers to their beasts. Huge fiery-eyed hounds with sharp teeth and leathery skin bounded toward Trystan.

My body was on autopilot, my feet racing toward him.

Rage. It was the only word to describe the emotion inside me. A burning rage, fueled by the men trying to kill us. Kill him. My blood bonded. My mate.

I thrust both palms outward toward the two hounds charging straight at him. A huge ball of crimson flame, five feet in diameter, shot forward and slammed into the creatures. They let out a cry I'd never heard in my life. A blood-curdling wail that seemed to linger as their flesh melted and bones disintegrated into ash.

Gods.

Pushing my right palm forward, I aimed it at another beast bounding toward Trystan. A wall of fire surged forward, slamming into the creature and the one right behind it. The beasts wailed and howled as the flesh melted from their bones.

Trystan's head jerked back at me. His eyes, black as night, shot me a look. A look that sent a wave of heat through my entire body.

Trystan turned toward the last beast as it bounded forward, its razor-sharp teeth snapping. In a blur, Trystan held his dagger toward the creature with his left hand, and with his right, punched the hilt with a blast of air. The dagger sailed forward, lodging into the beast's mouth. As it pounced,

Trystan dodged it. And as it sailed mid-air, Trystan wrapped his powerful arms around the creature's neck. With a sharp tug, bones cracked, and the massive beast went limp in his arms. Trystan effortlessly tossed it to the side, as if it weighed nothing.

Goddess above. He was incredible.

The forest was quiet. When Trystan's eyes met mine, his expression softened, and with a blink, his eyes returned to their gorgeous azure color. Running toward me, he wrapped me in his arms. "Are you hurt?" His eyes scoured my face.

"No, I'm fine. What about you?"

"I'm fine." His head tilted back, and his gaze went up into the sky. "Nyx," Trystan spoke aloud with authority. A few seconds later, the bird cawed somewhere above us in the still dim sky. Trystan closed his eyes, using Nyx's eyes to scan the surrounding area. I held his hand and kept my eyes peeled on the shadowed woods surrounding us.

"The area is clear," he finally spoke. "My men are coming."

I suddenly relaxed, my body trembling. The power I'd exuded left me weak.

Trystan immediately noticed, his eyes filled with concern. "Calla?"

"I'm just tired."

Without saying a word, Trystan wrapped an arm around my waist, then slid the other under my knees, cradling me in his strong arms.

The power inside me was much stronger than ever before. It was an extension of my mind—my will—but when it took over, I was no longer in control. My power was on autopilot with one purpose alone. To save and protect. And that's exactly what it did.

I'd gotten another taste of what my gifts could do, but I knew I was still skimming the surface. Through the roots, I could feel the men dying. I could feel their bones crushing. Feel them writhing in pain as their life was squeezed from them.

The wails of the beasts still echoed in my mind as the flesh melted from their bones and my flame incinerated them. My power was growing, but there was still so much to learn.

The problem was . . . we were running out of time.

"Good gods. What the hell happened here?" Kylan's voice spoke from behind us. "We heard screams and came running." He was dressed in his fighting leathers, his sword unsheathed. Brone, Andrés, and Feng also appeared in their leathers, weapons drawn, eyes scanning the tree line for any sign of our enemies.

"Where's Markus?" I questioned.

"He stayed back with the others," Kylan responded.

"Good." I was glad he was there to protect them in case anything happened.

Andrés stepped over a corpse coiled in roots. "Did you two do this?"

Trystan grinned. "Yes, we did."

"Shit. It's a massacre. There are at least twenty men and three hellhounds here," Brone exhaled, scratching his head.

"Five," I added.

Brone's dark eyes narrowed on me. "Five what?"

"There were five hellhounds. Two of them were disintegrated." I gave him a tired smile, then raised my hand and twiddled my fingers.

"Gods above. Remind me to never cross you,"Brone laughed, his eyes wide as he surveyed what was left of the hellhound corpses.

"I wish I could have witnessed this," Kylan said, coming up beside us.

"I'm sure you will, soon enough," I said sadly.

Trystan hugged me tighter to his body. "You're weak. You need to feed."

I closed my eyes and rested my head against his chest. "I'll be fine."

"Your powers are growing, and if you don't feed, you'll weaken quickly." Trystan sighed. "When was the last time you fed?"

"When I sealed the blood bond."

"That's not a proper feeding. We need to take you back."

"Dispose of the bodies," Trystan instructed his men.

"Gladly," Brone said, lugging a lifeless body by the arm, hurling it on top of another. Kylan, Andrés, and Feng did the same, and in no time, there was a pile. Kylan poured some liquid from a flask on top of them and was about to light a match when I interjected.

"Let me," I said. "There will be no smoke."

"Are you sure?" Trystan asked.

I smiled, raising a palm to the mound of bodies. A ball of crimson fire burst outward, instantly incinerating the men and beasts into a pile of ash.

Trystan's cadre stood with mouths agape.

"That was badass," Kylan muttered, and they all agreed.

Trystan proudly kissed my forehead. I wrapped my arms around his neck and closed my eyes as he carried me back to the cave.

Inside, the cave was warmer, and the aroma of meat and spices drifted in the air, causing my mouth to water. As we rounded the corner, everyone was sitting around a fire and all eyes were fixed on us.

Markus stood with a raised brow and wide eyes. "What happened? Is she injured?"

Nicolae also stood and headed toward us.

"I'm fine," I said. "Just a bit weak."

"We were attacked by a few dozen men with hellhounds. She used her powers, and the enemy was swiftly destroyed," Trystan said proudly.

"Dispatched?" Brone let out a barking laugh behind us. "These two single-handedly slaughtered twenty men and five hellhounds before we arrived."

Trystan glanced down at me with admiration in his smile. "I couldn't have done it without her. She was glorious."

I shook my head, having watched Trystan in action. "You were incredible. I've never seen anyone move like him—like the wind. He dodged every arrow shot at him."

Trystan's cadre smiled like they'd witnessed it before. "Our prince is a wonder," Kylan said. "Watching him fight is a rarity, because we usually do it for him."

"That's why I employ you," Trystan chortled. "So I don't have to get my hands bloody." Trystan's eyes moved to Nicolae. "You would have been proud of her. Watching her use her gifts, calling earth and fire, it was astounding. Her gifts are powerful, and they came so easily."

Nicolae looked at me with pride sparkling in his eyes. "Your gifts are maturing."

"They are," Trystan said. "But using them has made her weak. She needs to feed."

Nicolae turned and headed toward his satchel.

"How is our blood supply?" Trystan asked.

"Low," Nicolae replied, extracting a bottle from his bag. "This is the last of it."

Trystan turned to his men. "Someone needs to return to Carpathia to replenish our supply."

"I will take whoever is willing," Nicolae offered. "It will be the quickest and safest way."

Trystan faced his men. "Feng, will you go with him?"

Feng placed a fist to his chest and bowed his head. "Yes, prince."

Carrying me, Trystan set me down on the blanket we'd shared earlier as Nicolae brought over a half-full bottle of ruby wine.

"Finish it all," my grandfather said. "You have to be strong for what is to come."

Placing the bottle to my lips, I downed the entire contents in no time, letting the magic of the blood run its course. I was surprised the bloodlust wasn't as strong as it had been only months ago. I was adapting to this new body very quickly.

Closing my eyes, I relaxed into the buzz as the blood mended and strengthened my body.

My power had grown so much it drained me, and I didn't want to be put in that position again. If there had been more soldiers or beasts, I might not have been able to help Trystan. And that thought terrified me.

Nicolae took the empty bottle from my hand. "What I want to know is how those men found you? It hasn't even been a day since we arrived here. It can't be a coincidence."

"I don't know," Trystan said. "We know for certain that no one here is a spy."

"What if there is a magical tracer on one of us?" Melaina suggested. "My magic is strong, but I don't know how to seek out a tracer, especially a hidden one." She turned to Nicolae. "Could you find one?"

"I'm afraid not," he said, shaking his head.

Melaina let out a deep sigh. "There are powerful witches back in my hometown. I know they have specific locator spells that could locate a tracer."

"They would have to be willing to come to us," Nicolae said. "We cannot risk moving to a place where more lives could be put in danger."

"You think one of us carries a tracer?" Sabine questioned, worry scrunching her brow. "Do you have an idea of who it could be?"

Melaina peered over to me. She'd revealed to me she felt Brynna was carrying something dark inside of her since she was rescued from Morbeth. However, I would never speak that out loud. Brynna wouldn't understand, and I knew she would become defensive about it.

"It could be any one of us," I replied. "Any person who has been in contact with Roehl. Me, Trystan, you, or even Brynna."

Thalia stood up, crossing her arms over her chest. "If that's true, then no matter where we go, we aren't safe."

"No, we aren't," Nicolae breathed. "If there is a tracer on one of us, we are most certainly vulnerable."

Melaina strode over to Nicolae. "Could you transport me to Hale?"

"Yes, but we were supposed to get blood."

"The blood can wait," I said. "Our safety is our greatest concern. We can get the blood when you return."

Melaina faced me and Trystan. "I'll need some time to convince the coven. Give me a day, at most."

I sat up. A wave of anxiety hit me, wondering — "With both of you away, will the magical wards and glamour around the cave hold?"

"Yes," Nicolae replied. "And if you need me, Calla, just use our connection to call me. I can be back here in seconds."

His words gave me peace, but with this new possible threat, I felt like we weren't safe, even with the wards up.

Melaina packed her satchel, threw it over her shoulder, and strode over to Nicolae.

"We'll be back as soon as we can," Nicolae said before grabbing Melaina's hand and disappearing.

Leaning over, I rested my head on Trystan's shoulder. His arm wrapped around me, pulling me onto his lap.

Kylan turned away, a smile on his face. "I must say, I am relieved to see Trystan in his right mind."

"I agree," Feng said, taking a seat near the fire. "You two are a beautiful pair. An equal match."

"I also agree," Andrés added. "And I have to admit, I am a bit jealous."

Brone raised a hand to smack him but glanced at me with a sly grin before lightly placing it on his shoulder. "Princess Ivy has recently become available, brother."

Andrés burst out in a coughing fit. "Oh, hell no." His tongue shot out of his mouth as he made a retching noise. "That snaky bitch can slither back to Northfall and die for all I care."

"So, does this mean there will be a wedding in the near future?" Sabine added with a shimmering smile.

My heart plunged. *Wedding?*

A wedding was the furthest thing from my mind. We still had to deal with Roehl, and whatever lay behind the Red Wall of Morbeth. Everyone here knew that going into Morbeth was a suicide mission.

I glanced at Trystan and my insides warmed. If we did live through this, I was going to marry him. This beautiful, selfless prince who had embraced me before he even knew me. Who never gave up on me and kept fighting for me when I thought I was alone. He always showed up, always came to my rescue, protecting me and my loved ones, even when I turned him away. And even while he was under that vicious curse that made him despise me, a curse that fed him lies, telling him I was his enemy and would destroy him and his kingdom . . . even then, through the torturous pain it caused him . . . he fought through it, *for me*.

Trystan's arms tightened around me.

I knew from this moment on, I would hold tight to him and wouldn't let go. We were bound forever. Me and *my prince*.

I glanced over to Brynna who had an unreadable expression on her face. A look that made me wonder if she was happy for me and Trystan. Then suddenly, she snapped out of it. She looked at me with her signature sassy smile, crossing her arms over her chest. "You know there will be no debate. I am going to be your Maid of Honor."

I smiled back at her, then flashed back to those simpler days—only months ago in Sartha—and tears flooded my eyes. "You know I wouldn't have it any other way."

Brynna knew me better than anyone else. Even better than my own parents knew me. We grew up together and were practically joined at the hip since birth. From the time we started to notice boys, Brynna and I vowed that if either of us got married, the other would be their Maid of Honor. I would never go back on my word.

"At least you have Nicolae to give you away, since your parents—" Brynna caught herself, her expression saddening. "I'm sorry, Cal. I wasn't thinking."

I smiled and shook my head. "I know what you meant, and yes, I am thankful Nicolae is here. It's not the same, but it's close."

My parents. A pang of pain radiated through my chest at the thought of them. I visualized them together. Happy. I knew it was true because I had seen, had touched, and had spoken to my mother and Leora in the In-Between. Knew they were watching over me and that one day, when I did cross over from this realm to the next, they would be waiting to welcome me. And Nicolae.

Markus didn't say a word, but the smirk on his face also told me he approved in his own way, for which I was thankful. He knew my journey and had been there since I had arrived as a prisoner at Morbeth. Markus had seen what I had endured as Roehl's prisoner, and being the Head of the King's Guard, he had compassion for me. He saved me from that wretched place and was still here, protecting me.

I believed that even if my grandfather, King Romulus, had not given Markus the order, he still would have followed me. He was a strong and intimidating warrior, but I had been a witness to his softer side. A side he'd kept hidden. Kept protected.

I smiled at Markus, and he shook his head and smiled back. Actually, it was more of a smirk. I expected nothing more and nothing less, but I knew he would try to be happy, because he knew *I* was happy.

He also must have been relieved to know there were more warriors, especially the Prince of Carpathia who was now bound to me, along with his cadre, who had sworn to protect me. However, I wasn't the only one who needed protection. Brynna and Sabine were mortal, and both had become targets of Roehl. He knew how much they meant to me. He knew that if he captured them, I would do anything to get them back.

CHAPTER THREE

I STAYED IN THE cave, curled up in Trystan's arms, listening to Sabine and Brynna discuss the seasoning put in the stew they'd just eaten. I couldn't sleep, and one heavy burden resounded loudly through my mind and echoed through my chest. It twisted in my belly, making me feel nauseous.

Sixteen days.

We now had sixteen days until Roehl would kill the witches and guards who served his father in Morbeth. Sixteen days to figure out our next move.

I hoped, with every ounce of hope left inside of me, that Nicolae or Trystan would come up with a plan. If anyone could, I knew they would.

Markus's deep voice echoed through the cave. He'd been out hunting all night. "There are armed men in the wood bearing the sign of Morbeth."

His words hit me, confirming my fears. Confirming someone in our group had a tracer hidden within them.

Trystan's cadre jumped into action, snapping on armor, and fitting themselves with weapons.

I closed my eyes and focused on Nicolae. *"There are Morbeth soldiers in the woods. How much longer before you return?*

"Melaina is having a bit of trouble convincing her coven. She is meeting with another witch now. A relative of hers. With the wards we've put up, no one should be able to find you. At least not the exact location. Stay inside. Let me know if you need me."

"I will." I swallowed hard and turned back to Markus. "How many men are out there?"

"A few dozen."

"Roehl has likely used his dark mages to find us," Brone growled.

Kylan sheathed his sharp blade. "With Nicolae's magical stones placed around the cave, we should have been untraceable. They must have found a powerful locator spell."

"Nicolae said we should be fine. Melaina needs a little more time," I said.

"We can take them." Brone snarled. "Morbeth's men are no match for us."

Trystan's cadre, ready and waiting, stepped in front of him—in front of us—with fists over chests and heads bowed.

"Send us," Kylan said. "The sun hasn't risen yet. Send us so we can buy you all a little more time."

"No." I took a step forward, holding my hand up before Trystan could reply. "They're baiting us. Nicolae said they most likely don't have our exact location, so Roehl must be waiting for us to fight so they can pinpoint our exact location."

Trystan remained silent for a moment. "Calla is right. It's too risky right now. If I send you out, everyone in this cave could become an easy target. We'll have to sit tight until Nicolae returns with the witch."

Gods, I needed to learn how to transport. That would be a game changer. Nicolae said that I could do anything he could, so I would have to ask him to teach me when he returned.

We waited for what seemed like hours, and everyone in the cave was growing restless. Then suddenly, Nicolae and Melaina appeared with an elderly woman.

I saw a small resemblance of Melaina in her. The woman's skin was pale and freckled, and she had wild reddish hair that was pulled up into a messy bun. She wore a simple green smock and carried a small satchel over her shoulder.

"This is my aunt," Melaina said to the group. "She agreed to help us."

"Thank you." I walked up to the woman and held out my hand to greet her.

As soon as her hand connected with mine, her eyes snapped wide, and her legs faltered. Nicolae caught and steadied her, but her wide, green eyes fixed on mine.

"Who are you?" she whispered.

Beside me, Melaina giggled. "Excuse her," she spoke to me. "Just as I felt your power the first time we touched, she can too." Melaina stepped toward the woman. "Aunt Ophelia, this is Calla Caldwell. She is Incendian royalty, chosen by Helia the Fire Goddess. She is the future queen of Incendia and now blood bonded to the Prince of Carpathia."

Ophelia placed a hand to her heart. "Goddess above. In all my years, I have never felt power like yours. But I also sense a deep sadness. A sadness that comes with one bearing a heavy burden."

Melaina gave me a knowing smile. "Aunt Ophelia, can you tell if Calla has a tracer on her?"

Ophelia nodded and held out her frail, weathered hands to me. As I placed mine in hers, this time she was ready and steadied herself. Closing her eyes, she muttered a spell.

We all waited in complete silence.

I felt anxious, my insides twisting, wondering if I was the one who carried the tracer. If it was me, I couldn't stay with the group. I would have to leave to assure their safety.

After a few grueling moments, Ophelia opened her eyes. "She is clean. There is no tracer on her."

I let out a deep sigh of relief as Trystan came and slid his arm around me. He was tense, and I knew it was because he could also be a carrier of the tracer. While he was captured, who knew what Roehl had done to him, besides the starvation and torture.

Markus came running around the corner, after standing guard at the entrance of the cave. "The men are coming too close to the cave's entrance. The wards are holding, but we should leave as soon as possible."

Trystan strode toward Nicolae. "How long before you are ready to transport?"

Nicolae waved his hand over the fire and the flames died. As did the embers and smoke. "I'm ready. We just need to solidify a new location."

I couldn't help but smile and feel a great admiration for my grandfather. I was so glad he was here. If he wasn't, we would have been stuck in this cave.

But he also looked tired, and I knew he was still recovering from transporting all of us from place to place. The last large transfer was only a day ago, and today he'd transported

Melaina. That, and he'd given me the last of the blood supply. How was he able to recover?

I didn't want him to pass out again while transporting us. The last time, we were put in a very dangerous situation.

"We will go to the Isle of Aria. Do you know the place?" Trystan asked Nicolae.

"Yes, although I've never been there. It is another island off Carpathia. To the north. Am I right?"

Trystan smiled. "Yes, but are you strong enough to transport all of us?" He must have noticed the dark circles under Nicolae's eyes too.

"Yes, of course." I knew Nicolae would agree so we wouldn't worry, but I could see that he was weary, and hated that he had to do this alone.

I strode over to Nicolae and pulled him to the side. "You said I can magically do anything you can, right?"

"Yes, of course."

"Well, is there any way I can help you transport? With two of us, our odds double and we can get everyone to safety much faster."

Nicolae's expression was unreadable. Then, he grinned. "I suppose you could. But it does take a bit of practice and a lot of concentration. When I first started out, I ended up in a few unfamiliar places. Some, I still have no idea where I'd landed, and it took me a few days of trial and error to get back to where I'd started."

My anxiety rose. The last thing I wanted was to transport someone to an unknown place with no way of knowing how to return.

Nicolae placed a gentle hand on my shoulder. "I have no doubt you could do it, Calla. All it takes is a lot of concentration. And a bit of magic, of course." A smile blossomed on his lips. "Let me do the transporting this time, and as soon as we are settled in the new location, I will show you how it's done."

I nodded. His confident smile put me at ease.

I wanted to learn everything I could, because even if I wasn't able to master it all, I could still have a magical arsenal in my back pocket. Just in case.

Nicolae tugged me into his arms. "Thank you, Calla, for accepting me. You don't know how much it means to have a family after all these years. I've been alone for so long."

I hugged him back, equally thankful to have him in my life. I couldn't begin to imagine what it must have been like to be all alone for countless years, thinking you had no family. Living a life wandering from place to place, not knowing if those who murdered your family and destroyed your kingdom would come after you next.

But Nicolae survived. And instead of cowering, he became powerful. Without him, we wouldn't be safe in this cave right now. If he hadn't come for me in Morose Mountain, I would probably still be wandering somewhere on that frigid range, on the brink of death. He was the best ally I had, besides Trystan. He was my blood. He was family. And I had no doubt he would remain loyal until the very end.

"She is your mate now, Trystan," I heard Feng say behind me. He and the rest of the cadre had surrounded Trystan. "We must be extremely careful with our plans from here on out. Her safety, as well as yours, is now our highest priority."

My heart swelled with admiration for all of them, but my mind lingered on those few words Feng spoke. *She is your mate now.*

Mate.

When this all started, being mated sounded absurd and was the last thing on my mind. I had just turned eighteen and hadn't had much of a social life. But now, with Trystan, it felt right. It felt like I had finally made the choice that destiny had intended. To be bound to this beautiful soul. A soul intertwined with mine from the moment we entered this realm.

I smiled at Trystan and the world around me dissolved. His darkened eyes swirled with desire.

Kylan slapped a hand on Trystan's shoulder. "Focus, Prince. Sealing the mating bond should be the least of your worries right now."

Brone laughed a deep and boisterous laugh. "Even the strongest man alive cannot tether the pull of the mating bond."

"Exactly." Andrés fanned himself. "Those two will be horny as hell until they seal that bond. Gods, I am standing between them and am stifled from the heat."

I turned away, my cheeks flushing with warmth. "We should be leaving."

"I'm all for them sealing their mating bond," Sabine chimed. "It's been long in coming, especially after all they've been through."

"I agree," Brynna added. "Calla has finally found someone worthy of her."

"No!" Nicolae blurted, giving an awkward expression.

Everyone in the cave paused and looked at him. He straightened his back and crossed his arms over his chest.

"Why not?" Sabine threw her hands on her hips, ready for a dispute.

Nicolae let out a breathy sigh. "Because I am her grandfather and her guardian. I need to make sure her priority is staying alive. Not sealing a mating bond."

Gods. Could this be more embarrassing?

"Well, I think both should be a priority," Sabine added. Brynna agreed, nodding her head.

I cleared my throat. Loudly. "In case you have all forgotten, I am an adult now and have proven I can manage and protect myself. My life decisions are mine alone to make, right or wrong. And you can rest assured that every decision I do make, from here on, will be in the best interest of everyone involved. I will not be reckless with my choices."

Nicolae inclined his head to the side. "I agree you are more than capable. I am just concerned, knowing how strong the call of the mating bond can be. It could be a major distraction. A distraction we cannot afford, especially at a time like this."

"I also understand where you are coming from, but this concern should only involve Trystan and me. And we will not let it affect our current situation."

"No, we will not," Trystan spoke, suddenly standing beside me. "We know full well what is coming, and I will not allow the mating bond to be a hindrance. I assure you."

"I trust you both and your judgment." Nicolae let out a deep sigh and threw his hands up. "But once everyone has arrived at the new location," he said to me, "we will begin your transport training."

"I look forward to it," I replied, knowing he'd try to keep me busy enough to avoid sealing the mating bond.

But I had a goal. In sixteen days, we would be in a battle for our lives.

What if I didn't survive? The bigger question . . . what if I never sealed the mating bond with Trystan? That would be a sad tale. Calla Caldwell, Incendian Royal, chosen one of the Fire Goddess, mated to Prince Trystan Vladu of Carpathia—the most gorgeous man in Talbrinth and beyond—dies a virgin.

Death.

It was eminent. And I would pray to the goddess that it would come swiftly to Roehl and spare our group. I couldn't begin to think about losing any one of my friends. I had to stay focused. I had to believe we would all make it out of this alive.

"I'm ready," Nicolae said, breaking me from my thoughts.

"Who owns the island we're going to?" I wanted to know more about this place we would be seeking refuge.

"I do," Trystan said, grabbing hold of my hand and lacing his fingers through mine.

I glanced at him, still trying to wrap my head around the fact we had broken the curse and we were now blood bonded, something extremely serious and permanent to a pureblooded royal.

He leaned down bringing his lips close to my ear and whispered, "And now, it also belongs to you." His smile and the darkened look in those eyes caused a spark to ignite in my core.

I swallowed hard. "I can't wait to see it."

There was an incredible and undeniable pull between us, a powerful connection, even greater now that we had sealed the blood bond. I could feel it pulsing in the air between us. I could feel it in his touch, which seemed to stir the magic in my blood.

Nicolae stood in front of me and Trystan. "I will take you both first. But—"

I held up a hand to stop him. "Look, there isn't time to seal a mating bond. Not in the amount of time it'll take you to drop us off and transport the others."

Nicolae smirked, then placed his hands on each of our shoulders. In a split second, we went from the dark, dankness of the cave to twilight and a wide-open field filled with fresh air and freshly fallen snow.

CHAPTER FOUR

ISLE OF ARIA

HEAVENS ABOVE.

The Isle of Aria was glimmering like a million diamonds. The sun still hadn't risen, but it was yawning, ready to wake. The ground and surrounding trees were flocked with white. It was a winter wonderland, and I could only imagine how breathtaking it would be during the other seasons.

The cold air bit my skin, but before I could shiver, heat warmed my bones. Being an Incendian had its perks. I would never have to worry about being exposed to the winter elements.

Nicolae disconnected his hands from our shoulders and stepped back. "I'll be right back. I must deliver the others before the sun rises," he said before vanishing right before our eyes.

Trystan slid an arm around my shoulders. "I know a way the mating bond will not be an issue for us any longer."

"How?"

"We must seal it." His eyes darkened again. "Once we seal the mating bond, the overwhelming desire and pull to seal it will not be a major distraction. Yes, it will still be there, and I am told it will never leave, but it won't be as strong as it is right now."

His lips were so close I could almost taste them. His nearness making it hard to breathe.

Trystan already knew about me. He'd been stung by the purity ring that once adorned my finger. He would be my first. And my last.

"Come," he breathed. "I'll take you inside."

I looked around and didn't see a structure anywhere nearby. "Inside where?"

When I glanced at him, his eyes were studying me. "My father's mages put wards and a glamour over the property. The house is hidden, just as the castle in Carpathia is hidden from the mortals. Nicolae will have to unveil your eyes when he returns."

I blinked at him. "Can't you unveil my eyes?"

Trystan faced me, then leaned down and gently kissed my eyelids, one at a time. But after opening them, I frowned, still unable to see a house.

Trystan laughed. "Unfortunately, I cannot." His azure eyes were like liquid, swirling with emotion, making my chest tighten. His lips pressed against mine, his tongue delving deep between them. Heat ignited between us, around us, through us. His kiss melted me from the inside out, transporting me to a place far away. My mind was gone, floating on a cloud somewhere in the heavens above.

When he finally pulled away, I was left breathless, my entire body like putty in his hands.

"Hey, you two!" Sabine hollered, waving her arms in the air.

Trystan kept his eyes on me. "We will finish this later."

I nodded because his kiss had stolen all words from my lips.

Nicolae delivered Sabine and Markus and vanished. As soon as Markus saw us, he began trudging through the snow, directly toward us with a large gait. I quickly removed my hands from Trystan's shoulders and took a step back.

An instant coldness seeped between us, so I quickly reached out and took hold of Trystan's hand. He tugged me to his side and wrapped an arm behind my back, his eyes meeting mine as Markus finally reached us. "You're my mate now and no longer need Markus's protection. You should release him."

My heart hammered against my chest, so loud I knew they both heard it.

Markus shook his head. "My oath was made to the King of Morbeth. Not to Calla."

"I understand," Trystan said carefully, addressing Markus. "But your king is dead. You are no longer bound by his oath."

Markus's expression saddened. "I will continue to protect Calla until there is no longer any threat."

Trystan slid his arm from behind me and took a step toward Markus.

"As Prince of Carpathia, and her mate, I absolve you from your oath. It is now my duty to protect her from all harm. And I will do so until death."

Markus bowed his head and slammed a fist to his chest. "I understand, but I cannot and will not leave the princess. I will fulfill my duties until Roehl is dead. Until that day, I will remain close to her."

"Listen," I interrupted, stepping in between them. I could feel the tension growing between these two alpha males. "I am grateful to both of you, but I am not a fragile doll. I was given power to protect not only myself, but those under my care."

I turned to Trystan. "Markus will stay with us because he is an asset and an ally." I then turned my attention to Markus. "Today, I am giving you a new order."

Markus glared at me, then closed his eyes and bowed his head. "What would you have me do, princess?"

It took everything inside of me not to growl at him for calling me *princess*, but I straightened my back and took another step toward him. "I want you to keep Sabine and Brynna safe. Thalia too, although she can protect herself." I placed a gentle hand on his shoulder, as a friend. "I really need you to do this for me, Markus."

Markus paused and gave me an unreadable expression. Then, he exhaled, and his eyes softened. He bowed his head. "I vow to keep them safe."

I nodded, thankful this didn't go in another direction. "Thank you. Markus. You don't know how much their safety means to me."

Markus shook his head. "You're mistaken, princess. I do know how much it means to you, which is why I have willingly accepted your order."

Without thought, I threw my arms around his chest and hugged him. Markus stood stiff as a board, and after a few seconds, I felt his hand gently tapping my back. Knowing he wasn't a hugger, I stepped away from him and watched his shoulders relax a bit.

My heart swelled inside, knowing that this man—warrior and Captain of the King's guard—had become my friend and respected my wishes. I also had a mutual respect for him and would never take advantage of his kindness or what he risked being here.

I was less worried knowing he would help keep my mortal friends safe. I had no doubt that no one would do a better job than Markus.

Looking behind Markus's large frame, Nicolae reappeared with Ophelia, Melaina, and Brynna. Ophelia looked a little winded.

Nicolae glanced at us and uttered a spell that made me lightheaded. Blinking, I turned around to see a majestic mansion, three stories high, about a hundred yards in front of us.

He had unveiled our eyes.

"Come. Let's get everyone inside," Trystan said, leading the way to the mansion. I followed, knowing Brynna and Sabine despised the cold.

"This is your place?" I exhaled, catching up to him.

"Ours," he said slowly, taking my hand. "This is *ours*."

Suddenly, two large wooden doors with ornate carvings swung open. Three women and two men all wearing similar uniforms exited and formed a line to welcome us. As soon as they saw Trystan, their faces lit up.

"Prince Trystan, it's great to see you again." An older woman with salt-and-pepper hair tied in a tight, neat bun made her way toward him, wrapping him in a hug. "It's been a while since we've had any guests."

Trystan hugged her back, and I could tell that this woman was very familiar to him. "It's great to see you too, Fern. It's been too long. How have you all been?"

"We've been very well, thanks to the generosity of your family."

"That's good." Trystan turned to the others, and they all bowed their heads. "We will be staying for a few days. Please make sure my guest's needs are met."

"Of course," Fern said, dipping her head. "Please come. We'll show you all to your rooms."

As we made our way inside, Sabine gasped. "Goddess above. This place is incredible."

She was right. The inside of the house was luxurious with tapestries, rich furnishings and carpets, golden sconces, and glittering chandeliers. Everything was perfect and pristine, decorated in shades of gold and silver with large crystal vases filled with cream roses spread throughout the foyer.

In the middle of the foyer was a grand staircase that led up to the second and third floors.

I was in awe, gaping at the surroundings, watching Fern escort Markus, Brynna, Sabine, Melaina, Ophelia, and Thalia upstairs.

Melaina turned back to me, her arm wrapped around Ophelia. "My aunt is still recovering from an illness, so I am going to take her upstairs to rest for a bit. I'm glad she even agreed to come in this condition. She will work on the tracer spell when she is a bit stronger."

"Of course," I said. "Whenever she is ready."

I heard voices behind us. Trystan's cadre had arrived, along with Nicolae.

"Calla," Nicolae stepped inside, his eyes meeting mine. "Are you ready for your lesson?"

My eyes narrowed. "Are you up for it? You look a bit tired."

"I'm fine. I'll feel better once you learn how to transport. It will give me peace of mind, knowing if you are ever in a deadly situation, you will be able to escape."

"I will accompany you," Trystan said, coming up beside me. "I'd love to witness *my flame* in action."

My flame. I liked that. It sounded so endearing coming from him.

Trystan's lips turned up into a broad smile. He leaned closer, offering me his arm. "Shall we?"

I happily took it and followed Nicolae outside.

"Prince Trystan, can you suggest a place for us to practice?"

"The stable is probably a good place to start. It's covered and will give us privacy."

Trystan led me past Nicolae and headed toward the back of the house. Our feet crunched on the freshly fallen snow as we strolled down a small pathway lined with spruce and pine that led back toward a large stable.

The stable was just as grand as the one Shadow was housed at in Carpathia.

When we first entered, there were ten stalls, but only six housed thoroughbred horses. Three were chestnut, two bay, and the one that caught my attention was dark gray.

As soon as it heard us, the gray horse poked its head out and nodded. I made my way over and gently ran my hand down its forehead. "Hey, pretty—?"

"Girl," Trystan said, coming up beside me. "Her name is Storm."

"Storm," I said softly. "You're a beautiful girl, aren't you?"

Storm nodded a few times, making me laugh.

Outside one of the stalls was a bucket with apples and carrots in it. I walked over and took one of each before returning to Storm's stall.

As soon as the mare saw the treats, she began stretching her head toward me. "Don't worry. These are for you," I whispered. "Don't tell the others."

I thought I heard Trystan chuckle as I held the apple in the palm of my hand. Storm quickly snatched it up. When she was done, she nudged me with her nose, telling me she wanted more. "You've got spunk. I like you," I said, holding out the carrot. Storm bit off half, then returned for the other half after a few crunches.

"She's feisty, but fast as hell," Trystan said. "She can run like the wind."

"Whose horse is she?"

"Mine."

"Of course, she is." I ran a hand down her neck which was soft as silk. "She is beautiful."

Trystan came up behind me and placed a hand on my lower back, making my insides buzz. "She's taken a liking to you." Trystan reached over and scratched Storm behind her ear, and she reached forward, her nose nudging his chest. "She was wild, brought in by request from my father. For a long time, no one could touch her, let alone break her. But when I was younger, I was determined. I stayed on the island for a few months, and every day would come out to the stable to talk to her and feed her treats. After a few weeks, I felt I had gained her trust and that we'd formed a silent alliance, so . . . I saddled her.

"When I mounted her for the first time, she didn't buck like the others did. Instead, she took off running. I held on for dear life. I'd never ridden anything so fast.

"When she finally tired, I realized we were miles away from home. My father found us, and that's when he said she was mine. A gift from him to me. I'm the only one she'll let ride. No one else can even get close enough to put a saddle on her."

I smiled, hoping Storm and I would have a similar connection like I had with Shadow.

Nicolae cleared his throat, and for a moment, I had forgotten why we had come to the stable in the first place, and that he was still here. "Shall we start our lesson?"

"Yes," I said, kissing Storm on her nose. She nudged me again, making me laugh. "I'll be back, girl. I promise."

The back of the stable opened into a barn which housed chickens, a few cows, pigs, and even some goats. Each of their pens had access for them to go outside, which I thought was pretty awesome.

My nose tickled with the pungent animal smell permeating the area. I had been to too many farms before, so I wasn't a stranger to the scent, and it was one I liked to avoid.

Nicolae stood in the center of the barn with the chickens on one side, and goats on the other. "Calla, come stand next to me."

I did as he said and listened carefully as he explained the process of transporting.

"To make this spell work, you will need to think ahead. Focus on the location you would like to travel to and keep your mind locked on it. Any deviation, and you could end up lost. Or even in the middle of danger."

I swallowed hard, wondering if I should even attempt this. What if my mind took me to Morbeth? What if it delivered me to Roehl?

The thought had me second guessing myself.

"Hey," Trystan's voice spoke from behind. "You can do this. I believe in you."

I was thankful for his confidence. Inhaling, I held out my hand to Nicolae. "Okay, where should we go first?"

"Let's start with something easy. Transport from here to the entrance of the stable."

I looked at the area to which he was pointing. Fifty steps and I could be there, so it wasn't hard or intimidating.

I nodded and focused my attention on the entrance. Closing my eyes, I didn't feel my power. No warmth. No tingles.

My eyes slid open, and we were now across the room, at the opening of the stable, Trystan standing fifty yards away.

"Did I do that? I didn't feel anything."

Nicolae gave me a sheepish smile. "I did," he admitted, and I hung my head. "You are holding back, Calla. Come, let's try something else." He led me out of the stable and headed back down the path until we reached an area where we could see the landscape, far into the distance. The entire island was quiet. I liked that. No people buzzing around. No judging eyes.

Stopping, Nicolae pointed to where a single, bare tree stood out from all the rest. Its dark branches reached up and out, dominating the area.

"Focus on that tree. I want you to transport us there."

I hesitated. It was far, at least five hundred yards away. Doubt began to seep in when Nicolae stepped in front of me and grabbed hold of my hands.

"Don't doubt yourself, Calla. Your gifts, your elemental magic, can be altered, molded to how you see fit. They are *your* gifts, and *you* are their master. You control them. You wield them. You tell them what you want, and they have no other option but to serve.

"Just remember, these gifts were entrusted to you for a reason. You are Incendian Royalty, the only true heir to the throne. The Fire Goddess would not offer this power to someone she did not believe worthy. Trust in that fact alone and believe in your abilities. The Prince of Carpathia believes in you. And so do I."

I let his words seep down into my soul. Let them take root.

All this time, I felt like I had to prove myself. Like all these powers were dumped on me and had become a burden—my burden to bear. But they weren't a burden. They were a gift. A gift given to me, and only me. My powers were a blessing to help and save, not only myself, but my friends and my people. They were not a curse.

Still holding onto Nicolae's hands, I looked ahead at the tree and closed my eyes. I focused on the location and called to my power. I asked it to help me, to carry me and Nicolae to the location just under it.

There was a stirring in my blood, a warmth I could not explain. It was a calming warmth, almost like a gentle hug from my power, letting me know that it was there for me. That this was the first of a journey we would embark on together. A journey that would lead us to much greater things. If I believed. If I didn't doubt.

I felt Nicolae shift, and when I opened my eyes, we were no longer in the same spot. Glancing up, we were standing under the fifty-foot-tall tree. Gaping at Nicolae he nodded with the widest smile on his face, a look of pride in his eyes.

"I knew you could do it. I am so proud of you."

I shook my head in disbelief. "I did it?"

"It wasn't me," he said, holding his hands up. "I just came along for the ride."

Tears spilled down my face as I stepped up to the tree and placed my hands on its bark. I didn't even realize I had transported us here. Was it really that easy?

I faced Nicolae. "I never could have done this without you."

"Yes, you could have. I did nothing except instruct. The rest was you."

I glanced back to where Trystan was now standing and could feel his pride emanating through the air. Then I heard his voice through our bond. *"I knew you could do it. Hurry and come back to me."*

I couldn't help but smile and couldn't wait to return to him.

I took Nicolae's hand. "Could I ask you a question?" This was just a small feat. The tree was within my view. But what if I wanted to go somewhere I'd never been?

"Of course."

"How did you transport us here without ever being on this island?"

Nicolae smiled. "I knew where the island was, and earlier, Trystan had pinpointed the location of where the house was on a map. It was the map I focused on, and my magic took me exactly to where I needed to be."

"So, it really is locking onto a location and concentrating on it?"

"It's that simple," he said. "Now, take us back. I'm sure your prince is anxious to hear all about your first transport."

I closed my eyes, but my mind remained on Trystan. I focused on where he was and asked my magic to take me to him. Again, I felt my power hum through me, and when I opened my eyes, Trystan was standing a few feet away.

"I did it!" I exclaimed, running into his open arms.

Trystan caught me, wrapping me in a hug. "I am so proud of you."

"It's not as cool as riding in a wind funnel, though."

"Traveling in an air funnel is overrated. Ask my cadre." Trystan laughed, and the sound of his laughter and the warmth of his smile brought me so much joy. I never wanted to see his face riddled with agony or torment again. It nearly broke me.

"Want to take a trip with me?" I asked him, glancing back toward the tree.

"I would love to."

Nicolae gave me a nod of approval, so with my arms still wrapped tightly around Trystan, I focused on the single tree in the distance. This time, keeping my eyes wide open, I called to my power and was suddenly encased in a familiar, warm, and welcoming darkness. In seconds, that darkness dissolved around us, safely delivering Trystan and I under the tree.

It felt easy, too easy. Like transporting was done with no effort at all. Maybe it was because I had just fed, and my body had regenerated.

Inside, I felt my powers growing stronger every time I used them.

Trystan leaned over and kissed me. "This is a huge advantage," he whispered against my lips.

"Mmm," I hummed, pulling his lips back to mine.

Gods, the pull between us was growing stronger and stronger, especially being in such near proximity to him. My entire being craved his touch, his kiss, his closeness.

But Nicolae called me through our connection, making sure I remained focused. He had me practice my new transportation spell at least twenty more times, transporting them to different parts of the island. And each time, I completed the transport with almost no effort at all.

My magic was potent and every time I used it, I could feel it connecting, sinking deeper, growing stronger and blooming into something even more powerful.

By the end of the day, I was spent, but in a good way.

"I'm famished," Nicolae said, heading back to the house. "Tomorrow, we will train again. Tomorrow, we will use all of your elements."

"Then she will also have my guidance," Trystan said, reaching for my hand.

Air. It was the only element with which I had not really practiced. In Carpathia, Trystan wasn't able to help me, but after witnessing him massacre Roehl's men back in Carpathia and in the Whisper Woods, I knew it would be a major asset.

I'd never seen anyone move like him—like the wind. He'd shifted the air into weapons and shields. He was an incredible force, and I knew that together, now that our elements were connected and he was my mate, we had the potential to stop Roehl.

Trystan's voice spoke loud and clear through our bond. *"Tomorrow, I will show you how to manipulate air. But tonight, my flame. Tonight, you will experience something you have never experienced before. Tonight, you will burn bright for me."*

I almost unraveled with his words.

Goddess above.

CHAPTER FIVE

After a hot bath, I made my way downstairs, where everyone was gathered for dinner at a large, ornate dining table set with candles and fresh flowers. My companions were smiling, probably happy to be settled in proper rooms with running water and bathing rooms. I didn't blame them. My own room was just as luxurious as the one in Carpathia, only smaller. More intimate.

"Melaina, where is Ophelia?" I noticed she wasn't at the table.

"She's old and like I said earlier, still recovering from an illness. After checking you for your tracer, she felt a bit dizzy and off-balance. I gave her a potion that should help, and I believe after some rest, tomorrow she will have enough energy to check the rest of the group for any signs of tracers."

"No problem. I wish her well," I said, taking a seat next to Nicolae. "Just have her check those who have been in contact with Roehl."

Melaina nodded. "I'll do that."

Trystan was also missing, but I knew with this being one of his family homes, he was probably busy.

"Where are you?" I spoke through our bond, anxious to see him.

"I'm sorry. I had to take care of some business, but I'll be back shortly."

"Are you on the island?"

"No, I had to return to Carpathia, but I am on my way back to you now."

"Okay. Be safe."

"I will. And you as well."

"Calla, I would give one hundred gold skrag for your thoughts," Brynna said, her eyes scrutinizing me from across the table. "Where is your prince?"

"He had business to attend to, but he should be back soon."

"Business? Where?" Kylan spoke, his eyes sliding to the members of his cadre.

"He went to Carpathia," I said, a little shocked Kylan wasn't aware he was gone.

Kylan ran a hand through his thick raven hair. "He never told me he had business in Carpathia. Did he tell any of you?"

The cadre shook their heads.

What was he up to?

Fern stood at the entrance of the kitchen, instructing the others as they began to serve us.

Large gold goblets filled with ruby wine were set in front of each vampire, while plates of meat, vegetables, bread, cheese, and fruit were set in front of the mortals.

Melaina took a bite of the meat and moaned, her eyes rolling back. "What I said before still stands. I would rather die a mortal and eat real food than have to drink that disgusting stuff." She held out her fork like a dagger, pointing it at the immortals in the room. "And I mean it. Anyone who turns me will be spelled into a toad." She then aimed her fork at Brone.

"Hey," I said, snatching my goblet from the table. "Some of us never really had a choice."

"I know," she sighed. "And that sucks for you. But I do have a choice and would rather die than be doomed to drink bodily fluids for the rest of my immortal life."

Her words churned my gut, so I placed my goblet down on the table.

"Calla, you look like you're about to be sick," Brynna said, tossing me her napkin.

"It's her fault," I said, aiming my finger at Melaina. "Don't ever refer to my only food source as bodily fluids. I'm still new at this and now I want to vomit."

Brynna leaned forward, batting her long lashes. "Oh, but if it were Prince Trystan's bodily fluids—"

I threw the napkin back at her, my face flushing with heat, my eyes darting to Nicolae, who closed his eyes and shook his head.

Everyone at the table laughed, and I savored the sound of it, along with the back-and-forth banter between my mortal friends and Trystan's cadre. Laughter had been such a rarity these days.

Markus mostly remained silent, unless he was asked questions, but I knew he was also thinking about the time we had left and what was to come.

"I could live in a place like this," Brynna said, her eyes scanning the room. She had always loved the finer things.

Sabine nodded. "I could too." She then pointed at me. "Maybe we can all live together. This house is certainly big enough and secluded from . . . people. If I could live the rest of my life without having to deal with other people, I would live a happy life. Hell, I'd even join the staff here and work for my keep."

I didn't want to offend the staff waiting on us, so I replied, "Sabine, I see you finding a good man to settle down with who will give you lots of children to keep you busy."

"Maybe." Sabine shrugged and discreetly glanced over to Markus, who was taking a swig of his ruby wine. "Eventually, I'd like at least two kids. One of each."

I smiled, envisioning them together with two beautiful children. "You will make a wonderful mother."

Nicolae finished his ruby wine and pushed his seat back before standing. "Please excuse me. I am in need of a bath and some rest."

"Yes, of course," I said, knowing he was probably uncomfortable. "Sleep well."

"You all as well," he said, bowing his head as he made his way toward the grand staircase.

Anyone could see Nicolae was exhausted. The dark circles under his tired eyes gave it away. I didn't blame him for wanting to leave, especially with all the nonsensical banter between us.

"Do any of you have wives or families?" Thalia asked Kylan.

"No," he replied, swirling what was left of the ruby wine in his goblet. "When we became part of Carpathia's cadre, we took a vow to remain single for as long as we are under their employment."

"But—" Andrés interjected. "Being single and a part of Carpathia's cadre does have its perks. In our line of work, it's easier not to be in any commitment."

"What about you, Thalia?" Brynna questioned. "Don't you have anyone special back in Incendia?"

Thalia shook her head. "No."

Brynna's eyes narrowed. "None in the entire kingdom?"

"I was appointed as head of the guard. Because my main priority was the queen's protection, she made it impossible for me to have any kind of relationship."

"Gods, that bitch queen really sucks," Sabine said, then nudged Thalia on the side. "Now that you are free from the fake queen, and Calla is bonded to Trystan, you should consider courting Kai."

Thalia shook her head. "That is not a decision I can make."

"But if he asked—"

"I would say yes," she replied with a smile, stabbing a ripe strawberry with her fork.

Thalia and Kai would make a suitable match. I'd seen the way they interacted with each other in Aquaria, how they danced and looked happy together.

Speaking of Kai, I hadn't heard from him in a while. He didn't even know that Trystan and I had been blood bonded.

Kai. He was a hero. He was a great friend who had saved my life and came to my rescue whenever I called him, but I never saw us as anything more than that, and he knew it. Before he returned to Aquaria, he tried to reason with Trystan. Tried to speak to him on my behalf. He even tried to make him jealous, so I would look more appealing to him while he was cursed.

"Sea Star?"

What the—? Did I call him?

"Sea Star. I know it was you. There is no other, besides Nicolae, I have a connection with."

"Kai," I responded, not knowing what to say.

"Do you need to be rescued?"

"No." I laughed. *"I—I haven't heard from you in a while. I was checking in to ask how everything is going in Aquaria?"*

"Things are fine here. We have a second meeting with the heads of Sartha, Baelfast, and Hale tomorrow. Aquaris has already sided with us."

"That's wonderful news."

"It is. Things are moving forward," Kai said, sounding a little tired. *"How is Trystan, by the way? Is he still cursed and being an ass?"*

"No, he's not, actually." I paused. *"Kai, we broke the curse."*

"That's awesome! How did you do it?"

I couldn't lie to him.

"The only way we could break the curse was if—," I took a sip of my ruby wine. *"I sealed the blood bond with him."*

This time, Kai paused.

"Well, there couldn't be a better match," he finally said, sounding sincere. *"Besides, I know you chose him from the very beginning. And even though me, my parents, and my kingdom rooted for us, I know that Trystan is your true match. I cannot deny that. In Aquaris, when I saw the two of you together, it was*

obvious you were destined for each other. I could never make you look at me the way you look at him. I couldn't make you feel the way Trystan does. He is a lucky man to have you by his side. And you are equally lucky to have him. I am truly happy for you b oth."

My heart warmed inside, and a tear trickled down my face.

"Thank you, Kai. You don't know how much that means to me."

"I'm glad you feel that way. You are my friend, Sea Star, and I will always be here for you. Your grandfather is a hero in our kingdom. You will always be welcome here."

"Thank you, Kai. I will always be here for you as well."

"Hey, are you crying? You better not be crying, especially if Trystan is nearby. He'll get jealous."

"Calla, is everything okay?" Kylan questioned with a furrowed brow.

"Yes." I laughed, swiping away the wet on my cheeks. "Everything is fine."

"When will we see you again?" I asked Kai.

"I will try to catch up to you within the week. I'll be contacting you to let you know when I'm coming. Tell Trystan I said hey and he better be good to you."

"I'll tell him. Take care of yourself, Kai."

"Take care, Sea Star."

"Are you doing that talking thing with your mind?" Sabine questioned, tilting her head to the side.

I nodded but decided not to tell her with whom I was speaking.

"It must be with her prince," Thalia said, nudging Sabine.

"Yeah, you better spill those juicy details later," Brynna added, popping a ripe grape into her mouth.

"There are zero juicy details. You all need to find mates," I huffed.

"We aren't as blessed as you, princess," Brynna said with a little bite in her voice, plucking another grape from the table. "I have someone in Sartha." Her eyes went blank, distant, for a moment. "Well, I *did* have someone in Sartha."

"Claude Bentham?" I questioned, knowing he was the last person she was dating. "I didn't know it was that serious between you two."

"Yes, Calla. Claude Bentham, *the blacksmith*. He might not be a prince or a warrior, but he was kind and treated me well. He even told me that he loved me. And now, he probably thinks I'm dead." A single tear trickled down her cheek. Then her eyes snapped to mine, brewing with tears. "I was on my way home from Claude's house when I was knocked out, kidnapped, and put under a magical spell. There were days, maybe weeks, that were lost to me. I was in Morbeth with a wicked man I didn't even know existed. I did things, and things were done to me that I have no recollection of. Gods, Cal. Do you realize how messed up that is?"

"Hey, now. You aren't the only one who suffered in Morbeth," Sabine said, coming to my rescue. She'd been there, tending to my broken ribs and raw wrists in the cell.

"Sabine," I breathed, shaking my head.

Seeing Brynna so broken shattered my own heart. She was right. Everything that was done to her was done because she was my friend. Because she was associated with me and with my family. If not for that fact, she would still be in Sartha with her family, with Claude, if Roehl hadn't sent his men to capture her. I could only hope that soon this nightmare would end.

"I'm sorry, Brynna. For everything you endured. I wish I could turn back time. I wish I could go back and make things right."

Brynna closed her bloodshot eyes and shook her head, her face wet with tears. "I know it wasn't your fault. I—I'm still trying to deal with the death of my parents. I can't believe they won't be in Sartha when I return. If I'm ever allowed to return."

"You will return to Sartha, Brynna." I tried to speak the words with confidence, but I was still unsure what the future held for us. "Once this is all over, I will make sure you return to Claude and live a good life."

"I want to see him," Brynna said, her eyes pinned on me. "I have to tell him that I'm alive. I need him to wait for me."

"Seeing him is out of the question," Kylan interjected. "You are a target of our enemy. If you go to him right now, his life, as well as yours, would be in danger."

"Why me? Why would I be in danger? I don't even know the bastard. I have no connection with him. With all the magical people in this room, is there no way for me to talk to him for a few moments?"

Kylan shook his head. "Maybe you can send him a letter."

Brynna threw her napkin on the table and pushed her chair back before storming out of the room. But she paused and turned around, her eyes glaring. "I don't see any difference between this place and Morbeth. I am still a prisoner." She turned and ran out of the room and then up the stairs.

I moved to follow her, but Melaina stood and held out a hand to stop me. "Let me talk to her. She needs a bit more time."

As much as I wanted to console my friend, I knew that Melaina had been her friend and ear during her darkest times. "Okay," I said. "Please let her know that I love her, and I'm here for her."

"She already knows," Melaina said with a sad smile. "Your arrival in Carpathia was unexpected, and since then, her life has been chaotic, moving from place to place because men are chasing us. She just needs time to adjust and process everything."

I nodded and slid back into my chair while Melaina excused herself and headed upstairs.

"Calla, it's not your fault," Sabine finally said. "Brynna's gone through a lot, but she will heal. She is not the only one who has suffered the loss of both parents. You have endured the same, along with torture and pain since you left Sartha. Trystan and his men came to save you in Morbeth, but you insisted they take Brynna instead, realizing you might never be rescued again. You saved her life."

"I agree," Thalia added. "You are brave, Calla. The strongest woman I have ever known. You are a future queen and, like I said before, I will follow and fight alongside you because you bring hope to me and the future of Incendia."

"And Morbeth," Sabine added, holding up a finger. "Once Roehl is defeated, Morbeth will need a new ruler."

"Wait a minute. Once she seals the mating bond with our prince, she will become princess of Carpathia, and our future queen." Kylan winked at me.

My anxiety rose with all this talk of royalty.

"Oh, to bear the weight of kingdoms and crowns," Feng said with a knowing smile. "I have no doubt you will be a great queen, Calla, no matter where you choose to rule."

I buried my face in my hands, overwhelmed with everything—Brynna, this conversation, life. I didn't even know if I'd be alive in two weeks. Ruling a kingdom and wearing a crown was the last thing on my mind.

I remained at the table until everyone excused themselves and went upstairs to their rooms.

I was just about to stand when I heard . . .

"Calla, come to the room." It was Trystan.

"Are you there?"

"Yes. I am waiting for you."

Goddess above. Excited, I headed for the stairs, heart thrumming, pulse racing, and stomach twisting with butterflies as my mind recalled the words he'd spoken to me earlier. *Tonight, you will experience something you have never experienced before. Tonight, you will burn bright for me.*

I tried to walk casually up the stairs, but every fiber in my being begged me to run. Run the hell up the stairs as quickly as I could.

Taking the stairs two at a time, I finally made it to the door, panting. Placing my hand on the knob, I breathed in deeply and twisted.

CHAPTER SIX

INSIDE, THE ROOM WAS glowing with golden light from dozens of lit candles, along with hundreds of red and cream roses in crystal vases placed all over the room. At the far end, in one corner, Trystan stood. I stopped breathing at how utterly gorgeous he looked. He was formally dressed in his royal attire, a black cape draped over his shoulders, with a golden crown sitting atop his head.

But he wasn't alone. Standing next to him was an elderly gentleman with short, silvery hair, wearing a long black robe embellished with gold crosses on either side of his chest.

"Trystan?" I breathed, suddenly feeling out of place. I glanced down at my simple brown tunic and pants.

"Close the door, my love, and come to me," Trystan spoke tenderly, his hand outstretched.

Swallowing hard, I did as he said and made my way over to him, placing my hand in his. My eyes shifted to the man standing next to him.

"Calla, this is Father Matteo." The man bowed his head and smiled. "He is here because I know your family has a religious background. Your grandparents were preachers, and you wore the silver ring as a sign of your purity." Trystan rubbed his thumb over the finger where my purity ring used to sit. The ring that had burned his skin when we'd first met.

I must have had a confused look on my face because Trystan's expression turned to one of concern. "I brought Father Matteo here to join us in holy matrimony. If that is what you wish, before we seal the mating bond. This union is between us. A formality to give you peace of mind." His hands gently caressed the sides of my face. "After we deal with Roehl, I promise to give you the wedding you deserve. A glorious wedding fit for my queen."

Gods. I didn't know what to say. I was overwhelmed, knowing that this beautiful soul . . . this generous and adoring man had cared so much about my religious background that he would travel to Carpathia to bring a priest.

My lips quivered, tears brimmed and spilled down my face.

"Calla, have I offended you?" Trystan's brow furrowed. "I can send him back."

"No. No. This is perfect."

A smile caressed his handsome face. A smile that warmed me entirely.

"Shall we begin?" Father Matteo asked.

Outside of the large window in front of us, snow was gently falling, flocking the surrounding trees, creating the perfect wintery backdrop.

Candlelight glowed and flickered off the strong panes of Trystan's handsome face. His eyes, those piercing azure eyes, held mine the entire time we stood in front of the priest and exchanged our vows. Vows that were simple, yet powerful. An outward proclamation, before the priest and his God—the same God of my grandparents—joining our two separate lives into one.

Trystan slipped a hand into his pocket and pulled out a ring. A golden band that held a large oval shaped diamond with sapphire gems encircling it. He slid it onto my finger, and to my surprise, it was a perfect fit.

"Trystan," I gasped. "It's beautiful."

"It was my mother's ring," he said, holding my hand. "Before she passed away, she gave it to me. She said that if I ever found my one true love, I was to give it to her."

"Was this her wedding ring?" I didn't want something his father had given her. Especially since he'd literally banished me from his kingdom.

"No, it's not," Trystan said with a knowing smile. "It is a family heirloom, passed down from her great-great grandmother."

I held up my hand, admiring the beauty of the shimmering ring. "I don't know what to say. I don't even have a ring to exchange with you."

"Calla, you don't—" Trystan spoke, but I placed a finger to his lips.

"I have nothing but this." I stepped closer to him, taking his hands in mine. Looking up into his eyes, I found them swimming with emotion. "Trystan, we have endured so many challenges, yet through each one, you have remained by my side. Fighting for me. Saving me.

"From this day forward, I will take your hand and will never let go. You are my biggest dream realized. You are my hopes and my future. You are my safe place. You are my home. I may not have a ring to give you, but Trystan—my husband—I willingly and wholeheartedly give you *all* of me."

Trystan's lips quivered. Tears brimmed in those beautiful azure eyes. "My flame. For the rest of my life, you are all I'll ever need." Trystan wrapped his arms around me and pressed his lips against mine. It was a kiss filled with warmth and a deep-seated want.

Father Matteo cleared his throat, throwing us back into reality. "I believe I shall now take my leave," he said, removing his robe and placing it into a bag. Underneath, he was wearing pants and a simple shirt. "As to not draw attention," he replied with a grin. "I have known the prince for a great many years. I am honored to meet the woman he has chosen to be his wife." With that, he turned, bowed at the waist, and quietly left the room.

Wife. I was not only Trystan's mate, but I was now his *wife*.

Trystan captured my waist and tugged me against his solid body. "I need you to transport us someplace," he spoke against my lips.

I was breathless, my pulse racing, my heart hammering against my chest. Every cell in my body was drawn to his.

Seducing.

Begging.

Pleading for us to seal the mating bond—two bonded but not yet consummated.

I could barely think, let alone speak. But I managed a few words. "Where do you wish to go?"

"There is a cottage a few miles away. I want you to transport us there." His voice was rasped. His warm kisses continued down my neck, his teeth and tongue sweeping across my sensitive skin.

I gasped, my body arching into his. "I—I need a location. I need—"

Trystan paused and stepped back, allowing me a moment to catch my breath. He withdrew a folded parchment from his pocket—a map of the Isle of Aria.

"We are here," he said, his finger landing on a large red X on the map. "And I want you to take us here." His finger traced a course that ended at a smaller red X.

"I don't know if I—" I was muted by his mouth crashing over mine.

His kiss was fierce, but brief. Then he spoke against my lips. "You can do it, my flame. I trust you." He then pulled out a small vial of liquid and held it up to me.

I took the vial and twisted it in my fingers. "What is it?"

"A gift from Melaina. To avoid pregnancy. For now." His eyes studied my reaction. "It is a far too dangerous time for us right now, especially being hunted, knowing we are on the brink of war."

Taking the vial from his hand, I popped the top off and poured the bitter liquid down my throat. "Thank you," I said. "I agree with you. It would be brutal to even consider having a child at a time like this."

"But maybe in the future." Trystan shrugged his broad shoulders.

"In the *distant* future," I said with a smile. "I'd like to enjoy my husband for a while."

Trystan laughed and wrapped me in his arms. Handing me the map, I carefully examined it, remembering everything Nicolae had instructed me to do. After I'd memorized the location, I took hold of Trystan's hand and closed my eyes.

"Take me to the cottage," I said to my power. Hoping, praying it would obey.

A tingling warmth flooded my veins as my power carried us through darkness, through the folds of time and space, delivering us right outside a charming cottage made of white stone.

"I did it," I exhaled, proud of myself.

"I had no doubt you could." Trystan leaned over and kissed me again.

Looking up, puffs of white smoke billowed from a chimney. The inside of the cottage was glowing with golden candlelight.

"This is ours for the night." He bent over, swooping me into his arms. The quickness of it made me gasp.

Walking over to the door, he kicked it open and carried me over the threshold. I didn't care what the inside of the cottage looked like. My eyes were locked on my mate. My husband.

Trystan carried me toward a large bed sprinkled with red and cream rose petals and set me down. He removed his crown, setting it on the side table. Then I carefully watched him slip the cloak from his shoulders, letting it drop to the ground.

The air was stifling, and I found it hard to breathe.

Trystan's eyes of glimmering azure darkened, filling with lust. I sucked in a heavy breath as he stepped closer, his fingers trailing down my jaw. My neck.

"Are you ready for me, *wife*?" His voice was like the sweetest honey dripping from his lips. Sinful lips I wanted against mine.

"Yes," I breathed. I had never been more ready.

His fingers gripped the hem of my tunic and then slowly pulled it over my head. His mouth planting fiery kisses along my bare skin, his touch driving me mad, to the brink of insanity.

My fingers trembled as I found his shirt and began unbuttoning it. Trystan helped, sliding out of it, dropping it to the floor where it pooled around our feet with the other discarded clothing.

I placed my hands against his perfectly sculpted chest, tracing them over his tattoos. Those archaic symbols and swirls that marked his toned body.

Over his right shoulder curled a long, barbed tail that ended at his wrist. I needed to see where it began.

His muscles tensed as I dragged my fingers along his smooth skin. Slowly, I strode around him, his heavy-laden eyes carefully watching me. On his back was the most beautiful tattoo I'd ever seen. A large dragon with horns, scales, sharp teeth, and long talons, intricately detailed. There were swirls of air encompassing it. His gift. His element.

He suddenly turned and grabbed my wrists. "Enough lingering," he hissed, lifting me into his arms. I gasped as he dropped me onto the bed, his large frame hovering over me.

"I have been lonely, searching for my mate, living more than two mortal lifetimes waiting for you. The moment I saw the portrait of you and held it in my hands, I experienced something I'd never felt before.

"At first, I didn't understand the unbridled passion and need to find you. I questioned the tether that tugged at my soul, originating from a mortal that lived clear across the continent. And when I met you, the shy, innocent girl standing alone in the darkness, gazing up at the stars, I knew . . . I knew right then that I'd finally found you."

"Trystan," I breathed, but he placed a finger to my lips.

"I didn't want to turn you. But I knew Roehl had sent his men to take you and your family. I couldn't kidnap you and lock you away in Carpathia. So, the only thing I could do, the only thing I could think of to save you, was to claim you as my own. To turn you, so you would have a chance of surviving. And by the slimmest of chances, I left some of my blood in that flask, knowing that if you drank it and sealed the blood bond with me, Roehl wouldn't be able to touch you. But I left it in your hands. I wanted it to be your decision.

"After I bit you, I followed you to your cabin, knowing you would have to endure the change alone. I knew you were confused and frightened. So, I stayed and did what I could to ease your pain and help you through it. Hoping, praying to the gods that when it was over, you wouldn't hate me."

I shook my head. "Yes, I was confused and terrified because I didn't understand who you were, why you'd bitten me, and what was happening to me. But I never hated you, Trystan. I could never hate you. You kept your word and sent your cadre to protect me. You risked your life, and the lives of your men by coming into Morbeth, and again to Incendia. Even in Carpathia, you saved my life while the curse held you, telling you I was your enemy." I sat up on my elbows, his face inches from mine.

"I want you to know that I do believe in fate. I believe that long ago, you were created just for me." Hot tears streamed down my face. Down Trystan's face. I reached a hand up and touched his cheek. "I love you Trystan. I knew it the moment you showed up in Morbeth. When I saw your heart and realized what you had done, what you had given for me.

"I know Roehl knew it too. He knew the secret my heart tried to keep hidden, even from me. That it no longer belonged to me because it had already given itself to you."

Trystan's lips crashed down on mine, soft and gentle. The kind of kiss that carried you some place far, far away. I moaned into his mouth, and he echoed it, his kiss turning wild and unrestrained. The tether holding him back snapped, and the pull of the mating bond became overpowering.

"Don't move," he breathed, his fingers slipping down my waist, hooking into my pants. In one swift movement I was lying bare before him, the only thing that remained was the amulet around my neck and the ring on my finger. Trystan paused, his eyes drinking in my naked body before they snapped up to me. "You're so beautiful," he purred. My cheeks flushed under his heated stare.

His incisors lengthened, and his eyes went black as night.

"Don't be afraid, my flame. You will feel nothing but pleasure tonight."

An inferno raged in my core. The need to have him was overpowering. I could barely control my own urges.

I wanted him.

Craved him.

Needed him closer.

Trystan kneeled on the floor, his hands grasping my thighs. And then . . . then that beautifully sinful mouth pressed against my inner thigh, licking, and kissing a slow—much too slow—and torturous trail upward. My body shuddered with the contact and then — *He bit me.*

I gasped, but the prick of pain instantly turned to pleasure. Groaning, I writhed in his hands which pinned me down, not allowing me to move while his mouth inched higher, biting, and licking and kissing.

My body cried out, hands fisting the sheets, the heat inside my core threatening to consume me.

"Trystan," I gasped as he reached the apex of my thighs.

His dark eyes found mine, and then, he smiled, glancing between my legs. His one lick had me seeing stars.

"Mmm," he moaned. *"You're ready for me."*

He was going to destroy me. Utterly destroy me.

"Trystan." I begged through our bond. I needed him closer, against me. Needed to touch him. Feel him.

Trystan stood and unbuttoned his pants, letting them slide to the floor. My eyes widened, taking him in. Every rock hard, single inch of him was magnificent.

"Do you want me, Calla?" He spoke out loud.

"Yes," I said breathlessly. "I want you. *Now.*" It was a command. I was done playing.

Trystan laughed and situated himself above me. Then, he did something unexpected. Placing his wrist to his mouth, he bit down. Blood flowed from his wound.

"Drink," he said, offering it to me freely. This rare and precious gift of a pureblood prince.

Taking his wrist, I held it to my lips and drank. Drank from my mate, my husband. A wave of euphoria slammed into me, and *goddess above.*

I was burning inside. Burning with desire. His blood was potent—a drug, seductive and erotic, and I was afraid that if he touched me, I would shatter.

Disconnecting from his wrist, my mind and body was lost to the seductive power of his blood. It coursed through me, demanding for us to seal the mating bond.

Turning my head to the side, I gave Trystan access to my shoulder. The place he'd once claimed me. His lips touched that spot, kissing it ever so gently before his teeth sank deep into my flesh.

Ecstasy. It was the only word remotely close to describe the power that coursed through me. Suffused with his powerful essence, I groaned and clawed at his back. Needing to feel his skin against mine. But it wasn't close enough. It was never close enough.

Trystan moved, a sly grin rising on his lips before he captured my mouth. Opening to him, his tongue swept in and twirled around mine. His kiss turned wild and predatory, and then, he spoke through our bond.

"My flame. I claim you, body, mind, and soul."

Trystan slid inside me, torturously slow. I sucked in a breath, feeling a sharp pain, which caused him to pause.

"I'm fine." I exhaled, my vampire gift quickly healing me.

Trystan began to move, slowly at first. Torturously slow.

His darkened eyes pinned me down. "I am yours, Calla."

"And I am yours."

He moved faster, and I moaned, filling with absolute pleasure.

"I love you, Trystan."

"I love you, Calla," he breathed, his mouth capturing mine.

The sound of my name on his lips became my undoing.

Release ripped through me, and I cried out, my body encasing us in flame, intensifying the pleasure. Stars splintered and burst behind my eyes, shattering my entire being. Shattering us both.

And then I felt it. Felt that mating bond lock into place, sealing Trystan and I together. Forever.

Trystan rolled over and pulled my limp, trembling body against his, kissing the top of my forehead.

"How are you feeling?" he breathed, his eyes studying my face.

Glancing at him, into those bright, glimmering eyes, I smiled. "There is no word that could ever describe what I'm feeling right now." I shook my head. "How did I get so lucky?"

Trystan let out a soft laugh. "I am the lucky one." A sexy grin rose on his sinful lips. "Are you hungry?"

I shook my head, and the look in his eyes turned predatory.

"Why? Are you hungry?"

"I am," he purred, sliding back down my body, leaving a trail of hot kisses.

Gods and goddesses.

CHAPTER SEVEN

I WOKE TO RAYS of golden sunlight streaming through the cottage windows.

After a very long night, Trystan and I were satiated. He was sound asleep next to me, his breath slow, chest steadily rising and falling.

I found myself smiling widely from the inside out as I stared at him. I could literally sit and watch him sleep all day—he was perfect, in every way. Never in my life, would I believe that I would wake up in a fairytale. A princess, married to the handsome prince. A prince who was also a knight in shining armor, who would slay the world for her.

My heart swelled with warmth as I gazed at him. It was the first time I'd seen him so still, without worry or care. Over these past months, he'd carried such a tremendous burden. Mostly for the safety of me and my family, and now my friends. And now, this kind and generous man was mine for the rest of my life. I would never take him for granted. However long we would have together.

Trying not to wake him, I slowly slid out of the bed. Plucking Trystan's shirt from the floor, I held it to my nose and breathed in his wonderful scent before wrapping it around me and buttoning it up.

My bare feet gently padded across the slate floor as I made my way toward the kitchen, finally taking a good look at the inside of the cottage. It was an open layout, decorated for royalty in shades of silver, gold, and cream. I had no idea how Trystan had planned this, because there were fresh white roses set within large crystal vases throughout the entire room, and at least a hundred white candles that had burned out during the night.

"You're awake?" Trystan's sleepy voice was deep and husky.

I turned, and the sight of him, bare chested, unkempt hair, tangled up in the sheets—*goddess*—it took everything inside me to not run and jump back on him.

A smirk graced his lips, like he knew what I was contemplating. But we had things to do. An upcoming, inevitable war to plan, and a group of people who were probably up and waiting for us.

"There is a fresh bottle of blood on the counter. You'll need it for your training today." His brows rose, along with a smirk.

I let out a pitiful moan. "Can I skip training? It's our honeymoon."

"You know I would say yes, but no one else knows you are my wife."

His wife. I could get used to him saying that.

I sighed and made my way over to the bottle and poured two glasses of ruby wine, then carried them over to Trystan.

"This cottage is beautiful," I said. "Is it your family's?"

Trystan took the glass and drained it with one sip. "It was built for my mother, but she was never able to enjoy it. Because of her illness, my father kept her at the castle."

"I'm sorry," I breathed, knowing how much he cared for his mother.

"Don't be. I'm happy she is no longer in pain."

"I am too." I wished I'd had a chance to meet the woman who gave him life. She must have been just like him. Beautiful and strong.

"She would have loved you," he said, holding his hand out to me. I took it and sat on the edge of the bed next to him.

"My mother would have loved you, too. I know my father did, before he died. I knew he had already accepted you."

"He did?" Trystan's eyes narrowed on me.

"Yes," I said, my mind flashing back to the moment in Morose Mountain. The moment just before he died. "My father smiled at me, and that smile spoke so loud and clear. It told me that he loved me, and he was happy I had finally found someone worthy of my love, who loved me back. That you were someone he approved of."

Trystan nodded, his expression saddened. "I went to Aquaris to save your father's life, but in turn, he was the one who saved mine."

"My father loved me, more than life. He did what he did because he knew I needed you."

Trystan grabbed my hand and placed it over his heart. "If I have to, I will slay the world for you."

I fell into his arms, and he hugged me tightly. I felt so safe enfolded in his arms, I never wanted to leave.

"You look good in my shirt." He whispered in my ear. I looked up and saw a sinister grin as his fingers started to unbutton it. "But you look even better with it off."

Trystan lifted the bedsheet, and I lost all thought and reason.

"Come, my flame," he rasped. "Come and set me on fire."

CHAPTER EIGHT

IT WAS NOON WHEN we finally made it to the main house. Trystan had one of the servants bring my training gear and a warm coat, and I transported us back, delivering us right outside the front door.

"Your powers are stronger, even after our morning session," Trystan teased, kissing my neck.

"What about the ring?" I rasped, twirling it on my finger. "We can't let anyone know about the marriage. Especially Brynna. She would never forgive me."

Trystan removed his hands from my body and held out his hand. "How about I make it an official engagement? However, they will know we sealed the mating bond as soon as we step inside."

"They will? How?" My pulse started racing.

"The vampires will scent me all over you, and you all over me."

"Goddess. I hope they don't say anything."

"Do you expect anything less from my men?"

I couldn't help but feel anxious. "I really don't care what they think about the mating bond, but I do think an engagement will be perfect. My mortal friends will be looking forward to it and will be thrilled to be a part of it."

He tucked the ring into his pocket. "Then we will play our roles. I will get down on one knee, and you will act excited."

I smiled and threw my arms around his neck and kissed his lips. "I won't need to act."

"Mmm," he hummed against my lips. "I thought we were going to be discreet."

"We are," I said, stepping back. "I couldn't help myself."

When we entered the house, we heard voices in the dining area. It was lunch, so they'd all gathered. As soon as Trystan and I entered the room, they fell silent.

Trystan pulled out a chair for me, and then sat down, raising his brows at his men.

"What? No wise ass remarks this afternoon?" Trystan asked.

"Nope," Andrés said, taking a sip from his goblet. "We promised Nicolae that we wouldn't discuss your—" he paused, searching for a word.

Brone sighed and shook his head. "We promised we wouldn't discuss your mating bond at the dining table."

"Good," I huffed. "Our bond is private, anyway."

Andrés sniffed the air, a knowing smile grew on his lips. "But we can totally discuss it after lunch."

Gods. I rolled my eyes and sucked in a deep breath.

"I thought you would be in a better mood," Sabine giggled. "Drink something. You're cranky."

I gasped, my mouth dropped agape. "I am not cranky."

Sabine crossed her arms over her chest and gave me a pointed look. "Mmm-hmm."

Nicolae dabbed a napkin on his lips. "After lunch, we'll train."

"I'm ready." I also grabbed my goblet. This entire lunch was awkward. Every vampire in the room, including Nicolae, knew Trystan and I had sealed the mating bond.

"Calla, you're glowing," Sabine finally said, giving me a sheepish smile. I sighed. They all must have known. There was no use in hiding it.

"Am I?" I pressed my fingers to my cheeks.

She nodded. "Did you . . . sleep well? Or . . . at all?"

"You're pushing the boundaries of our bargain," Thalia whispered, nudging Sabine in the side.

"Where's Markus, Brynna, and Melaina?" I asked, noticing they weren't at the table.

"They're upstairs," Sabine replied. "Markus is probably sleeping. You know him . . . Mister Night Owl. And Melaina's aunt is doing her tracking magic on Brynna. They should be down shortly."

"I think we should wait until Brynna is here for the proposal," I said to Trystan through our bond.

"I agree. I'll hold on to it until the time is right. I might even surprise you."

"I love surprises."

Trystan grabbed the bottle of ruby wine in front of us. "Have another glass," he said, pouring some in my goblet. "I will not go easy on you today."

"Oh my," Sabine exhaled, fanning herself.

I laughed and shook my head. "Trystan is going to help train me. I'll finally learn how to manipulate air."

"Well," she waved her hands at me. "Drink up then."

"Any word from your father?" Kylan asked Trystan.

"No. My father is busy getting ready for the winter festival."

"Winter festival?" Sabine asked before I could.

"It's a huge celebration with music and dancing, lanterns and wreaths and lots of food," Kylan replied. "The castle in Carpathia throws the best celebrations."

I suddenly felt sad. I loved celebrations, but in Carpathia, the home of my husband, I wasn't even welcome. I was an outcast, who the king himself forced to leave. He banished me, saying I was a troublemaker, causing his son to neglect his princely duties.

What would he say, or do, when he found out we were married and had sealed the mating bond? I didn't want to think about it.

Anxiety was building inside. I had to stop worrying over things that weren't in my control.

Nicolae scooted his chair back and stood. "Are you ready?"

"Yes," I said, jumping up a little too quickly. Trystan gave me a side-eyed smirk, knowing I wasn't looking forward to training. But I would do anything at this point to keep my mind busy.

I looked over to Kylan who was slouched in his chair, elbow resting on the table. "What are you guys going to do today?" I asked. The sun was shining outside, so I knew they had to stay indoors.

Kylan let out a deep sigh. "I think I am going to take Markus's lead and head upstairs for a nap."

"Me too," Brone exhaled. "We rarely get days like these where we have nothing to do." He cupped his hand behind his ear. "Wait, I hear something."

Everyone turned to him, waiting for his response. Then, Brone rolled his eyes.

"Oh, it's just my bed calling. She's lonely," he said, a wide smirk curling on his lips.

I couldn't help but laugh out loud. "Brone, you need a woman."

"What woman would want this brute? He's angry and a handful," Andrés chuckled.

Brone sneered at him. "Your mouth will get a handful if you don't shut it."

"See what I mean?" Andrés was about to say something else when I interjected.

"I believe there is someone for everyone . . . including Brone."

Brone glanced at me, and I gave him a wink. He smiled and made his way out of the dining room.

"What about you, Feng?" I asked, noticing he was quiet, as usual, sipping on his wine. "Are you going to nap, too?"

Feng shrugged his shoulders. "I think I will finish my carving."

I remembered the carving he started the first time we'd met. "Will I get to see it when it's done?"

Feng glanced at me with surprise in his eyes. "If you like."

"I would love to."

"Then, of course."

"Rest up," Trystan said to his men, linking his fingers in mine. "You're all on night watch."

He then led me out of the house.

We didn't go to the stable to train because I'd be using all my elements, and I didn't think the chickens would appreciate getting roasted before their time was up.

On the island, nearly half a mile away, Trystan directed us to a small clearing where his men had trained a few times. When we arrived, it seemed like the perfect place.

The clearing was circular, about one hundred yards in circumference, hemmed in with thick spruce and pine trees.

"Go stand in the center," Nicolae spoke. "Trystan and I will stay here."

Snow crunched under my boots as I made my way out to the center of the clearing. The sun was shining, but there was a bite in the cold wintery breeze. Soon, my body adjusted to the temperature and began to warm.

I let my head fall back, soaking in the sun's rays. It felt wonderful and rejuvenating.

"You're a vision," Trystan said through the bond. *"Do well today, and I will reward you tonight."*

My insides heated as I glanced over to where he was standing with arms crossed over his broad chest. He gave me a sexy, dimpled grin.

"If you keep looking at me like that, I won't be able to concentrate."

"Calla," Nicolae hollered. "Let's start with something you know. How about water?"

He was really going to put me to the test today.

But first, if I was going to practice, I needed something to destroy. I took a knee and placed my fingers in the snow, melting it so I could touch the earth. About forty feet away, large roots shot up from the ground, twisting and turning, creating a root mannequin. It was a simple thought that manifested right before my eyes.

I turned my head to the side, a sly grin on my lips. Both Nicolae and Trystan nodded, with glints of pride in their eyes.

"Impressive." Trystan winked at me, setting butterflies to flight in my belly.

"Well done," Nicolae said. "Now, let's see what you've got."

Standing, I raised my hands in front of me, palms down. Flames enveloped me, the snow within a ten-foot radius melted until I was standing in a puddle of water. Fisting my palms, I extinguished the flames. Then, I called water, and one after another, water daggers came to me. Focusing on the root mannequin, I threw them. One by one, they hit their mark.

Feeling stronger than ever, I called a water sword into my hand while sprinting toward the root man. On instinct alone, I called to the air, thrusting my left palm down. A blast of wind had me shooting upward, over the root man. Forward flipping, midair, I landed on my feet directly behind it, then swung my sword around, and decapitated the poor thing.

Goddess. That was a rush.

"You are a force to be reckoned with," Trystan spoke.

Nicolae clapped his hands. "Well done, Calla. You executed that perfectly, using all four elements in one strike."

Wow, I guess I did. "I literally killed a stickman, who didn't move or fight back." I laughed. The water sword dropped into a puddle at my feet.

"Well, you looked absolutely kick-ass doing it." Trystan strode toward me, stopping a foot away. He took my hands and held them up in front of me. "Like all the other elements, air is already a part of you." He placed his palms over mine and closed his eyes. "Concentrate, my flame. Summon the air to you."

Closing my eyes, Trystan's power surged through me, through my palms and the rest of my body. It stirred in my blood, seeping deep into bone and marrow. The feeling was euphoric and exhilarating.

And then, the surrounding wind began to pick up.

"Trystan," I gasped.

"Open your eyes."

I did as he said, my eyes opening, fixed on his. I was mesmerized, bewitched by him. Bewitched by the swirls of silver in those azure eyes.

We were surrounded by a massive air funnel imbued with flame and water and bits of earth that sealed us off from the outside world. The sky darkened and lightning cracked above us, around us, through us. I was hyper aware of everything around me.

"What's happening?" I breathed.

"It's us. Our powers, together. A benefit of being mated," he spoke, a sultry smile lifting over elongated incisors.

We were one, our bond deepening and intensifying our powers. There was so much energy, so much power being exchanged between us that I could barely breathe. Trystan laced his fingers in mine, grounding me. His touch was calming, the eye in the middle of a raging storm.

"Don't be afraid, my flame. Embrace it."

I let go of the fear holding me back, letting it out with a breath, when suddenly we were lifted off the ground, rising into the air. Thunder roared and lightning cracked around us as air, fire, water, and earth spun around us.

Trystan's eyes turned black. I blinked, and everything in my own vision turned red.

Flame and wind coiled around our bodies, binding us, binding our power. It was fate. Trystan and I were meant to be. Air was a fuel to fire. It fed it. Nurtured it. Gave it strength.

The power between us was raw and potent, like nothing I'd ever experienced before.

"Together we are a storm," he spoke, his breath against my lips. "A fury that cannot be quenched."

There was a roaring in my ears, and then . . . I heard Nicolae's voice.

"Calla," he hollered through our connection. *"Calla, there is trouble. It's Brynna."*

My focus faltered, and Trystan grabbed me. *"What's wrong?"*

"We have to go back. Brynna is in trouble."

"Transport us," Trystan said. "Take us back to Nicolae."

I closed my eyes and in a split second, we were no longer floating in the wind funnel, but standing in front of Nicolae. Thalia was also there, on horseback.

I ran from Trystan's arms to her. "What's wrong?"

"Melaina's aunt did her witch thing and found a dark stain inside of Brynna. She suspects a tracer from some dark and ancient magic. When she tried to break the connection, it backfired, and she was badly injured."

A rush of fear surged through me. "Where is Brynna? How is she?"

"She is safe. She's terrified, but she's fine."

"Go," Trystan said to me. "Take her back."

I nodded at him, then touched Thalia and the horse she had ridden in on, focusing on the main house. Darkness surrounded us, and in a moment, it dissolved, delivering us right where I'd pictured in my mind.

CHAPTER NINE

THALIA SLID OFF THE horse as I ran inside the front door. Sabine was there, her eyes wide with fright and brimming with tears. Grabbing my hand, she hauled me into the kitchen. "Roehl knows where we are because he is using Brynna. What are we going to do? No matter where we go, he will find us."

I sucked in a deep breath, trying to calm my fraying nerves. "I don't know yet, but I can't leave her. I can't send her anywhere where she is unprotected. If Roehl finds her, he will take her and use her as bait against me. She's my best friend, Sabine. I can't let that happen."

"I know," she sighed, wiping the tears that had fallen down her face. "I'm just terrified. For all we know, Roehl could be on his way here, right now."

"We'll figure out a way, I promise," I said. "But I have to see Brynna first."

Sabine grabbed my hand. "She's upstairs in her room. Melaina's with her aunt." Sabine's eyes narrowed. "She's injured pretty badly, Calla."

I let out a deep sigh. Things were starting to spiral out of control, but I centered myself and headed toward the stairs. Melaina's room was closest, so I knocked on her door first.

"Come in," Melaina said, her voice soft.

Opening the door, I found her sitting on a chair, holding Ophelia's hand. Her aunt looked like she was sleeping. Her eyes were closed, a blanket over her chest and legs.

"How is she?" I whispered.

Melaina shook her head. "I knew there was something dark inside Brynna. I just didn't know it was that powerful."

I kneeled next to Melaina's chair, taking hold of her free hand. "What happened?"

Melaina shook her head, a stray tear trickling down her freckled cheek. "Ophelia performed her ritual, and I instantly knew from the look in her eyes, something was wrong. She pulled me to the side, but Brynna demanded to know the truth. So, my aunt told her what she found. There is a dark stain inside Brynna. A spell put there by Roehl. It's dark magic. A spell which was supposed to remain hidden, but sometimes, when spells are so powerful, they leak." Her worried eyes slid to mine. "Roehl knows exactly where Brynna is. He's known since she left Morbeth." She shook her head and closed her eyes. "I shouldn't have brought Aunt Ophelia here. She tried to remove the spell, but it was designed to fight back. It injured her, but I don't know how badly. We are in danger, even now. No matter where we go, he'll find us."

I had to see Brynna. I couldn't imagine the things going through her mind. We'd left on a bad note last night, I just hoped she wasn't still mad. I needed her to trust me, now more than ever.

"I'm so sorry, Melaina," I said standing, laying my hand on her shoulder. "As soon as Nicolae and Trystan arrive, we'll figure out a plan."

She nodded, turning her attention back to Ophelia, so I made my way out of the room.

My mind was a whirlwind, my chest tightening as I made my way to Brynna's door. Would she even let me in if I knocked? I decided not to give her a choice.

Stepping up to the door, I grabbed the knob and twisted, pushing inside.

I found Brynna sobbing in a heap on the floor, a knife pressed to her wrist.

"Brynna," I wailed, throwing my palm out. A burst of wind dislodged the knife from her palm and sent it hurling toward me. I caught it, as if it were headed to me in slow motion, then tossed it behind me. Running and dropping to the floor in front of her I wrapped my arms around her. "Brynna, what the hell were you thinking?"

"I can't," she sobbed. "I can't live like this, Cal. I have some freaking dark curse attached to me, that is leading that bastard directly to us. You're all in danger because of me."

"Don't ever try to take your life again. Ever," I said, tears rolling down my face. "I would never forgive myself, or you, if you killed yourself." I grabbed her by the shoulders and made her look at me. "Listen to me, we *will* find a way to stop him. I promise you. But you have to promise me that you will never try to take your own life again." Loud sobs ripped from her chest as she fell forward, into my arms. "Bryn, promise me."

"I promise," she cried.

I held her, stroking her hair, wishing there was a way for me to help her. Maybe Nicolae would have some answers.

After a few minutes passed, there was a soft rapping at the door.

"Come in," I said, still holding Brynna in my arms. It was Trystan and Nicolae.

"Melaina told us what happened," Trystan said, standing next to me.

"What do we do?" I questioned, glancing between the two of them.

Trystan took a knee. "I think the only option we have right now is to take her back to Carpathia. She was safe in the castle.

No one would dare try to break into our kingdom. Not with our guards and witches protecting the place."

"Would your father take her back knowing she's connected to me?"

"I am the future king of Carpathia, and she will be under my protection. I will make sure she has guards and maids watching her until we finish what Roehl started."

"I don't want to go back there," Brynna begged, grasping my shoulders.

My heart was torn, but I knew Trystan was right. Having her go back to Carpathia was the best plan we had. And with Trystan's assurance, I at least knew that Brynna would be safe there.

"Listen, Bryn. You won't be there for long. We will have to confront that bastard in fifteen days, and after that, I promise I will come and get you. I'll take you back to Sartha and hand deliver you to Claude."

Brynna shook her head. "What if he kills you? What will happen to me then?"

"Calla is my mate and under my protection," Trystan said. "I will not allow anything to happen to her."

"Neither will I," Nicolae added.

"See, Bryn. We will be okay. We just have to be apart for a few weeks, but after that, you and I will be able to heal and move on with our lives. Okay?"

Brynna leaned back, glancing down at her wrist. There was a red mark there, but she hadn't broken skin. "Okay," she whispered. "I'll go."

I was a little shocked I didn't have to fight harder to get her to go. Brynna was headstrong and always had to be right. But this time, with our lives on the line, she knew she couldn't win.

"Can I talk to you outside?" Trystan asked through our bond.

I glanced at him, tipping my head, then turned back to Brynna. "I'll be right back and when I do, I'll help you get your things packed."

Brynna nodded as Trystan offered me his hand, pulling me up to my feet.

Nicolae offered to escort Brynna down to get something to eat and I was again surprised she agreed. I twisted back to look at her and my heart fractured. I'd never seen her so broken. She was hollow, just going through the motions.

I had to believe things would be better. We just had to hold on, believing that we would win against Roehl.

What I didn't understand was if he knew where Brynna was, why hadn't he launched an all-out attack, catching us off guard? All I could think was that he still wasn't sure if he could defeat us. And those token men he'd sent after us were just a distraction, to keep us uneasy as he gathered his army and mages and powers to defeat us.

Roehl wasn't stupid. He'd seen my power. I'd gotten away from him twice, but I knew this next time would be the last encounter I would have with him. One of us had to die.

Would it be Roehl? Or me?

Outside, Trystan pulled me to the side of the house. "I only suggested this because she is your friend."

"I know," I exhaled, falling into his embrace. "And I know I won't be able to go."

"Not yet. But while I am there, I will try to meet with my father."

My eyes snapped up to him. "Are you going to tell him about us?"

"You are my wife, Calla, and that is not going to change. I am going to tell him that I have chosen you. You are my princess and the future queen of Carpathia. There will be no debate."

"What if he exiles you?"

Trystan laughed and hugged me tighter. "I am his only heir. No matter what my father thinks about me or my decisions, he would never banish me."

"Will Nicolae be transporting you?"

"Yes."

"I am going to speak to her first, but I really want Sabine to go with Brynna. They are the only mortals, besides Melaina. They have no way of protecting themselves from Roehl's magic. But I know Sabine. She'll fight me, tooth and nail, to stay."

"She will. But you'll have to voice your concerns. Just like you did with Brynna. Having them around will not only be a danger to themselves, but it will be putting us at risk too. It will be too hard to try to keep them safe while we are fighting our own battles. We need to make sure they are protected. And within the castle walls of Carpathia, they will be."

"You're right. I'll go talk to her now."

"I'll be taking Andrés with me. Kylan, Feng, and Brone will stay."

"I'm going to miss you."

"I'll make up for it tonight when we return."

"Then, I'll look forward to tonight."

Back inside, I went to find Sabine. She was with Thalia and Brynna at the table.

I walked into the room, and they all looked at me. Brynna still looked terrible, her blue eyes were bloodshot and void of expression.

"Sabine," I called. "Can I talk to you for a moment?"

She excused herself from the table and followed me across the foyer into a small sitting area. "What's up?" she finally asked, plopping down into a soft cushioned armchair.

I exhaled, not knowing how to ask her. Sabine shook her head and threw her arms over her chest. "Girl, I may not have known you as long as Brynna, but I do know what's going on in your mind. You are worried and want me to go to Carpathia to look after your friend, don't you?" My eyes widened, and words eluded me. "Calla, you've shown concern this entire time about keeping your mortal friends safe. I realize the situation is getting worse, and we won't be much good to you in battle. So, this time, I will listen." She angled her head at me. "That is what you were going to ask me, right?"

I let out a breathy laugh. "Goddess, I was so worried you wouldn't understand."

"I know," she snickered. "And if circumstances were different, I would go along with you. But I know Markus has also been worried. I have zero powers and can't fight to save my life. If I stayed, it would be for my own selfish reasons. That's not who I am."

"No," I breathed. "You are the furthest thing from selfish, Sabine, and one of the fiercest, loyalist friends I have. You risked your life to save me. Down in the dark cells of Morbeth, it was your blood that kept me alive and gave me hope. You also brought Summer, who assisted in breaking the binding on my power. You, my friend, have always been there when I needed you. You are my hero, Sabine, and I will never forget it."

Sabine stood to her feet and strode over to me, wrapping her arms around my neck. "I wish I could go with you, but I am thankful Trystan will protect you now, along with the others. I know they will fight bravely alongside you. Meanwhile, Brynna and I will be praying and waiting for your safe return."

"Thank you. We will need your prayers."

Sabine grabbed my arms, her expression turned serious. "So, between us, is there anything I should know about Brynna? Is she okay? Like, is the curse going to make her do crazy things? Should I be worried for my safety?"

I laughed. "No, she is fine. The curse is a tracer. It allows Roehl to know where she is."

"And you're sure we'll be safe in Carpathia?"

"Trystan has assured me that there will be guards on duty to watch you both, and maids to make sure you are well taken care of. Roehl wouldn't dare break into Carpathia. Trystan said their army is strong and so are their witches. He will make sure they all know about Roehl, so they will be making sure security is extra tight."

"Okay," she exhaled. "What about the rest of you? Roehl knows where you are right now."

"Once they return, we will also have to move. We can't stay here."

Sabine grinned. "Good, then I'll go get my things."

We met outside right after the sun had set. Everyone except Melaina and her Aunt Ophelia. The plan was for Nicolae to take Trystan and Andrés first, then come back for Sabine and Brynna.

Trystan held me in his arms. "I'll be back in a few hours."

Nicolae ambled toward us. "Calla, if anything should happen, get yourself to safety. You can transport now."

"Yes," Trystan added. "You are my priority. My men can take care of themselves. Do you understand?"

"I understand."

Trystan went to his men and gave them one order. To protect me at all costs. I just hoped the moving of Brynna to Carpathia would make Roehl think we were all moving.

"I'll see you soon, husband."

"Very soon, wife."

Trystan's lips raised in a sexy smile as Nicolae lay a hand on his and Andrés' shoulders. And with a blink, they were gone.

Sabine said her goodbye to Markus, then I wrapped both her and Brynna in one last hug. Brynna grabbed my hand. "Don't you dare die, Cal. I will never forgive you if you do."

"I will promise you this, I will fight and burn the world to ash to stay alive."

A smile cracked on Brynna's face. "Good. Because I need you." I gave her one last hug, then pivoted to Sabine. "Make sure she stays busy."

"We will have two weeks being in the castle. I'm sure we can find something fun to do." Sabine looked at Thalia who was standing behind me. "Take care of Thalia. She's one of our sisters now."

"Don't worry. Thalia is an Incendian. We are a lot tougher than you think."

Nicolae reappeared right in front of us, making Sabine gasp. "Goddess, I nearly peed myself." We all broke out into laughter as she hooked her arm in Brynna's. "Let's go tracer girl."

Brynna gave Sabine a narrowed glare, but Nicolae touched their shoulders and they vanished.

My heart ached for a moment, but I was also relieved because I knew that in Trystan's hands, they'd be safe.

"So, Calla," Kylan called from behind. "Want to train with us?"

"No thanks. I've already trained with Trystan."

Brone crossed his muscular arms over his broad chest. "Oh, so we're not good enough for you?"

"Quite the opposite. I'd like to keep my dignity and my limbs. I've seen you all train, and I don't think I could ever move like you."

"With your powers, you won't have to move," Feng noted.

"True," Kylan agreed. "I think you'd give us a good run."

I gazed into the cloud covered sky, tapping my finger to my chin. "Maybe if Thalia trains with me."

Thalia shook her head and took a step away from me. "No thanks. I'll watch."

"Okay, I'm in," I said. "Let me grab a quick drink and I'll be right out."

As I turned to head inside the house, Melaina burst out of the door. "Help me. My aunt is dying. Whatever curse Roehl put inside Brynna is killing her. I have to take her back to Hale. Her coven is the only one who can save her."

Markus was suddenly behind me. "Calla, don't you think about leaving," he growled.

"Markus, please. Not now," I said, grabbing Melaina's hand. "Take me to her."

We ran inside, up the grand staircase and into Melaina's room. Inside, Ophelia was lying in her bed, still, eyes closed, looking very peaceful. Melaina walked over and tugged down the blanket, revealing her aunt's chest and arms. Black spidery veins were slowly crawling up her pale skin.

I took a step closer when Ophelia's bright red eyes popped open. She gasped, grabbing and clawing at my arm.

"Help me," she moaned, her lips quivering. Then, her eyes rolled back, and she fell backward onto the pillow, unconscious.

"Calla, please," Melaina wailed, grabbing my hands, and falling to her knees. "Please, I have to take her home. I have to take her now or she'll die."

I promised Trystan that I would stay on the island, but I had to help Melaina.

Even though she swore she would never enter Morbeth, Melaina had risked her life, coming directly into that hellish place to rescue me. She also kept her word to me by taking Brynna to safety when Trystan had given her a direct order to bring *me* back.

There was no way I could turn her down. I had to help her. What would the witches in Hale think if we stood by and watched one of their own die? Trystan was the one who hired Melaina so it would fall on him, and as his wife and mate, I would not allow that to happen.

My father taught me that if it was within my power to do good, then I must do it. This was no exception. Our names and reputations were on the line, and all the witches in Hale would be watching. Judging. Would we stand by and let an innocent witch die—a witch who willingly offered to help us? Or would we do everything we could to save her?

There was no debate.

I knew what I had to do. I just had to let the guys know, even though I knew they would be dead set against it. I never expected them to understand. They had taken an oath to the Carpathian throne, and their prince gave them an order. To ensure my safety.

I was their main priority.

I wasn't going to tell Trystan or Nicolae, because right now, they were securing the safety of Brynna and Sabine in Carpathia. That was something that had to be done. It was a major priority for me, and I didn't want them rushing back, leaving my best friends unattended and vulnerable.

Besides, all I had to do was transport Melaina and Ophelia directly to Hale and transport myself right back. The only reservation I had was that I'd only practiced transporting one person at a time. I also never traveled further than the radius of the island. Hale was hundreds of miles away, and I knew this transport would be pushing my power and limits. Especially with two passengers. But I was willing to try, with or without the consent of Markus and Trystan's men.

CHAPTER TEN

"I'LL HELP YOU," I said, grabbing Melaina's hand. "But I have to go and talk to the guys first."

"Thank you," she sobbed. "Thank you."

Ophelia suddenly gasped for air, moaning. I watched those cursed black veins crawl even further up her neck, reaching her jawline.

"Hurry," Melaina pleaded. "Please hurry."

Rushing out the door, I spotted Trystan's cadre, along with Markus, down at the bottom of the stairs.

"Follow me," I said, reaching them, heading for the sitting room. They followed in silence. Once in the room, Markus closed the door and every one of them looked at Kylan, like he was their spokesperson. Kylan exhaled and took a step toward me, running a hand through his thick raven hair. His turquoise eyes landed on mine, begging, pleading.

"Calla, please. Trystan will murder us if we let you leave the island."

I had to remain calm, but I also had to stand my ground.

"Listen," I spoke. "Melaina's aunt will die if she doesn't return to Hale."

"We can take her. There is a ship on the far side of the island," Kylan said. "We can leave right away."

"She won't last a day. You know it'll take at least three days to sail to Hale from here." I faced all of them. "Nicolae has been training me to transport, and I've completed each one with no trouble. All I am asking is to allow me to take Melaina and Ophelia to Hale, deliver them safely, and come right back."

"Can you take one of us with you?" Feng asked.

I shook my head. "Nicolae can only transport two people at a time. If he can only take two, I won't risk the transport by taking any more than that. I want this to be as smooth and stress free as possible."

Markus stepped forward. "If you take them, you better transport your ass right back here. I'm serious, princess. You drop her off and head right back."

"I don't plan on staying. I just want to help Melaina, since she's been there for all of us."

"Are you going to tell Nicolae and Trystan?" Brone asked.

"No," I replied. "There is no need to bother them right now. They are busy getting Sabine and Brynna set up, and

Trystan had an important meeting with his father. It's totally unnecessary to bother him. Besides, I'll be back before they return."

Kylan was pacing the floor. "You underestimate how protective he is over you. If he finds out—"

"Don't worry about Trystan," I interjected. "If he were here, he would do the same. You all know he would. He will understand why I am going."

Feng walked up to me. "I agree that Trystan would understand." He bowed his head. "I wish you a safe and quick return, princess."

I reached out and grabbed Feng's hand. "As do I."

Markus shook his head, letting out a heavy sigh. "There and back. No deviating."

"I know." Thankful they were letting me go, I quickly headed for the door before they changed their mind. "Thank you for understanding."

Back in Melaina's room, Markus, Kylan, Brone, and Feng all stood against a wall, while I stood in front of Melaina and her aunt.

Kylan had found a map, so Melaina pinpointed exactly where we were supposed to go. Her hometown wasn't on that map, but she put a small circle around the exact area. Within her circle was a small town called Neverton, which sat on the outskirts of Hale, near the border of Baelfast.

Neverton was a town where witches dwelled and was heavily warded and veiled from the outside world. Melaina assured me that if we landed anywhere inside the town, we would be safe. Hearing that settled some of my anxiety, and the anxiety of the men in the room.

Kylan ambled toward me and whispered, "Are you sure you can do this?"

I nodded. I had to do this. There was no turning back now. "Yes," I said confidently.

My confidence must have shown, because Kylan gave me a knowing smile and placed a fist to his heart. "Then return to us safely, princess."

I gave him a nod, then took a knee on the side of the bed, taking Melaina and Ophelia's hands in mine. Closing my eyes, I pictured the map in my mind and focused on the center of the little red circle.

"Take us to Neverton," I said to my power.

Ophelia's bloodshot eyes snapped open, and she let out a bloodcurdling scream, digging her nails into my flesh as darkness enveloped us. The pain broke my concentration as we traveled within the folds of space.

When the surrounding darkness evaporated, I held Ophelia down as Melaina withdrew a small flask from her pouch and poured it into her aunt's mouth. In seconds, her eyes closed. She stopped fighting and went limp.

Taking in my surroundings, I had a feeling we weren't in Hale. We were in the middle of a dry and barren desert. The wintery air was chilled, but there was no snow on the ground, which was odd.

"No, no, no," Melaina wailed, shaking her head. Her hand gripped my arm, a finger aiming behind us.

In the distance was a massive wall spanning for miles. My breath punched out of me, and I suddenly felt sick to my stomach.

The Red Wall. *Goddess, help us.*

We weren't in Hale. We were near the border of Morbeth and were sitting in the middle of Dead Man's Land.

"Calla, you have to get us out of here. Now," Melaina urged, her eyes wide with fright.

I nodded, gathering my thoughts, focusing back on Neverton. On that red circle Melaina had drawn. Taking hold of Melaina and Ophelia's hands, I spoke to my power. *"Take us to Neverton."*

But the darkness never came.

"Why aren't we going?" Melaina wailed. "Calla, we have to leave!"

I couldn't feel my power. "My powers. They are suppressed."

Melaina muttered a spell and when it didn't work, her eyes grew even wider.

"Whatever it is, it's dark and powerful. My magic isn't working either." She stood and paced back and forth, running her fingers through her wild red hair. I'd never seen her this unhinged. "We have to call for help," she said, her eyes boring through me.

"Anyone I call will be stuck here too. I won't risk any more lives."

"We can't stay here, Calla! Roehl probably has a tracking spell locked on you right now." She was starting to hyperventilate, and her anxiousness was making my own stress grow.

I tried to call my power, again and again. And each time, I felt nothing. Not even a stirring inside. This was Roehl's doing. And his mages. It was the same spell they'd used on Morose Mountain.

"What the hell is that?" Melaina shrieked, pointing to the sky above the Red Wall. An ominous black cloud was heading in our direction.

"Roehl knows we're here," she cried. "If he catches us, we'll die. We have to leave."

Shit, shit, shit. This was exactly what I didn't want to happen. How the hell did I end up here? This was supposed to be easy. A quick transport to Hale and back.

The dark cloud was coming fast, nearly one hundred yards away. I had to think. There had to be a way out of this. I called to my power again. Demanded it come. But there was nothing. It was as if it were dead.

"Flint," I screamed both in my mind and out loud, remembering what Helia—the Fire Goddess—had told me. That he would come to me when I needed him most. *"Flint, I need you!"*

Melaina's hands were raised toward the cloud. "I can feel it," she said, her lips and body trembling. "It's the shadow of death. A dark and ancient magic that expels life."

I could also feel it. The frigid air was humming with an evil power. I could almost hear the whispers of death floating on the breeze, coming, promising eternal rest to every living thing in its path.

"Flint!" I begged. *"Please, come to me."*

I hadn't seen him since we'd left Nicolae's island and headed to Carpathia. He could have been anywhere.

"We're going to die," Melaina sobbed, dropping to her knees, covering her aunt's body with her own. She was giving up, and there was nothing I could do or say to help. I had no power and no access to it.

Was this it? Was our time up?

The dark cloud grew closer. I could feel the tendrils of wicked power vibrating from it, suffocating everything in its path. Sucking all life forces from the earth and air as it passed over.

"Calla, where are you?" Trystan's voice ripped through our bond like a tidal wave. I could taste his anxiety. Felt it rattle through my bones.

How did he know?

"Please, don't come," were the first words out of my mouth. *"Our magic is dead here. It's a trap."*

"Where the hell are you?" he demanded, his voice strained. *"Are you in Morbeth?"*

Could he see me? Was it the amulet?

"Calla!" Melaina wailed, gasping for air.

The cloud was upon us, surrounding us in darkness. I dropped to my knees as its dark power squeezed the air from my lungs and burned my skin. I couldn't breathe. Couldn't see. Couldn't move.

We were dying.

I could hear Trystan yelling through the bond. He was trying to find our location, but I didn't want him to come. He needed to live and be there for his people. For his men. And to make sure my friends were safe. I knew he would fight Roehl alongside Nicolae for me.

"I love you," I said through our bond. *"Thank you for loving me."*

Trystan cursed, and I suddenly heard Nicolae's voice also calling me. But I couldn't think. Pain wracked my body. I could feel my life force being drained from me, when —

A loud shriek reverberated around me. Opening my burning eyes, I witnessed a violent flame burst through the darkness. *Flint.*

I felt him enter my chest, and then, like a shockwave, my power returned. It roared through my veins and echoed through my blood and marrow.

Calling to my power, I threw my arms upward. Energy exploded from me, from my entire being. Fire and air and earth answered, detonating through the blackness surrounding us, through that wicked cloud. As if it were alive, the dark spell screamed and hissed as my power disintegrated it, until there was nothing left.

Flint exited my body as a firebird and took off into the sky, leaving a trail of flame behind him.

"I love you, Flint," I called after him. He let out another loud screech before shifting back into the black crow and flying away. My love for that troublemaking bird was growing stronger every time we came into contact. He had proven he was truly a gift from the Fire Goddess, showing up when I needed him most.

Melaina was lying across Ophelia, her body still. I bent down and placed my fingers under her nose. She wasn't breathing. Gods above. This couldn't be happening.

"Melaina, get up," I demanded. "Get up!"

She didn't move, didn't respond, so I pushed my palm against her back and felt a surge of power exit me.

Melaina's eyes suddenly snapped open, and she gasped for air. Coughing and coughing, she vomited black ooze, and then she passed out.

Grabbing hold of her and Ophelia's hands, I spoke to my power. *"Take us to Neverton."*

In an instant we were gone, folded within a calm and familiar darkness.

When that darkness dissipated, we were delivered right into the middle of a small town. Men and women and children stopped and immediately circled us, most with wide, cautious eyes. Gasps erupted and many raised their wands, pointing them at me.

"Is this Neverton?" I asked, desperate, to anyone who would answer.

"Yes," a girl around ten replied. Her wide brown eyes were affixed to my face.

I looked down and realized my body was encompassed in flame. With a thought, the flames extinguished.

"Help them. Please," I begged, looking at the wary faces. "Ophelia and Melaina are from Neverton. There was a curse on them placed by Morbeth's mages."

An elderly woman with a weathered face and white hair hobbled forward.

"Goddess," she gasped, before immediately giving orders to the others around her. Five men came forward, carrying both Ophelia and Melaina away, while a flock of women followed, all murmuring.

"Calla? Calla, are you there?" Trystan's voice was strained, calling through the bond.

"We're safe," I replied. *"We're in Neverton."*

"Gods, Calla. I thought something horrible had happened to you."

"Something horrible did happen. But we're okay now. I'll tell you all about it tonight."

"Why are you in Neverton?"

"When Ophelia tried to remove the curse from Brynna, it backfired. The curse was killing her. If I didn't bring her back, she would have died."

"Calla," he exhaled.

"I'm sorry I didn't tell you, but I knew you were working on the safety of my friends."

"You are my priority, Calla. You will always be my first priority," he said.

"And right now, the safety of my friends is mine. I couldn't jeopardize that."

Trystan paused. *"Are you sure you're safe?"*

"Yes. Melaina said this place is heavily warded."

"Stay there. Nicolae and I will come as soon as we are finished here."

"I can transport myself back to the Isle of Aria."

"No. I don't want you transporting alone. Wait for me. I'll be there shortly."

I agreed, but really didn't want to stay. I had promised the guys I would return quickly. They must have been going mad, wondering when I was going to return.

"Who are you, child?" The old woman's voice broke me from my thoughts. She had shuffled a few feet away from me, her cataract eyes fixed on mine.

"My name is Calla Caldwell." I answered with a smile, knowing she probably wanted more of an answer than that. Especially after witnessing my body on fire. "I am Incendian royalty and engaged to the Prince of Carpathia."

The woman held out her arthritic hand to me. Taking it, she hissed, but her grip tightened around my hand. "I knew you were special," she murmured. "I felt your power before you appeared." A sly smile raised on her lips. "So, you are the one who has finally captured the heart of the handsome prince?"

"You know Trystan?"

"Of course. Our town is indebted to him and his kingdom. When we were hunted by Morbeth's immortals, Trystan stepped in and helped us. His grandfather is the king of Hale, you know. Hale is the birthplace of his mother."

I nodded, remembering he told me about the arranged marriage between his father and mother, and that she was the princess of Hale.

"Trystan bargained with the king for this piece of land. He purchased it and gave it to us so we could start a new life. He also provided everything we needed to sustain a life here. He is a good man who will make a fine king someday."

"Yes, I agree. He will make a wonderful king," I said with a smile, my heart warming inside.

I was happy to have learned something new about Trystan. I suppose there would be many more stories I would hear because, like he'd said, he had lived two mortal lifetimes. He must have accomplished a lot during those years.

"Will Ophelia and Melaina be okay?"

The woman nodded her head. "Our best healers are with them now." She paused and squeezed my hand. "Will you stay for some tea? It is rare we get visitors from the outside, and none as special as you. I know the others would love to meet you."

I bowed my head and smiled. "I'd love some tea."

The woman wrapped her arm around mine and gave me instructions on where to go. Her home was a simple hut, nothing fancy, but it was hers and it was safe.

Inside, different smells of herbs permeated the air. There was a small fireplace, and a table that held old books, candles, vials, and many odd trinkets. In one corner of the room were countless herbs hanging from a low rafter, drying out. And in the other corner was a small bed.

"Fireheart, would you mind igniting the kindling for this old woman?" she asked, pointing to her fireplace.

I giggled at her words. "Of course." I placed a few logs and some kindling on the hearth and flicked a flame into it. In no time, a fire roared to life.

The woman brought over a tea kettle and hung it above the fire. "There we go."

"What's your name?" I asked, taking a seat at the small table.

"Hazel," she replied, lowering into the seat across from me. "Tell me more about this curse that ails Ophelia and Melaina."

I told her what had happened to Ophelia when she tried to remove Brynna's tracer, and how it backfired, so I decided to transport them to Neverton for help. Then, how we ended up in Dead Man's Land, with no powers and the Shadow of Death sent to us. And just in time, my firebird— my gift from Helia — came to save us.

She nodded, her face somber. "Why was there a tracer in your friend?"

I then proceeded to tell her about the decree from Roehl, and how he had sent hunters to find me and my parents, wanting to exterminate any threat to the throne. I told her about Brynna and how we had been captured and taken to Morbeth. How Trystan came with Melaina and his cadre to rescue me, but I made Melaina take Brynna back instead. Told her about that dark stain Melaina had picked up on Brynna. Ophelia had found it too, the tracer, and when she tried to remove it, it backfired. I also told her how Roehl had killed his father and was going to kill his witches and guards if we didn't go to Morbeth within fifteen days.

Hazel's gaze went distant, focusing on the flames in the hearth. "The mages in Morbeth have no morality. They seek out and practice dark, archaic magic that was banned long ago. Magic that breaches our moral codes."

"Can they be stopped?" I questioned.

Hazel leaned forward and placed her finger against my chest. "It can. You have the power inside to defeat it, but it will be difficult. Their dark magic is twisted. It steals your courage and makes you feel powerless. Their magic causes doubt, even in the strongest of minds. When that happens, it will lock up, making you feel like you have no power at all."

"What do I have to do?"

"Just be, child," she breathed with a smile. "Just be. Because the gifts you have been given were created for truth and justice. Never doubt your gifts, and rely on those around you, especially your prince. He is the strongest immortal in Talbrinth and beyond. He will be your strength."

I sighed, a tear trickling from my eye, knowing that's exactly what Trystan was for me. He was my strength and my support. He was everything I was lacking.

CHAPTER ELEVEN

HAZEL AND I SHARED tea, and then she asked me to escort her outside. Linking my arm in hers, I led her out her door, where a group of people were lined up. Hazel gently patted my hand, letting me know everything was okay.

"They are anxious to meet you," she whispered.

Hazel introduced me to the witches of Neverton, and I realized then that she was a leader among them. They gathered around us, welcoming me with warm smiles and flowers. Their expressions were sincere.

It was the first time I was truly welcomed warmly as an Incendian royal. It was the first time I felt accepted by an entire community. And not a normal community. These were people born with magic and had practiced it all their lives. They were looking at me like I was some kind of god, which I was far from. I felt like an imposter here. Like I still hadn't endured the test of time like many of them had.

"He's here," a child's voice echoed.

That's when I felt him, a warm caress through the bond between us.

The crowd split and when my eyes met his, I couldn't help but smile. Running toward him, Trystan opened his arms and caught me, hugging me tight.

"My flame," he breathed. "Let's go home."

Home. No matter where we were, he was home. He was my refuge, my safe place.

Trystan walked me over to Nicolae. "Give me a moment," he said, then turned and greeted the people. I watched their faces, watched how much admiration they had for him. They truly loved and respected him. This prince, their hero, who had saved them from enslavement and gave them a new start.

Nicolae wrapped an arm around my shoulder. "I heard you ran into some trouble," he whispered.

I nodded. "For a moment, I thought we were going to die."

Nicolae sighed, rubbing my arm, while Trystan's head snapped back. His eyes narrowed with concern. Then he turned back to Hazel.

"I wish Ophelia and Melaina well. I also thank you for accommodating my fiancé."

"She is one of us now," Hazel replied, "and will always be welcome here."

Trystan bowed his head, placing a fist to his heart. "Until we meet again."

Walking back over to us, Trystan wrapped me in his arms. Nicolae placed a hand on his shoulder and transported us back to the Isle of Aria. We landed on the outside of the front door.

"Nicolae, could I have a moment with Calla?" Trystan asked.

"Of course." He proceeded inside.

Trystan's lips were suddenly pressed against mine, one hand holding the back of my head, the other around my waist. His kiss was fierce and impassioned. When he pulled back, I was breathless, while his forehead rested against mine.

"Dammit, Calla. I was so terrified I couldn't think straight. When you didn't answer me—" He paused, raking his fingers through his thick raven hair. "I'm glad Nicolae was there to keep me from sending a wind that would rip the world apart."

"I'm sorry," I said, seeing the fear in his eyes. "How did you know?"

"Nyx," he breathed. "She took over my vision. I felt her worry as she passed over a desert. She has never done this before, so I could only assume she was heading to you, but I didn't know where you were. I assumed it was Morbeth."

"Dead Man's Land," I confirmed.

"How?"

I shook my head. "Right before we left, Ophelia screamed and clawed at my arm. I lost my concentration. I think, because I've been thinking about the upcoming battle with Roehl, I ended up there. It's the only explanation I can think of." Deep sobs ripped from my chest. "My powers were gone, and so were Melaina's. A dark cloud, a shadow of death, came from beyond the Red Wall and headed toward us. It surrounded us and was sucking the life from us. But Flint showed up. He awoke my power and broke the curse, and I quickly transported us to Neverton."

Trystan held me, stroking my hair. "I'm glad you're safe."

He didn't say anything else, probably knowing that I already felt like shit.

I wiped my face and tried to gather myself, knowing I'd have to face Markus and his cadre. But if given the choice, I would have done it again. Because Ophelia's life was on the line. Now, she was in the hands of her healers, and I knew that if anyone could save her and Melaina, it would be them.

"Come, let's get you something to eat." I nodded, knowing I was weakened from the poisoned cloud and my use of powers.

Inside, seated at the table were Thalia, Markus, Kylan, Brone, Andrés, and Feng. As soon as we entered, they all stood.

Thalia ran over and threw her arms around me. "Goddess, I was terrified something bad had happened to all of you."

I hugged her back. "Something bad did happen, but we fought through it."

Markus gave me a pointed look and was the first to speak. "The next time you decide to leave without us, I will chain you up."

I glanced at Trystan, who nonchalantly leaned against the wall. *"Are you going to say something?"* I asked through our bond.

He shrugged. *"You agreed to keep him as your guard. He was worried. Let him vent."* I hissed under my breath, making him chuckle.

"You could have died!" Markus growled. "And there was no one there to protect you."

I crossed my arms over my chest. "Yes, I could have died, but I didn't. Every single day Roehl is alive, we have to fight to survive. But, even alone, I proved that I am getting stronger and have been able to survive the dark magic Roehl has thrown at me."

"Next time, you will take one of us with you. I'm sure your mate will agree." Markus's eyes slid to Trystan.

Trystan moved away from the wall. "This was an unfortunate situation with a deadly mishap, but I understand why Calla agreed to transport Melaina and Ophelia. They were in need, and she offered her help. But I, as your mate," Trystan came and took my hand. "I would like to know if you are leaving the boundaries and protections we have in place to keep you safe."

"I promise," I exhaled. I knew they were all looking out for me, and I appreciated that. "By the way," I said, facing him fully. "How are Sabine and Brynna?"

"They are under heavy guard and have been given strict rules for the next few weeks. They have also been given two of our best suites and they will be well served. Sabine said to tell you she'll be just fine."

My heart swelled with happiness. I was so grateful knowing that they would be well taken care of in Carpathia. It gave me a huge sense of relief. "I'm glad. And what about your father? Did you talk to him?"

Trystan shook his head. "I didn't get a chance to discuss anything with him because of the situation. But I have a meeting with him in three days. I want you to come."

Anxiety knotted in my belly. "I don't know if that's a good idea. He literally kicked me out of Carpathia and made his men escort me to the dock."

"The king will have to accept you, now that you are blood bound and mated to his son," Brone said.

"Once he gets to know you, like we have, he will be thankful that his son chose you over that viper, Ivy," Andrés added with a grin.

"Thank you," I exhaled, but still didn't feel any better. I directed my finger at Andrés. "Hey, how did you get back?" I knew he'd traveled with Trystan and Nicolae to Carpathia.

Andrés rested his elbows on the table. "They dropped me off here before running off to save you."

I gave him a smirk. "I was in Neverton, already safe."

Andrés shook his head and let out a boisterous laugh. "I have never seen your mate in so much distress. He was ready to shred the atmosphere to get to you."

Those words made my insides fill with warmth. To know he was that concerned for me. I turned to Trystan with a smile. "Thank you."

Trystan grabbed my hand and led me to the table, then pulled back a chair and I sat. The servants came out with large goblets of ruby wine, setting them down in front of us.

"We really need to discuss our plan for Roehl. He's not sitting around waiting for us. That bastard is always planning, gathering his army, mages, and dark magic. He is going to draw us in for one purpose. To kill us."

Nicolae placed his goblet on the table and leaned forward. "We can't stay here. Roehl probably tracked Brynna to this location already."

"When will we be moving?" Kylan asked. "Brynna was moved to Carpathia, so wouldn't they think we also moved?"

"We don't want to take that risk," Nicolae added. "I have been looking into stronger magic to protect us. But that won't be enough. We will need help." He turned his attention to me and by the expression on his face, I could tell he was planning something I wasn't ready for.

Inhaling and exhaling deeply, I grabbed hold of Trystan's hand. "What is your plan?"

Nicolae swirled the ruby wine in his goblet. "We need to go to Incendia. We must overthrow their queen."

"You know she is connected to Roehl, right?" I wondered if Nicolae knew. "She's sleeping with him."

He nodded. "Which makes it even more imperative. We cannot have Incendia involved with this upcoming war. They have already suffered destruction by Morbeth's hand once, and I have no doubt Roehl is planning to do it again. He is keeping his enemy close and will sacrifice Incendia, our home, to make a statement."

"The queen has dark mages she keeps close to prove she has power because she is not an Incendian royal," Thalia spoke. "Queen Garinda is ruthless and will do anything to stay in power. Yes, she has rebuilt Incendia, but her people are suffering and are oppressed. They lack proper food and supplies, while she gluttonously fills her belly and easily throws out the waste. She keeps her thumb on them because she wants the people to rely on her. She thinks if they had everything, they would no longer need her." Thalia knew the queen best. She'd been raised by her.

Thalia's words set a fire ablaze inside of me. These were my people. Nicolae's people, and they were being oppressed by a psycho queen who wanted nothing more than power. To rule over a people who weren't hers to rule.

Helia had told me the people didn't trust or respect the queen. They feared her.

I was Leora's heir and Helia's chosen. I had to free our people. They were survivors, yet they were still trying to survive when they should have been thriving.

Nicolae was right. We had to overthrow the queen and take Incendia out of the equation. But in the back of my mind, I knew Roehl would retaliate. His grandfather had nearly exterminated Incendia, and I knew he would gladly finish it, to spite me and Nicolae.

Yes, we had to take out Incendia's queen, but once she was gone, the true heir—the chosen one—would have to rise.

Was I ready for such a task?

No. But this wasn't about me. This entire journey, the course set out before us, was so much bigger than just me. I was simply a participant in this dark and twisted game, having to make sacrifices and maneuvers toward one ultimate objective. To win. Because if I didn't, the repercussions of losing would be catastrophic. Not only to me, but to an entire race of people. My people.

I could feel my true purpose stirring in my bones, calling to me, making me restless. The time for peace was over. War was at our doorstep and my destiny, my true calling, was awakening. I couldn't stand by anymore. I had to heed the call.

"When do we leave?" I asked.

The entire room fell silent, all eyes fixed on me. It was then I realized I was on fire. Trystan squeezed my hand and a cool and calming breeze encompassed me, extinguishing my flames. I smiled at him, and he returned a sexy grin, sending the heat straight to my core.

"We see your passion." Kylan said. "But we need a plan. This isn't a simple mission. We are going to overthrow a queen."

"I agree," Trystan added. "Garinda will not bow without a fight. I'm sure she's upped her security after seeing Calla, knowing she is the rightful queen."

"And believe me," Thalia added. "She would not hesitate to kill you, rather than give up her throne. She truly believes Incendia is hers. She has never been in her right mind."

Feng leaned forward, tenting his fingers. "To be queen, doesn't she need to bear the marks of Incendian Royalty?"

"Yes," I said, then Thalia interjected.

"Queen Garinda's marks aren't real. They are false, as she is, created from her mages."

"Well, that changes things." Feng looked so calm and collected. He glanced at Nicolae, then me and Trystan. "We are not going there to overthrow a queen, but a common Incendian, and will be placing the true Queen of Incendia on the throne."

I gave Trystan a concerned look, knowing I was his wife and the future Queen of Carpathia. If I was to be the Queen of Incendia, how would this work between us? Was one Queen allowed to rule more than one country at a time? I wasn't sure how that would work since our countries were so far away.

"Don't worry, my flame," Trystan reassured through our bond. *"We'll work through this together, one step at a time."*

I wondered how he could be so calm. Because even now, I wanted to wrap my arms around him and transport him back to the cottage. The mating bond was still as strong as ever and I was having a hard time being so close to him.

Trystan's eyes, a shade darker, captured mine. His hand slowly slid up my thigh. *"You cannot imagine the things going through my mind. Tonight, my flame, we will set our bedchamber ablaze."*

His words ignited a flame inside me that would be impossible to extinguish. I fidgeted in my seat, unable to concentrate on what was being said.

"Are you okay, Calla?" Brone asked. "You're looking a little flustered."

"Yes," I breathed, tugging at the collar of my tunic. "It's getting really hot in here."

I gave Trystan a side-eyed glare. *"You need to remove your hand from my thigh, my prince, or I will combust. And all that will remain of your wife will be ash."*

I stood abruptly, my chair falling backward and hitting the floor. I had to get away from him. He was making it hard for me to think, let alone breathe.

Trystan burst into laughter, and it was the first time I'd seen him laugh so heartily, with a broad smile on his face. His men looked confused, but the sight of him made my heart grow even more, making him look even more handsome. It wasn't fair.

"Okay, what are we missing?" Kylan questioned, his eyes sliding back and forth between me and Trystan.

"Nothing." I spoke too quickly. "I've just had a very intense day. I need to unwind. Possibly some wine and a hot tub." I glanced at Trystan. *"Are you coming?"*

Trystan stood, so cool and nonchalant, excusing himself. "I will escort her back to the cottage."

"Wait." I placed my hands on Trystan's chest. "Can we go to the stable first?"

"Stable?" Thalia scrunched her nose. "Why would you want to go there?"

"I want to give Storm a treat. And, I'd like to ride her before we leave the island."

"You can't ride that horse." Brone burst into a cynical laugh. "She won't let anyone near her, let alone ride her. Except him." He aimed his finger at Trystan.

I crossed my arms over my chest and tilted my head to the side. "Wanna bet?"

"Hell yeah." Brone slapped his large hands on the table and leaned forward. "I'll bet twenty gold skrag you won't be able to saddle her, let alone ride her."

"I'll take that bet." I challenged. "It's safe outside so why don't you follow? The sky has darkened, and it's snowing."

Brone scooted his chair back and stood. As did the others.

"I have to see this," Feng said with a broad smile. "If she can ride that horse, she is truly Trystan's match."

Nicolae stood and gave me a slight bow of his head. "I'm going upstairs to rest for a bit."

"Of course." I smiled, knowing he probably wasn't used to so many people around. Nicolae had lived his life in isolation. "We'll see you at dinner?"

"Yes, and we can discuss our next move then."

I nodded then Thalia ambled toward me. "I think I'm going to sit this one out too. Sabine and I stayed up way too long last night and my body is begging for a nap."

I reached out and took her hand, knowing how hard it must be for her to be without Sabine. They had been inseparable since we'd left Incendia. "I hope it's a good nap."

"I hope you win," she whispered with a wink. "I'm placing my bet on you."

CHAPTER TWELVE

At the stable, Markus, Kylan, Brone, Andrés, and Feng stood behind me and Trystan. As soon as she heard us, Storm stuck her head out of her stall to greet me. She was eagerly waiting, her head nodding up and down.

I grabbed an apple from a cart and carried it to her, and she snatched the treat from my palm.

"Hey pretty girl," I whispered, slowly opening her gate. "You want to get out of here and go for a ride with me?"

Storm took a few steps back and whinnied. When I stepped inside, she nudged me in the chest with her nose, so I scratched the spot behind her ear Trystan mentioned she liked.

"Are you sure you want to ride her?" There was a bit of concern in Trystan's voice as he stepped beside me.

"I'm sure." I was confident, swallowing down the fear that had grown since we'd arrived in the stable.

I knew Storm and I had a connection, just like Shadow and I did. She wasn't a simple mare. She was a wild and free spirit, and I appreciated that about her. I think she knew it, too.

Trystan ran a hand down Storm's side. "Would you like me to saddle her?"

I shook my head. "I'll do it. It's an important part of us connecting."

He smiled and stepped back, but not too far, watching intently as I began to saddle Storm. As I placed the blanket on her back, Storm slowly pawed the ground, her head lowering. I knew what this language meant because Shadow did this every time I saddled him. This action meant Storm was expecting something. She wanted to run. She wanted to get out of this stall and feel the wind against her face, feel the pounding of earth under hooves, and awaken those strong muscles under her silky silvery coat.

I took my time, slowly and gently placing the bridal, bit, and saddle on her. Then, I took the reins and led her out. As she passed the men, she neighed and stomped the ground. They all backed up, Brone speedily moving in the opposite direction.

I giggled to myself, seeing this monster of a man so afraid of this horse.

"Whoa, girl," I said softly, running a smooth hand down her neck. She calmed down and followed me out.

The frigid breeze was enlivening, snow falling, and the ground covered in fresh snow. The temperature had remained below freezing, so there was no ice underneath for Storm to slip on. Nicolae said the wards were tight, and now that Brynna was gone, I didn't think we'd have to worry about Roehl tracking us. Right now, unless he'd found some powerful tracing spell, we were invisible to him.

"Which way do we go?" I asked Trystan, getting ready to mount Storm.

"She knows the way," he breathed, coming up from behind me and wrapping his arms around my waist. "Hold on tight and come back to me quickly."

Twisting back, I pressed my lips against his. "I will."

I tried to be as calm as possible, the men watching, waiting to see if this beautiful, wild beast would allow me to ride her.

I stepped in front of Storm and placed my hand on her forehead. "Let's show these boys how we do this, okay? I'm just your passenger. You take me wherever you want to go."

Storm pressed her nose against my chest again, then rested her head on my shoulder. This was a sign of trust. I wrapped my arms around her neck, hugging her, then slowly, calmly stepped over to her side.

All the men were silent. Kylan shook his head in disbelief. Feng nodded with a wide smile, while Markus, Brone, and

Andrés' eyes were wide and fixed on me and Storm. They were probably anticipating her to buck me off.

In one fluid motion, I slipped my boot into the stirrup and mounted Storm. She danced around, but I held tight to the reins.

"Whoa. We've got this girl," I whispered. Then, I nudged her sides. "Let's go!"

Storm reared, but I anticipated it, holding on. As soon as her front hooves hit the ground, she took off in a full gallop, her powerful legs stretching and pounding against the snow-covered ground.

Goddess she was fast!

Snow pelted and wind whipped against my face, but I embraced it.

Storm flew down a path lined with spruce trees that led to wide open fields that ended at the sea. The view of the landscape was magical, the gray sky sprinkling snowflakes on us.

Storm hadn't let up. I let her run. Gave her the reins, knowing this was what she was created for. What she craved.

Above us, a loud caw caught my attention. Glancing up, I spotted a black crow soaring directly above us. Another crow swooped down, joining it, and a smile spread across my face.

"Are you watching me, husband?"

"I am," he purred. I could feel his pride vibrate through our bond. *"Watching you with my horse, seeing how natural you are with her, is incredibly sexy. The men are extremely jealous."*

"Jealous?"

"Because my wild mare likes you better than them."

Suddenly, Storm stopped dead in her tracks. Her ears were pinned back, eyes wide, and she began pawing the ground.

"What's wrong girl?"

"Calla?"

"Something's wrong. Storm is agitated about something."

"Do you see anything?"

Sweeping the area, I saw nothing. No person or animal around for miles. *"There is nothing here. I don't know why she's stopped, but something is obviously bothering her."*

"Turn around. Come back, now," Trystan ordered.

There was a loud whizzing sound in the air, and I felt a thud that jolted me.

In shock, I glanced down, watching blood exit from a wound on my side to which there was no weapon. I went to press my hand against the wound but moaned as my hand hit something lodged into my side that I couldn't see. There was an invisible shaft.

I felt along the shaft and realized I'd been struck by an arrow. The pain was searing and nearly unbearable.

Another whizzing sound, and I was struck in the thigh and again in my shoulder. I let out a pained scream but could barely breathe. The areas I'd been struck were like hot pokers being pressed into my flesh. Burning. The pain was so excruciating I could barely think.

Grabbing Storm's reins, I turned her around and bumped her sides with my legs. She took off galloping. Then, suddenly she stopped and reared. This time I wasn't prepared and flew off her, my back slamming into the ground. The tip of the arrow pushed straight through the back of my shoulder to the front.

Storm took off like the wind.

I screamed. *"I'm hit. They're here but they are invisible."*

"Protect yourself. Immediately!" That's all he said. But I could feel fear and concern in his voice. He must have seen what happened through Nyx's eyes.

Although I was weak, I immediately called my flame, and it wrapped around me in a dome of protection. Reaching down, I wailed as I yanked the invisible arrow from my thigh. As soon as it exited, it became visible. My bloodied fingers trembled as I held the arrow tipped with silver.

If one had hit my heart, I would probably be dead. I had to pull the others out.

The arrow in my shoulder had pushed through my front, so I focused on the one embedded in my side. The wound was turning black, poisoned by the silver tip inside of me.

Touching the shaft, I nearly blacked out. The pain was excruciating.

Arrows battered my fire shield, dissolving instantly. But I was growing weaker, and so was my shield. Outside I could hear Flint screeching across the sky, but he was also fighting an invisible enemy, and I was worried about him and Nyx.

"Flint, take Nyx and leave." I hoped he could hear me and would listen.

"Calla, you fight. Don't let them take you," Trystan roared. *"I'm coming."*

Gathering whatever strength I'd had left, I let out a scream, yanking the arrow from my side. Darkness threatened to fill my eyes, but I fought to stay conscious. If I passed out, my flame would die, and whoever was outside would take me.

"Help!" I called to Nicolae through our connection. *"I'm injured. I don't know how much longer I can hold on."*

"Calla, where are you? Can you transport?"

"No. I have a flame protecting me, but it's failing."

"Tell me where you are!" Nicolae's voice was frantic.

The sky above had darkened. Thunder roared and lightning snapped. Through my fire dome, I saw a violent tornado heading toward me.

My breaths were short and shallow. *"Follow the dark cloud"* I said to Nicolae.

Trystan was coming, his rage reverberating through the atmosphere. I could feel his power seeking me out, felt it enter my failing fire dome. His intoxicating scent curled around me, attempting to comfort me.

Outside of my shelter, I heard the voices of men, but I couldn't see them. Their invisible forces continued to batter my fiery shield, trying to get in.

I was failing. My body was wracked with pain and trembling. My palms were throbbing. I couldn't hold the shield much longer. The excruciating pain in my shoulder, side, and thigh radiated through my entire body as blood poured from the wounds.

I wasn't healing.

Why the hell wasn't I healing?

I could barely keep my eyes open, my consciousness dangling by a thread. Then, I felt a vibration around me. Through weary eyes, I saw my shield of flame dissolve. This was it.

Waiting for a death blow, a blazing wildfire encircled me. I was suddenly swooped up into Nicolae's arms as tears streamed down my face.

He'd come. Just in time.

Nicolae's eyes were pure onyx as he whispered a spell. I saw a ripple in the air, but nothing happened. With eyes narrowed and jaw set, Nicolae roared the spell again. The air rippled once more, the wall of invisibility faltered, but stood firm.

Closing my eyes, I concentrated on Nicolae's spell, sending what was left of my power to him. Placing my palms against his chest, I watched the flames in his eyes grow and the muscles in his jaw tighten. He spoke the spell one more time, and I watched a blast of power surge through his fire dome, shattering the spell of invisibility, instantly revealing the men attacking us.

There were at least a hundred men in the field, and beyond them, docked just outside of the island, were two ships. One bearing the flag of Morbeth. The other —

Goddess, no.

On the other ship, from the peak of the gaff, flew the flag of *Incendia*.

My heart cracked in two as I watched it wave in the frigid wind.

My people had traveled to this shore to hunt and kill me.

But I couldn't blame them. They were following the order of their queen. She'd fed them lies that I was the imposter and wanted to kill them. That I wanted to do them harm. Which was the same lies the Lethe curse fed Trystan.

The queen of Incendia not only sent my people to kill me, but she'd also aligned herself with my enemy. That sealed it for me. Garinda had to be taken out. Soon.

"Don't leave," I breathed, knowing Nicolae would transport me to safety.

His eyes had locked onto the ships — to the flag of Incendia fluttering in the wind. He knew. And his heart was probably just as broken as mine. Two outcasts wanted dead because of an age-old vendetta.

"Help him," I breathed. Trystan was alone.

Nicolae's dark eyes met mine, a smile rising on his lips. "He doesn't need my help."

I couldn't take my eyes off of the raging storm that was now upon us.

A deep growl detonated through the air, which had turned even colder. Wind whipped violently around our dome, ripping across the entire field. My eyes found the dark funnel of wind, and through the mist and lightning, I saw him.

Trystan was poised in the center, a deadly calm. A hostile glare visible in those black as night eyes. Bared teeth revealed elongated incisors, his arms extended to his sides. Lightning cracked from his fingertips and thunder erupted around him.

Trystan thrust his hands forward and black wisps of air shot out, coiling around the men surrounding us. With a flip of his wrist, screams echoed as men were thrust miles out into the sea. Countless arrows were shot at him, but none could penetrate the powerful air shield he'd raised.

And then, Trystan's voice, as cold as death, roared through the atmosphere. "You dare come here and attempt to kill my mate?" Another violent growl ripped from his lips, reverberating through my chest. "For that, you will all die."

The wind became deafening. Screams echoed around us, bodies were thrust skyward before slamming to the ground. Bones snapped and cracked, crushing under tremendous bursts of wind.

Master of air, Trystan's power was palpable.

He was a beautiful nightmare, death incarnate. An immortal creature filled with rage and vengeance. I watched in complete awe as he ripped through the field like a raging storm until there was nothing left but silence and stilled, broken bodies.

"It's over," Nicolae exhaled. "We have to tend to your wounds."

Nodding, I closed my heavy-laden eyes. And then, I sensed *him*. His powerful scent enveloped me, while Nicolae placed me in his strong arms. Without opening my eyes, I knew they were the arms of my mate.

Knowing I was safe, I finally let go and fell into darkness.

My tired eyes slid open, trying to focus on my surroundings.

"You're up," a handsome voice spoke off to my side.

Attempting to sit up, I sucked in a sharp breath as excruciating pain shot through my shoulder and side. Trystan, sitting on a chair next to my bedside, leaned over and gently helped me lay back down.

The arrow in my shoulder was gone, and I was glad I was unconscious while it was extracted.

Glimmering azure eyes hovered above me. My friend. My hero.

"You're weak." His voice was also weary, as were his eyes. He looked like he hadn't had much sleep.

"How is Storm?"

He let out a breathy chuckle, shaking his head. "Storm is fine. She took off, and is now back in her stable, unscathed."

"Good," I exhaled. "And Nyx?"

"They are all fine." His lips curled into a smile. "You need to rest and feed."

"I can't. The thought of drinking blood turns my stomach."

Those beautiful eyes narrowed while a sexy smile pulled on his lips.

"I wasn't going to give you donated blood."

My eyes narrowed as Trystan slowly raised his wrist to his mouth. Incisors lengthened and then . . . he bit down. When he pulled away, the sight of crimson on his lips set a fire ablaze inside of me.

Leaning closer, Trystan pressed his blood-wet lips against mine, his tongue delving into my mouth, giving me a taste. *Gods.* His blood was pure power.

A moan escaped my lips, and my body reacted, making my back arch.

"Do you want more?" he purred, making me writhe.

"Yes."

Trystan let out a soft growl then pulled back. His wrist had already healed, so he bit it once more and willingly offered it to me. Like an addict, I grabbed hold of it and pressed it to my mouth. My teeth, sinking into his soft flesh.

My eyes rolled back as his sweet blood burst into my mouth and poured down my throat. All the pain instantly subsided and my mind was set adrift, sailing into a place of pleasure only he could take me.

Trystan groaned as I fed from his precious blood. It was like drinking pure magic. Its power flowed through my entire body, healing, strengthening, and pleasuring every part of me.

Trystan slowly raised my shirt, his fingers trailing to the spot the arrow had entered my side. His touch was electric, his blood euphoric.

I suddenly became overwhelmed with sensations. They were so strong I had to unlatch from Trystan's wrist. Closing my eyes, I rode the high, no longer feeling any pain.

"My flame," Trystan whispered, his breath feathering against my cheek. "What do you need?"

Heat shifted in my core, spreading like a wildfire through the rest of my body.

My eyes snapped open, my fingers reached forward, grasping the fabric on his chest, tugging him closer.

"You," I breathed. "I want you."

His eyes darkened, and a wicked grin spread across those sinful lips. "I am more than happy to oblige."

CHAPTER THIRTEEN

BEFORE THE SUN ROSE the next morning, we all gathered at the dining table for breakfast, waiting for Nicolae and Markus to join us.

"You're looking well." Kylan's eyes scanned my face. "Unfortunately, we arrived shortly after the devastation."

"That's because someone left us behind, rushing to save his damsel in distress." Andrés' head inclined to Trystan.

Trystan raised his glass to him. "You all know the rules. Time waits for no man, especially when a damsel is in need of saving." His eyes met mine, soft and swirling with emotion. "Even more so when that damsel is your mate."

Andrés fanned himself. "You two need to stop looking at each other like that or everyone in this room will need to leave for a cold bath."

Brone smiled, leaning back in his seat, also assessing me. "You do look much better this morning, princess. Last night you looked like death had come knocking on your door."

I grinned and tilted my head to the side. "And now, I've proven I can survive with three silver tipped arrows in me."

Andrés let out a loud breath. "I don't know how you did it. I would have been down on the first arrow. I have a very low tolerance for pain."

My eyes widened. "And you're an assassin?"

Andrés threw me a sly grin. "It's because I'm fast and can avoid injury."

Brone smacked Andrés on the back of the head. His head flew forward, his forehead smacking the table with a loud thud.

Andrés growled, his narrowed eyes snapped to Brone. "What the hell?"

Brone pointed his large finger at him, rolling with laughter. "You aren't that fast, little man."

"You're an asshole. I wasn't ready."

Brone shrugged his broad shoulders. "An assassin should always be ready." Andrés threw a punch at Brone, but Brone caught his fist midair, twisting it to the side. "Like I was saying . . . always be ready."

"Would you two knock it off," Kylan exhaled, shaking his head. "This is what Feng and I have to put up with, day in and day out."

I smiled. "I love their playful banter. It helps lighten the mood, especially during these dark days."

Andrés pointed to the red spot on his forehead. "Does this look like playful banter?" His fingers rubbed the welt that was slowly healing, then he smiled at me. "Though, I'm glad it helps."

Nicolae and Markus both strode down the stairs with serious expressions on their faces.

I wanted to talk to Nicolae about what we'd seen off the shore of the Isle of Aria—the ship from Incendia. I wanted to know what he was thinking when I saw the dismal expression on his face.

We had less than two weeks to meet Roehl, but I had a feeling we would be meeting him much sooner than that. This had to stop. We couldn't give him any more time to plan. We had to attack when he least expected, like his grandfather did to Incendia.

Nicolae and Markus took a seat and Fern immediately brought them goblets filled with ruby wine. They both looked at me, their eyes assessing. I smiled, straightening my back, showing them I was fine.

"Good morning," I chimed, giving them a bright smile.

Markus gave me a smirk.

Nicolae gave me a warm smile back. "Good morning. How are you feeling?"

"Better than ever."

"That's good to hear." Nicolae's eyes slid to Trystan. "I know it's obvious, but we cannot stay here." Then his eyes met mine. "Our next move will be to Incendia."

My heart twisted in my chest knowing that the trip to Incendia was coming. I just didn't know it would be this soon. Trystan reached under the table and took my hand, gently squeezing, letting me know everything would be okay.

"You saw the ship off the island," I said to Nicolae as a statement, not a question. He gave a sad nod. "Do you have a plan?"

Nicolae's chest rose and fell with a deep sigh. "Not yet, but the queen must be taken out. She will bring Incendia to complete and total ruin if she continues. Roehl despises the Incendian people, and has a deep-seated hatred for Leora, who stole his father's heart. He blames her for his mother's death. Right now, he is using the Incendian queen, and when she is no longer needed, he will dispose of her along with the rest of Incendia. Of that, I have no doubt."

Trystan squeezed my hand again, his tired eyes fastened on mine. "Your people had survived a brutal attack, and since then, have remained broken and held down by the queen. Incendian legends speak of a phoenix—one who will rise and bring renewal and hope." Trystan turned in his chair to face me. "You are the phoenix, Calla, chosen by the Fire Goddess.

You are the true heir of the Incendian throne. The time has come for you to rise from the ashes and take your rightful place." He took my palms and pressed them against his chest. "And as your mate, I will stand and fight at your side, until death claims me."

"As will I." Markus slapped a fist to his chest.

Thalia placed a hand over her heart. "And I."

"As will we," Kylan said. He, Andrés, Brone, and Feng also slapped their fists against their chests.

Nicolae smiled at me. "You're my family, and I have vowed to protect you until death. I will gladly fight alongside you for our people—both in Incendia and Morbeth."

Tears brimmed and spilled down my face as I looked at my grandfather. My husband. My friends. I didn't know what I did to deserve their loyalty, but they also had mine. We may not have had an army, but I knew we were a force to be reckoned with.

"We leave tonight," Nicolae said, breaking the awkward silence. "We will attack before sunrise, when the queen is most vulnerable."

"Will we be transporting straight from here to the palace?" Feng questioned. "I just want to make sure I am ready mentally as well as physically."

"No," Nicolae replied. "We will transport somewhere closer. There is a small islet off Incendia. A place we can stay and prepare for the attack, while remaining undetected."

A thought popped into my mind, and I glanced at Thalia. "What about the Crag? Would we be able to transport instead?"

Her eyes lit up. "Yes."

Trystan rested an elbow on the table. "What's the Crag?"

"It's the mountain where the Fire Goddess dwells. The entrance of the cave is lined with protective runes, so I think it would be safe to transport there."

"It is safe," Thalia confirmed. "There is no spell on the mountain, especially the Crag. Garinda's mages verified that whatever power dwells there has blocked all of their spells. The Crag is also a few miles from the palace."

My heart began to thrum in my chest as I turned to Nicolae. "When the time comes, you and I can transport everyone straight to the Crag, and then into the palace." I turned to Thalia. "Thalia, will you be able to show us exactly where the locations are on the map?"

Thalia nodded with a wide smile. "Yes, I can. I also know where the guards are positioned around the island, and where the queen's mages live."

"Thank you, Thalia." Nicolae stood from his seat.

"Of course," Thalia replied. "Like Prince Trystan said, the people of Incendia have been oppressed and are waiting for change." Her eyes met mine. "I'm glad I'll get to be a part of it."

"I'm glad you are too, cousin." My words made a smile rise on her lips.

"I'll go retrieve the map." Nicolae excused himself and headed toward the stairs but paused and turned back to us. "Get ready. We leave for the Crag as soon as the sun sets."

Everyone at the table agreed and seemed to be in good spirits. If we did this right, we could make it out of this unscathed. We had everything and everyone we needed to make this work, but we couldn't underestimate the queen, or Roehl. They must have been preparing, knowing we would eventually overthrow the false queen. I had witnessed the fear and hatred in Queen Garinda's eyes the moment she laid eyes on my tattoos. She knew she was the imposter, and I knew she wouldn't go down without a fight. She would guard the Incendian throne at all costs.

After seeing the Incendian ship off the Isle of Aria, I knew she would do whatever it took to take me down, even sending our own people to kill me.

Who knew how many Incendians had died because of her? Trystan killed them to protect me. If he hadn't come when he did, I would be dead. Even Nicolae wouldn't have been able to hold off that many men by himself while trying to protect me.

This was getting out of hand. We had to stop her. Too many lives were lost at the hands of Roehl and now Garinda.

She had lied, not only to me, but to her people. When I first arrived in Incendia, I remember what she'd told me the night she invited us to dinner. *"Morbeth destroyed us once, and we will not allow that to happen again. You, stepping foot on this island, have already put every citizen at risk."* In front of the people, she blamed me, while she was in bed with the enemy all along.

Brone leaned forward on his elbows. "If you become Queen of Incendia, what will happen between you and Trystan?"

"Nothing will change," I said. "Once Garinda is overthrown, changes will be made in Incendia, but for the better. I only want what is best for the people. For them to thrive and grow without fear. They at least deserve that much for all they've been through."

I watched tears brim in Thalia's eyes. She had also been a victim of the oppression. Because the queen knew she was related to royalty, she kept her close but still under thumb, making her Captain of the Guard—to serve and protect her.

Not for long. Thalia also needed a place to live out the rest of her life in peace.

I took hold of Trystan's hand and spoke through our bond. *"I need to speak privately with Thalia."*

"Of course." He leaned over and pressed a soft kiss to my forehead.

"Thalia, can I speak to you for a moment?" I asked, standing, and pointing to the sitting room.

She nodded, then stood and followed me.

Closing the door, we sat down on armchairs seated side by side. I looked into her eyes, those beautifully different colored eyes that I had once seen in Melaina's scrying bowl. We were destined to meet, and she had become more than family. She was a powerful ally.

"Did you need something?" she asked.

I nodded, trying to find the best words. "Once the queen is taken out, I want you to consider ruling Incendia in my place."

Thalia's eyes popped wide open in shock. She shook her head and for a moment, her words were stuck. "No. No. No. There is no way I can rule Incendia. I am not qualified."

I knew my statement had thrown her, so I had to comfort her. "There is no one better qualified than you." I reached over and took her hands in mine. "The queen raised you. You know the people and they trust you. Because you were Captain of the Guard, you also have the trust and loyalty of the guards. You are much better suited for ruling Incendia than I am."

"Calla, I cannot rule. Because I left with you, my trust and loyalty have been shattered with the guards and the people," she said, her voice shaking. "You are the chosen one. The people won't regard anyone unless they are Incendian Royalty. The true heir to the throne."

I nodded, but I wasn't going to give up. "If that is the case, I could appoint you as my regent, to rule in my stead while I am away. I cannot rule Incendia when I am going to be princess of Carpathia. But I need someone I can fully trust, who will make sure the land and the people thrive in the future." I sighed, knowing this was a lot to throw at her. "I know it's overwhelming right now, but it will be a brand-new experience for all of us. And we will all be there to help each other."

Thalia sighed, and I could see the indecision in her eyes. "I don't know how I feel about being in a position with that kind of responsibility."

I squeezed her hands. "Just think about it. You don't have to decide right now. Okay?"

She let out a long, loud breath and gave me a nod. "Okay."

We stood, and I wrapped my arms around her. Thalia hugged me back, and I could feel her body trembling.

It was a tremendous responsibility to throw on her, but I could see how much she loved and respected the people. I just wanted to let her know how I felt so she would have time to let my words sink in, and really take time to process them. I had no doubt that if she chose to help, she would rise to become a great and powerful ally.

Even I had no idea how to be a princess, or a queen, let alone run a kingdom. But we would have to make it work, one way or another.

CHAPTER FOURTEEN

MY HEART ACHED KNOWING we were leaving the Isle of Aria. It would always have a special place in my heart because it was the place Trystan and I were secretly married and had sealed our mating bond. Maybe one day we would return and spend more time here. In peace.

Back in the cottage, I donned my favorite outfit. The one Trystan had given me when my adventure first started. Black tunic, black pants, and black boots. I held the cape from Sabine in my hands.

Sitting on the edge of the bed, I traced the threaded flames on the inside, remembering when she had given it to me. We were running in the woods, somewhere in Morbeth, trying to get to Crimson Cove, where we'd met Sebastian and his crew.

So much had happened in such a short time, and now, here we were, ready to overthrow the Incendian queen in a few hours. A woman ruling a kingdom that didn't belong to her.

The bed sank down next to me as Trystan took a seat. "What is going on in that beautiful mind of yours?" He wrapped a comforting arm around me.

"Too much," I smiled. "I was thinking back to the beginning of all of this. It seems like a distant memory, but it wasn't so long ago."

He gave me a sad smile. "No, it wasn't."

I looked up into those beautiful eyes that always gave me a sense of peace and stability. "I'm glad you came to Sartha to find me. And I'm glad you were the one who turned me. Since then, you've stayed by my side."

"Coming to Sartha was something I was compelled to do. It was a feeling, an immense pull I couldn't ignore."

"But you could have. You could have ignored that feeling and left me to die." Tears brimmed in my eyes. "I never truly knew or felt love. I'd seen it in my parents, but never thought I would ever find someone who would complete me." I wiped the tear that trickled down my cheek. "But now, I know exactly what love is. It's you, Trystan. It's you, coming to Sartha on a gut feeling and saving me. You, who I could always count on to be there every step of the way to help me through the darkest of times. My heart. My heart has never felt this way. Like it wants to burst because it cannot contain the love I feel for you."

Trystan's eyes swirled with emotion. He pushed me back onto the bed, his mouth crashing onto mine.

There were no words to describe what it felt like to seal the mating bond. It was much more than a feeling. Much more than a pull. It was an immense and powerful joining of two beings who were destined for each other.

The emotions, the senses, were multiplied by hundreds, if not thousands, when he was near. It was like our souls had merged, entwining, and fusing together. When I looked at him, I felt nothing but affection, devotion, and a tremendous respect for this powerful being. He was fiercely protective, but with me, he was kind, filled with warmth and tenderness. Because of that, the upcoming battle tightened my chest with worry.

"What's wrong?" Trystan pulled back, his eyes narrowing on me, probably sensing my apprehension.

"I'm afraid," I breathed.

"Of what?"

"What would happen if you were taken from me. Roehl knows you are my greatest weakness. He cursed you once, and I am terrified of what he is planning to do."

"Don't worry about me, my flame." Trystan leaned down and kissed my forehead, nose, lips. "Roehl will get what is coming to him. I will make sure of that. And no matter what happens, we will be together. Always."

"You have to promise me you won't die. My heart will never recover from that loss."

Trystan smiled. "Don't worry about tomorrow. Focus on the now. Focus on me. On us." Trystan pressed his lips to my shoulder, and then, his teeth sank into my flesh. I moaned, feeling only pleasure. His neck was bare, open to me. My incisors lengthened, so I pressed my lips against the spot where his shoulder and neck met, and then sunk my teeth into his flesh. Trystan let out a low growl, a growl that reverberated to my core.

His blood was addicting. It was intoxicating. It was erotic. *Gods.* I couldn't think. I could barely breathe, as both of us were latched onto each other.

The feeling had taken me to another level, back arching, and toes curling. I knew he was there with me.

I wanted him closer. Bare skin against mine.

Clawing at his shirt, Trystan unlatched, and unwillingly, I did too. The high, the ecstasy. In moments, we were both bare, our lips still wet with each other's blood.

"I love you, wife." Trystan situated himself above me, and with one movement, sheathed himself inside me. "You're mine."

I moaned as pleasure ripped through every part of me. "I'm yours."

"Forever," he breathed.

"Forever."

With eyes locked onto each other, he began to move faster. And in that moment, so incredibly intimate, Trystan took me to a place where, together, we rattled the earth's foundation and shattered the stars.

Before the sun had set, we gathered in the foyer. Trystan, Kylan, Brone, Feng, and Andrés were dressed in fighting leathers, as was Markus, who wore the leathers he left Morbeth in. Nicolae, Thalia, and I wore dark pants and tunics.

"Nicolae, do you think we can transport three at a time?"

"I'm sure we can, but I don't want you to risk it. Two is safe. We need to keep our strength up, and our supplies are limited."

Trystan stood next to me with a sexy grin, his fingers feathering against mine. *"You have more than enough supply right here,"* he spoke through our bond, rubbing the spot I'd bitten him earlier.

Gods. My face flushed with heat as he let out a soft laugh.

"I need to know what just happened," Andrés blurted, pointing between me and Trystan.

Brone glared at him. "Why?"

"Because our prince is chuckling, and Calla is turning bright red." Andrés rubbed his hands together. "It must be good."

"It was nothing," I said, looking at the window, embarrassed that my face was so revealing. I had to change the subject. "The sun has set. We should get going."

Andrés exhaled loudly and shook his head in disappointment.

Nicolae came in with his satchel. "I will be taking Feng and Brone, and you will take Markus and Thalia."

Thalia held out the map, and both Nicolae and I studied it.

"What if you and I linked together? Would we be able to transport everyone at once?"

Nicolae paused, considering my question. "Again, it is likely we could do it, but I have reservations because it is something I have never done before."

"Then how would we ever know if it is possible? If we can do this, that means we could transport everyone to the castle all at once. No one would be left behind." I looked at Trystan, who nodded in approval. "I know we can do this."

Nicolae smiled. "If you believe we can, then I will too."

I walked over to Trystan and took hold of his hand and held my other hand out to Thalia. Everyone else grabbed hands, and we stood in a large circle with Nicolae on one side and me on the other.

"You've got this." Trystan gave me another dose of his positivity.

My eyes fastened on Nicolae while my mind focused on the Crag. I couldn't lose concentration, no matter what. I'd been there before, so I knew it would be easier for me to focus on the entrance.

Nicolae gave a slight nod, and our powers combined, humming through our joined hands. In moments, darkness folded in around us and when it unfolded, we were standing directly outside the entrance of the Crag.

CHAPTER FIFTEEN

INCENDIA

"You did it," Thalia chimed, giving me a quick hug.

Nicolae stepped forward, his eyes sweeping over the ruins around the rim of the cave's entrance. I realized this was the first time he'd set foot on the Crag. The last time he was in Incendia was when he was an infant, carried away to safety in the arms of Leora's handmaiden. I could only imagine the thoughts running through his mind right now.

"Come," Markus urged. "We should get inside."

Thalia and Markus took torches from the entrance, and I lit them with my powers before we headed into the dark cave.

As we passed the entrance, I felt the same surge of power flow through me as I did the last time I had come here.

"Did you feel that?" Nicolae exhaled, looking a little dazed.

"Feel what?" Kylan was on guard, scanning the area.

Nicolae held his arm out to balance himself against the cave wall. "I feel—"

"Unbalanced?" I added, knowing exactly what he was feeling. "Like the ground is moving beneath us?"

Nicolae nodded, his eyes wide. "Yes."

"I don't feel anything," Kylan replied.

"Neither do I," Brone added, his brows knitted together.

Thalia paused and faced Nicolae. "Only Incendian's can feel the power here. It flows directly from the Fire Goddess."

Trystan turned my palms over, his eyes illuminated by my glowing tattoos.

Thalia smiled widely. "That proves Calla is the chosen one."

"That's badass," Andrés blurted, his eyes on my palms. "Why isn't Nicolae's tattoo glowing? Or Thalia's?"

"While I am an Incendian Royal," Nicolae explained, "only a female can be chosen. It has been this way from the beginning."

"Ahh." Andrés nodded, his eyes still frozen on my palms.

"Follow me," Thalia said. "The inner cave is large enough for all of us to rest."

"Because we aren't from Incendia, are we safe here?" Brone questioned, pausing near the entrance.

"Yes," Thalia replied. "As long as you don't pass the inner ruins, you will be fine. Only the chosen ones are allowed beyond that point."

Brone didn't move. He stayed frozen in place. "What happens if someone were to pass the ruins who wasn't the chosen one?"

She shrugged. "I don't know. Those not chosen, who have traveled beyond the inner ruins, have never returned." She turned and started moving down the corridor.

Markus slapped a hand on Brone's shoulder. "You'll be fine. I made it to the middle with no problem."

Trystan grabbed hold of my hand and I was thankful for it because the power flowing through the cave put me off balance. Following Thalia through the rocky tunnel that led us deep into the mountain, it felt like forever before we finally reached the larger, open cavern.

As soon as I stepped inside, the runes on the cave walls began to glow gold, illuminating the room. Nicolae, Trystan, and his cadre glanced around, taking it all in.

"I am assuming that is the area we can't enter." Brone pointed to a tunnel on the far wall of the cavern that led to the Fire Goddess.

"Yes. This is as far as we go." Thalia walked over, placing her torch in a holder on the wall. Markus did the same on the opposite side. "Because Calla is the Chosen One, she has awoken the runes. They have alerted the Fire Goddess. She knows Calla is here."

Everyone made themselves as comfortable as they could get on a dirty cave floor, except for Nicolae. He stood, slowly walking around the cave, taking in every rune. I gave Trystan a nod and stood, making my way over to him.

"How are you doing?" I asked softly.

Nicolae turned and smiled, those golden eyes shining as brightly as the runes on the wall. "A little overwhelmed," he said, looking back down the tunnel we'd traveled, with a distant look in his eyes. "I have spent my entire life in hiding from a threat I was told decimated our island. I never thought I'd set foot on Incendian soil again."

I grabbed hold of his calloused hand and felt the power surge between our palms. "Neither did I," I whispered. "But then, I never knew the story of Incendia or that it even existed until months ago."

Nicolae gave me a knowing smile. "I can see how confusing that would be." He ran the fingers of his free hand through his mahogany hair. "I guess returning was inevitable. I was born here and always felt a connection to this place. Like there had always been an invisible thread attached to me, tethering me to Incendia."

I nodded again but couldn't imagine what his life must have been like. How many years he'd had to live in isolation and on the run. It must have been a lonely life. An exhausting, burdensome life filled with worry and fear.

I hoped, one day, I would get a chance to hear his story. I wanted to know more about him, because growing up, I knew nothing at all.

I traced my finger along a rune on the wall and watched it glow even brighter. "It was Leora's wish for us to find each other and return to Incendia to take our rightful places. She cherished the land and her people. She unlocked our powers so we could answer her call, and whether we feel like we deserve this or not, we are her heirs. This is our kingdom, and these are our people." I could feel the destiny inside of me awakening. War was coming. It was at our doorstep.

Nicolae released his hand from mine before wrapping me tightly in both arms. "I cannot be prouder of you, granddaughter. You have grown so much in the short time I've known you. You've witnessed, dealt with, and faced death right in the face, and when most would have crumbled, you have only become stronger." His smile suddenly turned solemn. "I wish I'd had the chance to meet your father. If I had only known he was born — that he was alive — things would have turned out much differently. I also know it wasn't by chance. Fate had chosen a different path for him. And for you." He offered me a sad smile, but I knew he was still struggling with the fact he had a family he never knew existed. "Even though we don't understand why, fate brought us together. For such a time as this."

"Yes," I agreed. "For such a time as this."

"I hope to spend a lot more time with you in the future."

I couldn't help but smile. "I look forward to it. We have a lot of time to make up for."

"We do," he exhaled, a sad smile curling on his lips. "But first, let's stay alive and finish this." He held out his hand to me, so I took it, and we shook.

"Deal."

A sudden gust of wind burst through the tunnel we'd entered from. Everyone jumped up and readied for whatever was coming toward us. A loud screech reverberated off the walls, and I knew it was Flint before I saw him.

He sailed toward me in his firebird form, then swooped up into the cave, circling, before landing on my outstretched arm. Everyone stared at this rare creature in his true form. He was magnificent, a mythical being only a few witnessed. And he was my pet.

"What are you doing here?" I questioned, gently rubbing his head. He closed his eyes and leaned into my hand, like he was enjoying it. "Did you come to see me, or your creator?"

Flint let out a deafening screech before taking to flight again. He shot down the forbidden tunnel and disappeared.

"He answered that pretty quickly," Kylan laughed.

"You said the Fire Goddess gave him to you?" Feng questioned.

"Yes," I answered, watching Flint appear again at the entrance of the tunnel. He screeched at me before flying back down the pathway, like he wanted me to follow.

I didn't feel a need to follow him. I'd already met the Fire Goddess. Besides, it would be rude to pop in uninvited.

"Come to me, Chosen One, and bring your mate," a voice spoke. I knew that voice. It was Helia. *"I would like to meet your prince."*

I turned to Trystan, my eyes widened.

"What's wrong?" he asked, rising to his feet.

"Helia wants me to come to her."

He nodded. "Then you must go."

"But she wants you to come with me."

"Wait." Kylan rose and stepped beside Trystan. "I thought only the chosen were allowed beyond the runes."

Because I was clueless about the rune rules, I shrugged, and everyone looked at Thalia. But her expression mimicked mine, also filled with confusion.

"It's true. It's what we've been told since the beginning." She shook her head with a worried look in her eyes. "We've been told that only the chosen were allowed to enter. And it is also true that those who went past the runes without the markings of the Chosen One, never returned." She hesitated, her brow crumpling. "But if the Fire Goddess is asking for him to come, then maybe you should take him."

"What if it isn't her?" Markus said from his spot on the ground. "What if it's Roehl? He has been gathering dark mages. What if he's trying to get Trystan to walk past the runes so he will never return?"

I began to doubt. What if Markus was right? What if Roehl had found a way to get inside of my head? If it was true that no one could enter but the Chosen One, then I wouldn't risk it.

Thalia shook her head. "No. With all the protective runes and the power of the Fire Goddess shielding this area, I highly doubt that Roehl and his dark magic would have any power here. The queen's mages are old and are said to be two of the strongest, anywhere. If they cannot cast magic here, I doubt Roehl and his mages can. Plus, how would he be able to communicate with Calla now that their blood bond has been broken?"

"She has a point," Feng agreed. "Besides, I trust Calla to know the difference. I know she would never put our prince in harm's way."

I felt a warmth in my chest and an overwhelming sense of peace. *"Do not fear, Chosen One,"* Helia spoke again. *"Your mate is safe here and I will assure his return. Unharmed."*

"It is Helia," I said with confidence. Trystan moved to my side, and I gazed lovingly into his eyes. "I have no doubt it's her. She wants us both to come."

"Then I will accompany you." Trystan took hold of my hand. "It wouldn't feel right to let you go alone, anyway."

"Are you sure?" Brone stepped in front of us, his hand midair, like he was uncertain if he should stop us or not.

I didn't blame him, or any of them for their concerns. They were here to protect their prince.

I nodded, giving him a reassuring smile. "I cannot explain to you how I know it was the Fire Goddess that spoke to me, but I do know, without a doubt, it was her. She told me Trystan is safe and she has assured me he will return unharmed."

Brone's eyes bore into mine, like he was trying to read my thoughts. Then his expression softened, and he stepped out of the way.

"Be safe," he said.

Trystan laid a hand on Brone's shoulder. "I trust her with my life. We will return soon."

He then led me toward the entrance, and without pause, stepped over the threshold. I followed directly after him.

The tunnel was dark, so I called my flame. It filled my palm, illuminating the entire area.

Trystan broke the silence. "So, what exactly did the Fire Goddess say to you?"

I hugged his arm tight. "She wants to meet my mate."

"I never thought, in all my immortal life, I would meet a goddess." His lips curled into a smile. "Other than you, my flame."

I laughed out loud. "I am definitely not a goddess."

"You are mine," he said, his eyes sparkling in my firelight. "From the moment we sealed the mating bond, I vowed to worship none other than you."

"Trystan," I breathed. My heart thrummed loudly inside my chest, warmth filling it entirely.

My knees buckled as I took another step, power surging through my entire body.

Ahead of us was the open cavern, with a gaping hole in its center filled with blue fire. It was the portal that led to Helia.

Trystan grabbed me by the waist, steadying me.

"Are you okay?" he asked. He seemed unaffected.

"Yes." I had to catch my breath. "There is so much power in this room, it's hard to breathe."

He gave me a sly grin. "I thought it was my words that affected you."

I pressed a gentle kiss to his lips. "They did. Everything about you affects me, my prince. In the best way possible."

"Come to me," the Fire Goddess spoke.

"She wants us to come," I said, drawing Trystan toward the vast crater filled with blue flames. As we came near, those flames tumbled out of the hole and twisted around our feet.

Trystan threw me a side-eyed glance. "Is this safe?"

I nodded, knowing this place did appear a little daunting.

"Do you trust me?" I asked.

"With my life."

I took a step closer to the edge, and he held me back. "What are you doing?"

"We have to jump."

He hesitated for a moment, then straightened his back and stepped beside me. Turning to him, I draped my arms around his neck, while his arms curled behind my back.

I peered into his handsome eyes, filled with warmth and trust. A trust that made my heart want to burst, because right now, he was placing his life in my hands.

Even I was a bit uneasy, especially after Markus had put that fragment of uncertainty in my mind. But I knew it was the Fire Goddess because when she spoke, her words wrapped around me with truth and light. Whenever Roehl spoke to me, I felt only dread and darkness and that black smudge that lingered afterward.

But Trystan, my prince, had come without pause because he trusted in me.

"Together?"

"Always," Trystan uttered, pressing his lips against mine.

And then . . . we jumped.

CHAPTER SIXTEEN

We fell through the portal of endless blue flames. My stomach twisted, wondering why the Fire Goddess had called us. Was she upset because I had set off the runes in the Crag? Was she busy when they had alerted her?

I waited, wondering if she would appear like she had the last time. But she didn't. Instead, Trystan and I landed in the dwelling of the Fire Goddess in the Celestial Realm.

It was just as bright and magnificent as I remembered.

We stood on pristine white marble floors inlaid with gold veins, a shimmering mist at our feet, still dazed and still in each other's arms. Trystan's eyes swept the area, widening on the large gold vases filled with red roses.

"Are those —"

"On fire?" I giggled. "I believe they are."

"I just wanted to make sure," he exhaled. "I suppose it's fitting for the Fire Goddess to have flaming roses."

I laughed as we walked, hand in hand, past white columns that reached upward toward the brilliant blue sky, toward the grand dais where Helia was sitting on her throne petting Flint, who was now perched on a golden staff beside her.

"There you are." I narrowed my eyes at him.

"Welcome," Helia spoke. Her eyes, the color of molten lava, met mine.

I paused, forgetting how mesmerizingly beautiful she was. Her features were soft and perfect, her bronze skin flawless. She was wearing a fitted crimson dress over her long and slender frame. Fiery red hair tumbled over her shoulders, the ends flickering in blue flames. Atop her head circled a crown of gold fire.

When her eyes met Trystan, she stood and smiled, her aura glowing brightly.

"Goddess." Trystan placed a flattened hand to his chest, bowing at his waist.

Helia stepped down off her dais and glided toward us. "I am deeply pleased you are here." Those molten eyes slid to me. "So, this is your prince."

I turned to Trystan, my heart fluttering. "Yes."

Helia came within a foot of me, placing a gentle hand over my chest. "The prince has captured your heart, Chosen

One. I have seen how deeply you've put your trust in him." Her molten eyes shifted to Trystan. "And I've also seen the measures you've taken, how far you've gone, to keep her safe."

There was a glimmer in Trystan's eyes, and then . . . Flint screeched loudly, making my ears ache. Helia sighed, then twisted back to the firebird.

"Yes, yes. You have also kept her safe. I told you to stay near her, but you've been wandering with the prince's crow, flying all over Talbrinth, haven't you?"

Flint screeched again, making Helia turn to face him. "From here on, you will remain near her. A dark and violent evil is coming, so you must always keep her in your sights. Do you understand?" The firebird replied with another screech, making Helia nod.

Could she truly understand him? Of course, she could. She was the goddess who created him.

Helia pivoted, her eyes shifting between me and Trystan. "You two have sealed the mating bond."

My eyes widened. I wasn't sure what to say because she had caught me off guard.

"We have," Trystan replied. "Calla is my mate and my wife."

Helia inclined her head to him. "I am glad fate has chosen you, Prince of Carpathia. Calla will need someone to stand beside her, an equal who will accept her power and place in this life."

Trystan bowed his head. "She is my life. I will give everything to keep her safe and make sure her destiny is fulfilled."

Helia's molten eyes slid to me with a glowing smile and a look of pride in her eyes. I knew she was impressed with him. Who wouldn't be? Trystan was perfect.

"Stand in front of me and join your hands together."

I looked at Trystan, who took hold of my hands, linking his fingers in mine. Helia reached down and took our joined hands in hers, holding them in front of us.

"Today, I give you my blessing by imparting to you a gift. A gift no other mates have been given. A gift that could change the course of your future, if used at the appropriate time."

Helia closed her eyes, her body encompassing in flame. It was the most amazing thing I had ever seen, and it made me wonder if I looked like that when I called my flame.

Looking into Trystan's eyes, I had no idea what to expect. What kind of gift would the Fire Goddess give that I didn't already have?

Helia's gold and red and blue flames coiled around mine and Trystan's joined hands, moving upward around our wrists, arms, and then encompassing us entirely. I felt her power, felt it surge through my blood, bones, and marrow. Felt it strengthening my own power.

Trystan's hand gripped mine tighter, his azure eyes narrowing as he looked at me.

I could feel Helia's power surge between our connected hands. Something was happening. Something I had never felt before or could explain.

Closing my eyes, I let go. Let that power consume me until I couldn't breathe, and my legs buckled beneath me.

Falling forward, Trystan caught me, enclosing me in his arms, holding me steady. I felt his power. His cooling breeze, tempering the inferno raging inside.

Helia finally let go and stepped back, her power still buzzing in and through us.

Still wrapped in Trystan's arms, I glanced at Helia, and she gave me a blooming smile.

"Apart, you are both powerful. Together, you will be an unstoppable force." She glided back up to her dais and sat on her majestic throne. "I've done this because your lives have been sealed by the mating bond, and also because I've seen the love and loyalty between you."

"What exactly did you do?" I asked.

"I have given you access to each other's power."

Trystan looked down at his palm. He now had a tattoo like mine.

"You are twin flames, and your power will be doubled as long as you are together, linked to one another."

Her eyes narrowed on me. "I have watched you grow and use your gifts. Remember, do not doubt yourself. You can do much more than you think. Up until now, you have only skimmed the surface of your powers."

Skimmed the surface? I had killed men. Drowned them with monstrous waves, crushed their bones with roots, and opened the earth to swallow them whole. What more could my powers do?

I didn't want to be known as a murderer. I was just defending myself. Defending those I loved.

"You will need every bit of power to go up against the Prince of Morbeth. He has built an army that is infused with dark magic. They will be hard to kill."

"How many?" Trystan asked.

"Ten thousand," she replied, her expression dismal.

"We have come to overthrow the queen," I said. "We will soon have Incendia's army."

Helia's molten eyes filled with sadness. "I'm afraid you are too late. The false queen has taken Incendia's army. They are sailing on the Sangerian Sea as we speak, heading to Morbeth."

My heart was crushed. "Does the army know where they are heading?"

Helia shook her head. "They do not. She told them they are going to war to fight against Morbeth. But Morbeth's mages will be waiting with their magic, to infiltrate the minds of the men as soon as they dock. They will be forced to serve Morbeth."

"No," I breathed. "We can't let that happen. We have to reach them before they get to Morbeth."

"How?" Trystan questioned. "We cannot transport to a ship we have no location for."

There had to be a way.

"Kai," I spoke out loud. "He can help us. He can find the ships and let us know exactly where they are."

Helia gave me a smile.

"Isn't he in Aquaria?" Trystan asked.

"Yes. But he told me he would be coming to meet us soon. I'll contact him."

Closing my fist, I called to him out loud, so Trystan and Helia could hear. Only, they wouldn't be able to hear his response.

"Kai, are you there?"

"Hey, Sea Star. Is everything okay?" he replied.

"Yes, but we need your help."

"Where are you?"

"Incendia," I said. "It's a long story, but we came to overthrow the queen. We just found out she's gone, sailing somewhere in the Sangerian Sea with the Incendian army. They are on ships heading to Morbeth where Roehl's mages will be waiting to use magic on them, to make them fight for him."

"And you want me to help?"

"Yes," I answered. "We need to know where the ships are so we can transport there."

"He won't be able to give you exact coordinates." Trystan's arms were crossed over his chest, his expression one of concern.

"He's right. It's a risk you cannot take," Helia added.

There was more than one way for us to be transported, and since the ships were in the Sea — Kai's terrain — he should be able to find them easily. "Kai, can you afford to bring some men with you to take us to the ships?"

"Of course. How many men will you need?"

"There are nine of us."

"Sea Star, you are traveling to ships filled with Incendian men ready to fight. Do you need me to bring a small army?"

My mind whirled and my stomach twisted with his question. But I would not spill any more Incendian blood. We had already killed those that had come to the Isle of Aria. I wasn't going to allow any more to die.

"No. I am going to take care of the queen, and once she has fallen, the army will have to submit."

"Are you sure?"

"Yes. I am positive."

"Okay," he replied, but his voice sounded unsure. *"Be ready at the Incendian shore. The same place I saved you the last time."* He let out a chuckle. *"We should be there in about two hours."*

"Two hours? Aren't you in Aquaria?"

"I am." He let out a breathy sigh. *"You're right. I can be there in two hours, but my men might need a little more time. Give us three hours."*

"Three hours is perfect. Thank you, Kai. We'll see you then."

"Tell Trystan to keep you out of trouble until we get there."

"I will not," I huffed. "Besides, there is no trouble here. The trouble is sailing to Morbeth."

"Fine. See you soon, Sea Star."

"See you soon."

"I will send you back to the others," Helia said, petting Flint. "Three hours is not much time to prepare." She glided back to us and held out her hands to me. "I wish I could help, but I cannot. My hands are bound when it comes to dealing with issues of the mortal world. The best I could do was bestow the gift to you and your prince. Think of it as a wedding gift from me."

"Thank you, Helia," I said bowing my head.

Catching me by surprise, Helia moved toward me and wrapped me in a hug. "I have never felt more protective over a Chosen One. I suppose it's because you were unaware all this time of your powers and of Incendia. But you have surprised me, and I am proud you are my representative." She moved to Trystan. "Prince of Carpathia, your powers have been tied to

Calla's and so has your life." Helia's expression turned staid. "If one of you dies, the other will die as well."

"What?" I was suddenly filled with a rush of anxiety.

Was this gift worth it? Trystan couldn't die. He was the future king and only heir to the throne of Carpathia. He had to survive.

"If that is the case, then I will make sure we both live," Trystan said, fisting his hand over his heart, bowing his head. "If she dies, my life will be forfeit anyway. Now that I have found my mate, I would not want to live a life without her."

Helia's smile widened, her aura brightening. "I can see why my Chosen One has fallen so deeply for you. Take care of her. She is the last of her kind." Those molten eyes slid to mine. "Unless you see fit to bear another heir."

I swallowed the huge lump in my throat. "Maybe in the distant future."

Helia laughed, her aura blooming with color. "Then, stay alive, Chosen One. Your people will need you."

I nodded, knowing war was coming. We now knew Roehl had gathered an army of ten thousand and was ready to fight. We had to be ready.

I wondered if Trystan would call his army in Carpathia to help. I doubted his father would allow such a thing, but our sands of time were running out. We needed to gather our allies.

"Remember, the gift I bestowed works only when you are together," Helia said. "Stay close to each other. Twin flames burn the brightest."

With a single touch, Trystan and I were standing back in the cavern, next to the portal filled with blue flame.

Trystan raised his left hand, observing his new tattoo. Then, those glimmering azure eyes met mine as he fisted his palm, offering me his arm. "Shall we?"

I hugged his arm tightly as he escorted me back down the dark corridor.

CHAPTER SEVENTEEN

THE MOOD WAS SOMBER as we stepped into the cavern. As soon as the group saw us, they jumped to their feet.

"You're back!" Thalia ran up, her expression a mixture of happiness and relief, mimicked by everyone in the room.

Kylan also strode toward us. "I am relieved to see you both. Alive."

"Did you think I wouldn't return?" Trystan laid a hand on Kylan's shoulder.

Kylan shrugged and let out a deep sigh of relief. "After hearing the tales, I was a little worried. So, did you meet the Fire Goddess?"

Trystan nodded. "I did."

Andrés' popped up to his feet. "Tell us about her. What was she like?"

"I will tell you everything, but first we have news," Trystan said. "The queen is not in Incendia. Nor is the Incendian army."

"What?" Nicolae's brow crumpled with concern. "Where are they?"

"They are sailing to Morbeth," I said sadly.

"Why to Morbeth?" I could feel Nicolae's frustration.

"From what the Fire Goddess said," Trystan explained. "The queen told the army they were gathering to fight Morbeth, alongside other countries. But their ships are not set for Baelfast. They will arrive at Crimson Cove where Roehl's dark mages will be waiting. They will put a curse on Incendia's army, and they will have no choice but to fight for Morbeth."

"Gods," Nicolae exhaled. "So, we missed our chance?"

"No," I replied. "Kai is on the way with some of his men. They will take us to the ships, so we must make it to the shore in a few hours. This will be the perfect time to strike. The queen would never expect us to find them out at sea."

Nicolae nodded, gathering his satchel. "When should we leave?"

"I think we should head down as soon as possible."

"I know a place close to the shore where we can stay until Kai arrives," Thalia added. "It's where the guards stay, so there might be a few stationed there. But if most of the army is gone, it shouldn't be a problem."

"I'll take care of the guards," Nicolae said. "I can transport and quickly immobilize them."

Markus stepped forward. "Take me with you. I can help. It's always good to have an extra pair of eyes watching your back."

Nicolae gave him a curt nod.

I could tell Nicolae was so used to doing things alone. Being with others, especially in a group setting, was new to him. He was still reserved and gaining trust, but he would have to adjust. Just as I was. Especially if our future entailed wearing crowns and ruling kingdoms.

Gathering our things, we met in the center of the cavern. Thalia drew a simple map in the dirt and showed Nicolae where the guards were stationed, in a small shelter just off the shore. Nicolae snatched my wrist and pulled me to the side.

"If I don't come back in five minutes, come with reinforcements," he whispered.

My stomach twisted in knots. A lot could happen in five minutes, and from experience, five minutes was a lot of time for someone to lose a limb or a life.

"I'm coming with you," I said.

"No. You should stay here with the others."

"My power is strongest here in Incendia. No one can match it. I am coming with you."

Trystan came up behind me. "If you're going. I'm going with you. There is no debate."

Markus shook his head. "This was supposed to be a simple assignment."

I gave him a smirk. "Oh, it will be."

"Wait," Kylan interjected, sheathing his sword. "Why can't we all go together, since half of you are already going? We will stand back until you clear the area."

"We might as well," Nicolae sighed. "But the sun will be out. You will need to keep your cloaks on."

Thalia stood on my side, while the others donned their cloaks. "The area near the shore is dense with trees, so those who cannot be out in the sun, won't be there for long."

"If everyone is ready, we should go." Nicolae's expression was grave, even more so after we'd told him what the queen's plans were.

Everyone gathered in a circle and held hands. Again, I kept my eyes on Nicolae, and when everyone was ready, he nodded. I called to my power and could immediately feel how much stronger it was here. Or maybe it was the fact I had just visited the Fire Goddess.

Focusing on the map that Thalia had drawn in the sand earlier, I asked my power to take us to the spot she'd pinpointed. This time, darkness came and went in a matter of seconds, delivering us safely to a spot right off the shore.

"There," Thalia whispered, pointing to a small structure hidden within the trees.

Nicolae placed a hand on Markus's arm, and they disappeared. I grabbed hold of Trystan's hand and in a split second we were inside the structure.

Two men turned to us and froze.

Nicolae was about to throw his power at them when I jumped in front of him with my arms wide. "Wait! Don't hurt them!"

Nicolae dropped his hands, but Markus and Trystan stepped forward, ready to defend me.

"Princess?" Everett breathed, his eyes wide as if he was looking at a ghost. "H-how are you here?"

"Who are they?" Nicolae's voice was low, guarded. His eyes darkened, hands out to his sides.

"They are the queen's guards," I replied. "But they are not loyal to her. They took care of us while we stayed here."

Both Everett and Callum froze in place, their arms up in surrender.

"It's okay," I said, turning to them. "They won't hurt you."

"I can't believe you're here," Everett said. "We were told you were killed after you left Incendia."

"Because that's what the queen wanted you to hear," I sighed. "I came here to deal with her, but found she is no longer in Incendia."

"No, she's not," Callum answered, his sandy blonde hair in disarray, and light brown eyes bloodshot, like he'd been up all night. "She has taken our army and is sailing with them to a place between Baelfast and Morbeth. Morbeth has threatened to destroy Incendia, so the queen ordered the men to get on the ships, where they will sail to join allies who will help us fight against them."

I shook my head, aghast at the massive lie the queen had spun. She was just as cunning and wicked as Roehl. They both had no regard for the lives of their people. Narcissistic pricks.

"She is not taking Incendia's army to fight against Morbeth," I explained to Callum and Everett. "She is taking them to join forces with them. Prince Roehl will have his dark mages waiting to put a spell on the men when they dock. It will force Incendia's army to fight with Morbeth. Not against them."

"That can't be. She wouldn't do that." Callum looked utterly confused.

"How many men did she take?" I questioned.

"Five hundred and forty," he replied. "She left a handful back to guard the city." He paused, letting out a frustrated breath. "How do you know this is what she plans to do?"

I wondered if they would believe me. I didn't care. They had to know.

"The Fire Goddess told me. Your queen is not looking out for Incendia. In fact, she is in bed with the Prince of Morbeth."

"What?" Everett gasped, turning to Callum with a horrified expression. Watching these two men looking like they were about to unravel made my heart ache.

"Did you truly see the Fire Goddess? Did she really say those things?" Everett looked at me with disbelief. He was one of the guards who had escorted me to the Crag the first time I went.

"I did. She wants what's best for all of Incendia. The only way to do that, is to take out Queen Garinda. Which is why we are here." I turned and looked out a small window, one that overlooked the sea. "We came to the shore to wait for the Prince of Aquaria's arrival. He is going to take us to the ships so we can stop the queen and save Incendia's army. But I'm afraid the men won't be able to see the truth. They are blinded by their loyalty to the queen."

"Princess, you have our full support," Callum said, bowing his head. "Whatever you need."

"Yes," Everett added. "Anything."

Thalia stepped inside the small shelter, and Everett's jaw slacked agape. He slapped a fist to his chest and bowed his head. "Thalia, I thought you were dead."

Thalia gave him a smirk. "Do I look dead to you, Everett?"

"Of course not. But they said all those who left with the princess had died."

"Who said that?" Thalia stomped closer to him, eyes narrowing, hands fisted at her sides.

"The castle guards spread the word. Those closest to the queen."

A growl rumbled in her chest. "The queen wanted everyone to believe the princess was dead because she was terrified. Terrified that the true blood heir of Incendia had returned to claim the throne." Thalia turned to me with a steadfastness in those blue and green eyes. "Today, a new queen will rise, and she will carry us to glory. She will rescue Incendia and its people from the slough they've grown accustomed to. She will bring the queen to ruin, and a new Incendia will rise."

Everett dropped to a knee in front of me, throwing his fist over the center of his heart, head bowed. Callum did the same.

"We pledge our service to you, Queen Calla," Everett spoke.

Nicolae smiled, his eyes beaming with pride. Markus was leaning against the wall behind me, a grin on his face.

I shook my head, about to say something when Trystan grabbed hold of my hand. *You are their true queen. Let them honor you.*

I felt I shouldn't have been the only one they honored. I stepped over to Nicolae.

"I want to introduce Prince Nicolae Corvus to you. He is Princess Leora's only son, and my grandfather." I smiled at Nicolae. "He has returned to help save Incendia."

Both Everett and Callum's eyes jerked toward him. Everett stayed on his knee, his fist still over his heart.

"It is an honor to meet you, prince."

"Yes," Callum said, bowing his head again. "I grew up hearing stories of Leora's son. The lost prince who survived the attack. The prince who was also heir to King Romulus of Morbeth." His eyes rose to Nicolae. "Is it true?"

"It is." Nicolae folded his hands behind his back. "I am Princess Leora and King Romulus's firstborn son."

Both Callum and Everett looked like they were going to pass out.

"Here," Thalia said, pouring and handing them each a glass of water. They accepted and drained their glasses quickly.

"What can we do to help?" Everett asked, rising to his feet. "The queen left us here because she knew our loyalty was to you."

"That was stupid of her to leave you," Thalia spat. "You and Callum are the best swordsmen in Incendia."

I glanced between Nicolae and Trystan, but both shrugged. I guess whatever decision I made was up to me.

"What gifts do you have?" I knew Incendian men also had a gift from the Fire Goddess. Nicolae had more than one, but he was a direct descendant of Incendian royalty.

"Callum and I are both trained to fight, and both have the gift of fire. It's not as strong as the females, but it works when we need it."

Thalia stomped her foot, her hands fisting at her sides. "Once the queen is gone, changes will be made. Female Incendian's will be trained to fight, as it has been from the beginning. We will no longer be oppressed."

Callum and Everett agreed, nodding their heads. "And the men will gladly be there to fight alongside you. As it has always been."

I could see that Thalia was already rising to the challenge. I knew she had it in her. She just needed to believe in herself.

"What would happen if you left your post?" I asked Everett.

"The mages have shielded the city, so it is protected. Incendia will be safe if we leave."

"If I ask you and Callum to come with us, would your families agree?"

Everett smiled warmly. "Our families will understand. They know what it means to be a guard and what our duty entails to the Incendian throne. They would be honored if they knew we were supporting our true queen."

Kylan, Feng, Brone, and Andrés stepped into the shelter, and it suddenly became cramped.

"I'll be back," Nicolae said, stepping outside.

"I'm coming," I said, grabbing hold of Trystan's hand and pulling him with me, leaving the room for the ones who had to stay out of the sunlight. Thalia also remained with Everett and Callum. It must have been good for her to be back with those she'd grown up and trained with.

Outside, the trees were thick, just as Thalia had said. Sparse sunlight dappled the sandy ground.

Trystan and I followed Nicolae to the shore. It was a tropical paradise.

The sun was bright, shimmering off the crystal clear, aqua blue water, making it glimmer like diamonds. Opposite of the wintry months that had now taken over Talbrinth. I assumed it was pleasant here because this was home to the Fire Goddess and her people.

There was a gentle breeze blowing, birds chirping, and the sound of waves rolling back and forth along the shore. It made me want to sit down and soak it all in. Incendia was paradise.

Nicolae stood with his arms out in front of him, and I could barely hear the murmur of a spell. A dark cloud began to grow and spread across the sky, concealing the sun. This time I welcomed it, knowing it wasn't Roehl's doing.

"How are you doing that?" I asked, walking up to Nicolae.

Nicolae dropped his arms to his sides and gave me a lopsided grin. "It starts with a spell, and then a thought. Magic will bend and fold to your will if you believe in it."

"So, I could do that too?"

He tilted his head toward me. "Of course, you can. You possess the power of every element inside you. The power of the world is in your palms."

Trystan wrapped an arm around my waist. "We will be traveling to ships that are filled with Incendia's army, ready to fight for Garinda. We must be extremely careful on how we approach them."

I nodded, wondering how this would play out. It was supposed to be easy, transporting to her palace, slipping into her chamber, and taking her out quietly. Now, she was surrounded by an army.

Them, leaving on ships to join Morbeth was something we weren't prepared for. First, we had to figure out which ship the queen was on. Then, we would have to find out where she was on that ship. Not to mention the mages who were likely with her.

When — and if — we succeeded, we would have to try to gain the trust of the men. Men who were fed lies about me. Men who thought I was the enemy and were told I was dead. Even Everett and Callum had a hard time hearing the truth. How was I to convince an entire ship?

"Don't worry, my flame. This is just another obstacle we will overcome." Trystan's comforting words and gentle touch never ceased to take my breath away.

"Grandfather," I said. At first, he didn't respond, then he twisted back to me. His expression made me wonder if I'd done or said something wrong. "Is everything okay?"

"Yes," he said, shaking his head. "I'm still adjusting to that name. . . *grandfather*. It will take some getting used to."

I felt a little embarrassed. The last thing I wanted to do was make him feel uncomfortable. "Should I call you Nicolae instead?"

"No, I like you calling me grandfather. It makes me feel connected. Like we're family."

"We are family." I felt warmth in my chest as I looked into his familiar golden eyes. Eyes that immediately reminded me of my father.

"We need a plan before Prince Kai gets here," he said.

I nodded. "I know you have a spell that can make you vanish. When we board the ship, would you also be able to glamour me and Trystan?"

He shrugged his shoulders. "I don't know. I have only used the spell on myself."

"Why don't you try it," Trystan said, stepping away from us.

I narrowed my eyes on him. "Where are you going?"

"To watch. Someone needs to see if it can be done. I'll be right here."

I held out my hand to Nicolae. "Shall we try?"

Nicolae took my hand and with a wave of his hand, he disappeared. The only thing I could see was a nearly invisible shimmering outline of him.

"Can you see us?" I called out to Trystan.

"No," he hollered back.

I let go of Nicolae's hand and looked down at my hands. I was still invisible, so I started to step away from him.

One. Two. Three. Four. Five. Six.

On the seventh step, my body reappeared. Taking another step toward him, I became invisible again.

"There is a radius," I noted. "Seven steps away from you and we will become visible."

"Then, it is too risky to cast this spell on more than two others."

"Then you will take me and Calla," Trystan said. "The others can wait in the water, off the sides of the ships for our command."

Nicolae agreed. "We will have to stay together. Our goal will be to locate the mages first. They are our greatest threat, and when disposed of, we can go for the queen. Once she has been subdued, I will alert the others and have them board the ships. With two princes and their Chosen One, the Incendian army will have no choice but to listen."

It seemed like an easy plan. But we all knew that there were so many things that could go wrong.

For now, we would have to sit and wait for Kai.

CHAPTER EIGHTEEN

"We're almost to the Incendian shore," Kai said through our connection.

"Okay. I'll gather everyone."

"Kai's almost here," I said to Trystan and Nicolae. "I'm going to get the others."

Standing and dusting off my pants, I started back toward the small structure hidden within the trees. Nicolae kept the cover of dark clouds over the sun, so everyone else could join us.

Standing on the shore, we watched a huge wave of water crest, and out of the top, seven men rose, with Kai at the center. It was an incredible sight to see the Aquarian men dressed in their armor. They rode a wave in and then jumped off onto the sandy shore.

"That was impressive," I said.

"I like being dramatic. I knew you'd like that," Kai said, coming over and wrapping me in a warm hug.

"Hey now," I said. *"I'm blood bonded to another."*

"So what?" Kai gave me a smirk. *"You're my friend and a friend of my kingdom. Besides, I need to keep Trystan on his toes."*

I shook my head and laughed as he released me.

"Kai," Trystan said, holding his hand out to him. "It's good to see you, brother."

"You too," Kai replied, raising his brow. "Especially now that you're . . . you. If you didn't break out of it, I would have been forced to kick your ass and take your girl."

"You could never kick my ass." Trystan gave a sinister grin, slapping a hand on Kai's back. "And you need to find a mate of your own, my friend. Calla's mine."

Kai let out a deep and pitiful sigh, dropping his head. "I thought I found the girl of my dreams, until I realized you had gotten to her first. You sneaky bastard."

"What are you doing?" I narrowed my eyes at Kai.

Trystan grinned and inclined his head to the side. "It was fate, my watery friend."

Kai turned to me with a wicked grin. *"I'm paying him back for the way he treated you on the island. I'm also going to make sure he deserves you, because you deserve nothing but the best, Sea Star."*

"He only acted that way because he was under the Lethe curse. You know that."

"I do. But it broke my heart to see how heartbroken you were. If it is within my power, I will make sure he never makes you feel that way again."

"Thank you. He does deeply regret it."

"He should," Kai said, then slapped his hands together and turned to the others. "So, what's the plan?"

Nicolae quickly went over the plans so everyone was on the same page. Kai was a little ruffled that he couldn't go with us on the ship, but I assured him that me, Trystan, and Nicolae would be safe, and I would call him if we needed his help.

Turning back, I noticed both Everett and Callum looked nervous. I didn't want them to feel like they had to come because I'd asked them.

I pulled them to the side. "You can stay here if you feel uncomfortable. You don't have to come with us to the ships. We can come back and get you."

"No," Everett replied. "We need to be there. Callum was there when they boarded the ships. He knows which one the queen and mages are on. And we both agree that we can help get the men to see the truth."

It was comforting to know there were Incendians who believed in me and were willing to help overthrow the queen. "All right. Let's go."

Kai agreed to take Callum and Everett, while his men took the others. I could tell that Thalia was a little disappointed. I knew she wanted to ride with Kai, but she did her best not to show it.

Stepping in, I ran my palms over the top of the water, feeling a jolt of power. There was a reason why water was the second element tattooed on my palm. And here, right off the Incendian shore, I could feel the water power pulsing through my fingertips, waiting to be released.

Trystan and Nicolae stepped in, on either side of me.

"Are you okay?" Trystan asked, slipping his hand into mine. When our palms touched, I felt another surge of power that threatened to buckle my knees.

This time it was different. A direct link between me and my mate. His power entered me, a cool and calming caress. When his eyes met mine, I swore I saw a bit of gold swirling within.

"That was a rush," he exhaled.

"We are still on Incendian soil. The power is much stronger here."

If we stayed close, like the Fire Goddess said, I knew we would get through this.

Nicolae came and took my other hand as we waded further out until the water touched our chests.

"Follow me," Kai said to his men. "It shouldn't be long before we find the ships. They all have the same routes." He then turned to me. "You think you can keep up, Sea Star?"

I gave him a smirk. "Don't worry about me."

Kai, Everett, and Callum sank under the water. We did the same, and as soon as our heads went under the surface, I put an airtight seal around us. Suddenly, we were off, right behind Kai. But it wasn't me propelling us forward. It was Trystan.

"Relax and save your energy," he said. *"I've got this."*

My hero. *"Thank you."*

"You can thank me later."

"It will be my pleasure."

We jettisoned through the water, extremely fast, but my eyes quickly adjusted so I could see everything. Every detail ahead of us and below.

Since Trystan powered us, I took it upon myself to do the steering, avoiding any sea creatures in our way. Nicolae remained quiet, his eyes keenly focused ahead, probably making sure I was doing a good job.

"I see two ships ahead," Kai said. *"We will arrive in about twenty minutes."*

Straining my eyes into the dark water, I saw nothing.

"Are you sure? I don't see anything."

"Yes, Sea Star," he said sarcastically. *"They are miles ahead, but I can spot the ripples in the water."*

Ripples? How the hell could he see ripples? I strained my eyes to see what he was seeing, but still couldn't figure out what he was looking at.

Either way, I trusted him. He lived in the sea. He knew it better than anyone else.

"Kai spotted the ships. We should be there in about twenty minutes." I said to Trystan and Nicolae.

"Good." It was the first word Nicolae spoke since we'd left.

It was then I realized how tense he was. His hand was gripping mine so tightly it was becoming numb. His eyes were fixed ahead, and his face was hard like stone.

He was afraid.

When we got within a few miles, I finally saw what Kai was talking about, and how the ships affected the water current below them.

My breath quickened and my heart began to race inside my chest, knowing what we were about to do. This wasn't a simple task. This was monumental. We were about to overthrow a queen.

I just hoped that the men on those ships would come to accept me. All I wanted was their safety and wellbeing, and for them to live and strengthen Incendia.

"I am going to take Callum and Everett up quickly to see if they can spot the ship the queen and her mages are on," Kai spoke.

"Okay. Be safe."

"I always am."

We waited anxiously as Kai, Everett, and Callum slowly broke the water's surface. Kai made sure to stay as close to the ship as he could so they wouldn't be detected.

Each second felt like forever as we waited. And then, they dropped back under the water.

"They said it's this ship," Kai said, pointing to the one nearest them. *"But there is a twenty percent chance it isn't."* He shrugged and made a face that made me laugh.

"Kai said it's the ship closest to them. They are eighty percent sure."

Nicolae sighed. *"Well, it's better than zero."*

"If it's not the right one, it shouldn't be a problem. One of you can transport us to the next ship," Trystan said.

"Of course," I exhaled.

I was still trying to learn and hone my gifts and realize the extent of where and how to use them. But between me and Nicolae, maybe this would be easier than we thought.

"I'll transport us to the ship," Nicolae said.

I wasn't even ready when we were suddenly invisible, standing on the bow. There were men spread out all over the deck. Some were sitting, some lying down, and a couple leaning over the side, heaving into the water below. I gagged, hoping my friends under the water would avoid that.

Most of the men looked exhausted, like they'd been at sea for a while. The air was frigid, and the sun was still concealed by Nicolae's dark cloud. The Incendians didn't look like they did much sailing or enjoyed it. I didn't imagine they left their island much. They were self-sufficient, depending on their land and sea to provide whatever they needed.

After a quick scan of the ship, I didn't spot the queen or her mages. I also didn't expect them to be out on the open deck.

"We have to find them as quickly as possible," Nicolae whispered, tugging my arm.

I laced my fingers through Trystan's as we zig-zagged through bodies, making our way across the deck to a door that led to the rooms. The men didn't have a clue we were here. They didn't even glance in our direction as we passed by.

When no one was looking, Nicolae carefully opened the door to the cabins and walked through with Trystan and me in tow. This was harder than I thought, not knowing which room she would be in. She could have been in any one of them.

Continuing down the narrow corridor, we heard voices and loud footsteps. Two large men came toward us, blocking the entire hallway. There was no way to avoid them other than backing out. But behind us, the door swung open and another man, followed by two others, walked through the doorway.

Before I could panic, we were suddenly behind the men who were headed toward the exit, and it took me a second to figure out that Nicolae had transported us.

Goddess, I was so thankful he was here.

Moving down the hallway, Nicolae stopped in front of one of the doors. *"I can feel power behind here. It must be the mages,"* he said through our connection.

"Are we going in?"

"Yes. Be ready."

I squeezed Trystan's hand. *"Nicolae thinks the mages are in this room. We're going in. Be ready."*

"I'm ready. Let Nicolae lead. Don't do anything that could get you hurt."

"I won't." Hearing his concern and how protective he was over me made me love him even more.

"Let's go." Nicolae opened the door, and we rushed in. Two older women in dark cloaks stood against the far wall. They must have sensed us because their arms were up, hands outstretched, facing us.

My power was stifled as their dark power filled the room. It was suffocating, and I found myself gasping for air.

We were suddenly visible, each of us choking as whisps of black power shot toward us and wrapped itself around our necks. Nicolae was struggling, his feet dangling as the power yanked him upward, hanging him from the neck.

"Nicolae!" I screamed.

He was obviously weak, and I hadn't noticed. Our rations of blood had been low, and he probably hadn't had enough to recover from all the transporting to the Crag, the shore, and the ship. Not to mention the cloud cover and invisibility he held over the three of us.

I reached my hand toward Trystan, but he was just out of reach. I felt the darkness coil tighter around my neck, and then I watched one of the mages raise her other arm. I was pulled up by the neck, my legs dangling. I clawed at the whisps of darkness, but there was nothing to hold on to. My airway was pinched shut, and I was losing consciousness.

"Flint!" I bellowed in my mind. *"Flint, I need you again. Please."*

The corners of my eyes were darkening.

Glancing over, I watched Nicolae's eyes roll back and his arms go limp. On my other side, Trystan was struggling, also losing his battle. My eyes were about to close, when the portal behind us shattered and a streak of fire entered the room, shooting straight into my center.

Power shot through me like a bolt of lightning. Flames detonated from my body, the dark magic wrapped around my neck instantly disintegrated.

Rage burned within, turning my flame to crimson.

One of the mages dropped her arms and fell to her knees, and Nicolae's body instantly plummeted to the floor. He was unconscious.

"Spare me, Chosen One," the mage whimpered. "I beg of you."

The other mage kept her arms up, keeping Trystan in her snare.

"Let him go," I demanded, my voice as sharp as a two-edged sword. "Now!"

The mage gave me a smirk, and that was it. I threw my power at her. A huge crimson ball of flame shot from my palm and slammed into her center. The mage flew back. The power that hit her was so strong her body went crashing straight through the ships outer wall. She let out a blood-curdling scream as her body dropped, hitting the water below.

"That was one of the mages," I told Kai. *"Take her out."*

"With pleasure," he replied.

I ran over to Trystan, who had fallen, but was already up, standing on his feet.

"I'm fine," he choked, rubbing his neck. "Tend to your grandfather." He made his way over to the mage, who was still face down on the ground.

"Where is your queen?" he demanded.

"She is under a sleeping spell. She wanted us to wake her before we arrived."

"Which room?" he demanded.

"I'll take you, but you must promise to spare me."

Trystan glanced at me. "*She could have killed Nicolae, but she didn't. She released him.*"

"*I agree. But we'll have to watch her closely,*" I said, and he nodded.

I kneeled next to Nicolae. His eyes were closed, but his chest was still rising and falling. Thank the goddess.

I slid one hand under the back of his neck, and raised my wrist to my lips, biting into it. Holding my wrist over Nicolae's mouth, I let the blood fall onto his tongue and down his throat. After a minute, his golden eyes fluttered open.

"What happened?" His voice was raw.

"You passed out," I said. "You were weakened because you haven't fed." I gave him a pointed look. "Are you one of those, *Do as I say and not as I do, role models*?"

He offered me a weak grin. "I suppose I am."

Trystan came and stood beside me, holding the mage by the arm. She was older, with stringy salt and peppered hair, maybe five feet tall, with weather worn skin and a slight hunch in her back. She cowered at his side, her eyes aimed at the floor.

"We have to go," Trystan urged. "The men will be breaking down the door soon."

I turned back to Nicolae. "Can you move?"

"Yes, but I'm weak. You'll have to transport us."

Voices were bellowing outside. The men were checking the rooms and it would be moments before they got to ours.

"Which room is she in?" I asked the mage.

Her eyes stayed on the floor, but her finger pointed further down the hall. "The last door on the left."

I had no idea how I could transport us to a room I couldn't pinpoint. I'd have to guess and ask my power to take me to the queen.

The voices were louder, and footsteps pounded right outside our door. I grabbed Trystan's arm and Nicolae's hand just as the door opened.

A man's dark eyes caught mine, widening as I transported us.

CHAPTER NINETEEN

"Enemies are on the ship," a deep voice shouted as we appeared in another room.

Spinning around, I spotted a female lying still atop a bed. A blanket was pulled up to her neck.

I'd done it. I'd found the room.

Garinda was sound asleep, just as the mage had said.

"Quickly. They're coming," Trystan urged.

We hurried over to the bedside, but as soon as I reached out to touch her, Garinda's body vanished.

"What the hell just happened?" I growled. My head snapped to the mage.

She fell to her knees and begged. "It wasn't me. It's a failsafe spell Prince Roehl's mages placed on her. If anyone but us were to come within ten feet of the queen, she would be transported directly to him."

Nicolae's eyes narrowed. "That means Roehl knows exactly where we are. We must leave now."

"What about the mage?" Trystan asked, his hand still grasping her arm.

"I will serve you, my queen." Her voice trembled. "Don't leave me here. Prince Roehl will kill me if you do."

Trystan narrowed his eyes and shook his head. "We can't trust her."

"Calla, we have to go," Nicolae urged.

"Please, don't leave me," the mage pleaded, her cataract eyes watering.

I wasn't sure if I was making a wrong decision, but knowing Roehl's wrath firsthand, I couldn't bear to leave her, knowing she would be tortured. "We'll take her with us, and drop her off in Baelfast," I said.

Trystan sighed but lifted the mage to her feet. "If you try to hurt her, I will kill you," he growled, his face set, eyes darkened.

"I would never hurt the Chosen One," she muttered. "Never."

The door busted open, and men charged in. Nicolae rushed over, throwing his arms out and grabbing us. Suddenly, we were back in the water, and I quickly put an air bubble around the four of us.

"What happened?" Kai asked.

"Kai, can you do me a huge favor?"

"That depends on what it is."

"I need you to take everyone, including the mage, to Baelfast."

"Why didn't you kill her? The other one was dead as soon as she hit the water."

Gods. I must have killed her when I threw my power at her.

"This one seems to be sorry. She said she was forced to use her magic against us. I still don't know if I trust her, so keep an eye on her."

"What are you doing?" Trystan asked me.

"I'm asking Kai to take everyone to Baelfast. I need to stay and let the men on the ships know what happened."

"I'm staying with you."

I turned to him and smiled. *"I know. I planned on keeping you with me."*

Kai's luminous blue eyes narrowed. *"What are you planning, Sea Star? Why aren't you coming to Baelfast with us?"*

"The men on the ships need to know what's going on. They have no leader now that Garinda is missing."

"Missing? What happened to her?"

"She's with Roehl. I'll explain everything to you later. We cannot stay here. It's not safe."

"We're here to help you, Calla." Kai shook his head. *"I won't leave you here alone."*

"I won't be alone. I'm taking Trystan and Nicolae with me."

Kai glanced at Everett, who was talking to him. *"Your Incendian guards want to know what's going on. Should I tell them?"*

"Yes, that's fine. I don't want them to wonder."

"We need to go back to the ship," I said out loud to Nicolae.

"I know. But I'm afraid I'm still too weak to do anything. I need to feed."

"What about the mage?" I asked through our bond. *"Can't you take a little from her? Just enough until we get to Baelfast?"*

Nicolae's eyes slid to the mage. Her eyes were wide, like she was terrified, so I took her hand. "My grandfather needs to help me explain to the men on the ship what happened, but he's weak. He needs to feed."

Those dark eyes finally slid up to mine. "He can have my blood," she said. "I'm an old woman, though."

"I don't think that matters. He will only need a little."

The mage nodded, then pulled up her sleeve, holding out her bare arm in front of her.

Nicolae looked at me and I nodded, so he took her wrist and placed it to his lips. He bit down, and the mage didn't flinch. She stayed still, eyes pinched shut.

When Nicolae was finished, he pulled away and wiped the blood from his lips. His golden eyes were brighter, and the dark circles under them were not so pronounced.

"You look better," I said.

"I feel better."

Nicolae ran a fiery finger down the place where he'd bitten the mage, and the marks disappeared. Her wound had completely healed.

"Thank you," he said, and she nodded.

"You can heal people?"

"Superficial wounds," he said. "I haven't tried it on anything fatal."

The mage lowered her sleeve. "My sister is dead, isn't she?"

Goddess. The other mage was her sister?

"Yes," I answered, but I wasn't sorry. She was killing Trystan, even after I gave her a chance to stop.

The mage's eyes saddened. "If you like, I can help. Take me to the ship. I can convince the men you are the true heir."

Nicolae shook his head. "Why would you do that?"

"Because Garinda treated my sister and I poorly. She is cruel. She stole us from our families in Northfall and forced us to work for her. We were starved and tortured until we gave in. We had to. We had no other choice. She said if we didn't serve her, she would kill our family."

Gods. She and Roehl were meant for each other.

"I'm sorry," I said.

My eyes shifted to Trystan who was still reserved, and I didn't blame him. He'd probably seen his fair share of people who had betrayed him.

Kai spoke through our connection. *"Calla, your Incendian guards insist on staying with you."*

"It's too dangerous. Roehl could be coming, and I want to keep them safe."

"They think they can help. They know the men on the ships personally. But if they stay, I will have to stay too, since I'm their ride." Even from a distance, I could see him wink.

Maybe having them would be an advantage. *"Fine. But if they go, Thalia will want to go too."*

"And what's wrong with that? They are Incendians."

This was quickly becoming a lot more complicated than I had anticipated. We needed to get this done quickly. *"Stay here for now,"* I said to Kai. *"We'll take the mage, and I will let you know if I need you to bring Everett, Callum, and Thalia up top. Okay?"*

"Fine. Just let me know."

"We're going back up to the ship," I said to Nicolae, Trystan, and the mage. "They will be riled up after what just happened, so we'll need to be extra careful."

"They've been brainwashed by the queen," the mage said. "But I believe once they see and hear the truth, that you are alive and the true heir to the throne, they will have no choice but to follow you."

I had to try. I had to make them see the truth. That the woman who had been ruling them all these years was not their queen. She was an imposter.

"We need to make a move now," Trystan urged. "Every second we wait is a second closer to Roehl arriving."

I nodded, and in seconds, we were back on the bow of the same ship, but this time we were visible.

"There they are!" one of the men hollered, aiming a finger at us.

Just as I expected, all the men on deck assumed we were the enemy. They charged forward with anger on their faces, drawing swords and nocking arrows.

"Stay here," I said.

Flint had never left. He was still there. I could feel his power coursing through my veins.

"My flame," Trystan spoke, concern laced his voice.

I rested my palm against his chest. "It's okay. I need to do this."

Trystan nodded and stepped back, placing his trust in me. I also knew he would be right there to protect me if anything went wrong.

Turning to the men, my body encompassed in flame, and the ship went dead silent. The men stopped in their tracks, their eyes widened. All except for one, who let his arrow fly.

I held out my hand. As soon as the arrow touched my palm it disintegrated, turning to ash.

"Fire Goddess," one of the men cried out. His sword fell from his hand as he dropped to his knees.

Murmurs quickly carried through the men on the deck. One by one, they dropped their weapons and fell to their knees, their foreheads touching the ground.

"Goddess," they chanted. "Forgive us."

"I am not the Fire Goddess," I said. "But the Fire Goddess has chosen me." I held out my fiery palms to face the men. "I am your true queen, heir to the Incendian throne."

"How is it so?" One of the men near the front spoke, his head still bowed. "Queen Garinda is our queen."

"She is not your queen," the mage spoke from behind me. "Garinda has been lying to you. She is not from the royal bloodline."

"What about her tattoos?" Another questioned. "She is Incendian royalty."

"They are fake," the mage replied. She moved next to me, and all the men's attention snapped to her. They knew the mage. She'd been with the queen for countless years. "Garinda forced my sister and I to place the tattoos on her palms. All of her displays of power were done by me and my sister. They were fabrications. Illusions created by us to blind you from the truth. That she is not royalty."

"How do we know you aren't lying to us? Where is the queen?" another man shouted.

"Yes! Where is our queen?" the others repeated.

"She is with the Prince of Morbeth," the mage replied.

Her eyes went milky-white as she raised her arms and muttered a spell. She was scrying.

There was a shimmer in the air, and then, the queen's face appeared. It was as if we were looking into a portal created by the mage. Suddenly, Roehl came into view, his lips pressing against Garinda's. My chest tightened and stomach soured at the sight of him.

Then, Roehl's head suddenly snapped back, his eyes were glaring at the mage, as if he knew she was spying on him. His crimson-rimmed eyes went completely black, his face twisted with rage.

There was a sudden shift in the atmosphere that made my insides knot. Before we knew what was coming, thunder roared above us, and a lightning bolt cracked across the sky, striking the mage. She fell to the ground writhing and screaming, her skin blistering.

"It's a dark omen! We're under attack." The men began shouting and running for cover.

Nicolae took a knee, trying to help the mage, but her cries suddenly fell silent, and her body went limp. Her eyes were open, but there was no longer life within them.

"She's gone," Nicolae said, running his fingers down her eyelids, closing them. "We have to go."

An ominous dark cloud was forming, coming quickly toward us.

"I can't leave the men," I said. "They will die."

"We must. If we stay, *we* will die," Nicolae urged, grabbing my shoulders. "Roehl needs them alive. We cannot transport five hundred men. If I could, I would. But it's not possible."

"I can't leave them." Tears welled in my eyes, knowing that every man on these two ships would be cast under a spell and used to fight against me.

"Kill her!" the men bellowed. "You've brought danger to us all!" Arrows began flying, but I put up a fire shield to protect us.

Trystan grabbed my arms and pulled me against him. "We will save them later, Calla. I promise. But we must leave for now. We will not die today."

I nodded, tears rushing down my face. He was right. We weren't ready to fight Roehl or his mages right now. And we were in no position to save the men on these ships.

A sudden surge of power sent Flint into the sky. His fiery body shifted back into the crow as he took off, flying in the opposite direction of the cloud. I took it as a sign that we were to leave too.

Nicolae grabbed our wrists and transported us off the ship and back into the water, where I quickly put an air bubble around us.

"What happened?" Kai asked.

"Roehl is coming. We have to leave."

"Are you okay?"

"Yes. Do you have somewhere safe for us to go?"

"I do." He said, giving me a warm smile. *"Follow me."*

Kai shot through the water, and everyone followed. Trystan used his power, and I held on, my heart crushed. We'd failed our mission. The queen was still alive and now, the Incendian army would be under Roehl's spell.

Gods, I wish I could turn back. But like Nicolae had said. We needed to do this right. If we ended up staying and dying, the men would become Morbeth's slaves forever and Incendia would finally fall to ruin.

"Your people will be rescued, my flame. I assure you. You will have my full support."

"Thank you." I hugged Trystan's arm and rested my head against his shoulder. He pressed a kiss to my forehead before focusing on the water ahead.

I thought Kai was going to take us somewhere above ground in Talbrinth, but instead, we went deeper into the dark depths of the sea where the water was much colder.

At the bottom of the sea was a large formation of rocks, the size of a mountain. We weaved through a few tunnels until I saw a shimmer in the water, the size of a doorway. It was a portal. Kai set down next to it and he, Everett, and Callum walked through.

The rest of us did the same.

As we stepped through, we stood in an underwater dwelling that reminded me of the inside of the palace in Aquaria.

"What is this place?" Thalia asked, her eyes roaming the inside of the underwater home, soaking it all in.

"My parents own this place. It's their secret getaway," Kai said, turning with a lopsided grin. "So, let's keep this a secret, huh?"

"Like any of us can get down here without you, anyway," Thalia snickered, which made him laugh out loud.

"We need to get blood," Kylan said to Trystan.

"Yes. We are near Merchant Port. Go to our distributor."

Kylan bowed his head. "Me and Brone will go if someone can take us topside."

"I can take you," one of the Aquarian guards said. He was the one who had brought Kylan down.

"Thank you," Trystan said with a bow of his head. "Be safe, Kylan."

Kylan placed a fist over his chest, then he and Brone followed the man back out.

Kai led us to a large sitting area, decorated with statues of mermaids and the sea god. There was also a fountain in the center that overflowed into a large glass aquarium filled with colorful fish. The seats were shaped like clam shells but were plush and very comfortable.

"Do you have places like this throughout the sea?" Andrés asked.

Kai took a seat and leaned back, crossing a leg over the other. "We do have rest areas, but none as big as this. They're meant for overnight stays."

Nicolae was quiet, and I noticed he still looked exhausted.

"Kai, do you have a room where Nicolae can lie down?"

"I'm fine," Nicolae said, but his expression showed otherwise. His skin was pallid, his eyes heavy.

"Nicolae, we have six rooms upstairs. The first five are guest rooms, so you are welcome to any one of those. They each have bathing rooms, so feel free to soak in a tub and relax."

"Do it," I urged Nicolae. "We don't know the next time we'll be able to rest in a place like this."

Nicolae finally leaned forward on his chair and gave me a grin. "Thank you, Kai. I will take you up on your offer because my granddaughter won't relent until I do." He stood and gave us a nod before he made his way to the staircase.

"It's only because I care about you and want you to be healthy. I want you to be around in the future," I said loudly.

Nicolae twisted his head back at me and smiled, his eyes glassy. "I will see you all later," he said with another bow of his head before heading up the stairs.

I knew he was touched by my words. He probably never had anyone care about him, except Leora's chambermaid and the farmer's daughter. But now that he was in my life, I would make sure he knew he belonged. That he was loved.

"So, give me the details. What happened on the ship?" Kai asked. "Where's the mage?"

Everett and Callum sat up. This directly affected them too and I know they wanted answers.

"She's dead," Trystan responded.

Kai rolled his eyes. "I figured she was dead, but I want the details. How did she die?"

"She was telling the men on the ship the truth about the queen, showing them through a magic portal of air that Garinda had aligned herself with Roehl. But Roehl somehow knew, and in moments, dark magic surrounded us. The mage was struck with a bolt of lightning." Trystan shook his head. "It was tragic. At least she didn't suffer long."

Kai leaned forward, his elbows resting on his knees. "You said Roehl was coming? How do you know?"

"A dark, ominous cloud grew in the distance, heading our way," I explained. "I could feel Roehl's wicked energy in the atmosphere. It makes my skin crawl."

"Was the cloud like the one we saw in Incendia?" Thalia asked.

"Yes. But this one felt darker. Much stronger."

Thalia's brow furrowed. Everett and Callum remained quiet, but I could see this conversation was a lot for them to take in.

"He must have gathered the mages from the Forest of Murk," Markus said. "They are ancient hags, wicked to the core. They practice forbidden magic, ancient, dark, and incredibly powerful. I witnessed one of them suck the soul right out of a man, leaving nothing more than a withered shell." Markus shook his head. "They were the ones who created the Lethe potion."

"How can we defeat anything like that?" Andrés asked.

Markus let out a deep sigh. "You can't."

"*We* can't," Trystan added, those glittering eyes sliding to me. "But Calla can." I opened my mouth to speak, but he shook his head. "Everyone in this room knows it's true. Even the Fire Goddess herself said you are more powerful than them."

"He's right, Sea Star. I also believe that."

Trystan gave Kai a side-eyed smirk after hearing his term of endearment for me.

"Listen," Kai added. "You have the backing of Aquaria, Aquaris, Sartha, Hale, and Baelfast. After hearing that Roehl murdered his father, they turned against him. They also agree that sending out a death decree on Nicolae and his bloodline was an abuse of his power."

"That's amazing," I said. "Nicolae will be thrilled to hear that."

Kai slouched back in his chair, crossing his arms over his chest. "It wasn't hard to convince them, given the current circumstances in Morbeth. None of the kingdoms want to be involved in another senseless war. The last one cost too many lives. It took a lot of work to rebuild Talbrinth, and some countries are still struggling because of it."

I felt overjoyed to know that the other vampire kingdoms would no longer see Nicolae as an outcast. He would be able to come out of hiding and show everyone who he truly was. A prince of Incendia, and hopefully, the future King of Morbeth.

Trystan wrapped his arms around me in a warm embrace.

"The time is coming much sooner than we expected," I said. "Once Nicolae is rested and fed, we will have to plan our next move. A move that will change our future . . . for better or for worse."

"You are all welcome to make use of the rooms upstairs," Kai said. "Rest up while you can."

Feng stood. He had been quiet this entire time, but I knew he was soaking up every word of our conversations. "I will take you up on that offer."

"Me too!" Andrés popped off his seat.

Markus stood and stretched his muscular limbs. "I'm always up for a nap."

"Callum and I will share a room," Everett said. Callum nodded, and they both made their way up the stairs.

"Are they lovers?" Kai asked, pointing at Everett and Callum.

"They are cousins."

"Ahhh. I wouldn't be against it if they were. I just noticed how close they were."

I nodded and shot him a smile.

"Thalia, there is one room left," Kai said. "It's the master, and you are welcome to it. Why don't you go get some rest?"

"I'm fine." Thalia aimed her finger at me. "Why don't you and Trystan take the room? After all the crazy things that happened today, I'm sure you both could use some rest."

The offer was too good to pass up. I not only wanted, but needed time alone to muddle through my thoughts and try to make sense of what had happened on the ship.

I stood and grabbed Trystan by the wrist. "Let's go."

Trystan didn't hesitate, and immediately rose to his feet. "I guess we'll take the room," he said to Kai. "Thank you for your hospitality, my friend."

"Always," Kai said, giving us a jealous smile. He then turned his attention to Thalia. "Are you hungry? We have real food stocked in the kitchen."

"I am starving," she said, hopping up from her seat, her face blooming with a smile.

Kai offered her his arm and bowed to us. "Rest well."

CHAPTER TWENTY

Upstairs, Trystan walked into the bathing room, and I soon heard water running.

"What are you doing?" I asked, leaning in the doorway.

"Drawing you a hot bath."

I blushed, watching him roll his sleeves up, pouring scented soap into the steamy water and swirling it around with his hand. *Gods, he was sexy.*

"You don't have to do that for me."

Those beautiful eyes snapped up to me, stealing my breath away. "No, I don't need to. I want to."

When the tub was filled, he stood and strode toward me like a predator seeking its prey. He captured me against the wall, his arms locking me in on either side. He leaned in, his lips a breath away.

I could barely breathe, as he pressed a kiss to my neck.

"Your bath is ready, my flame," he whispered.

His mouth was suddenly on mine, his tongue sweeping across my lips, delving deeper. My mind and body went numb as he stepped away, grasping the hem of my tunic, pulling it over my head and tossing it aside.

His lips pressed against my chest, slowly leaving a hot trail of kisses down, down to my breasts. Trystan's mouth and tongue were like magic, causing my eyes to roll shut and head to fall back.

"Trystan," I moaned, pleasure ripping through me.

He continued to undress me until I was completely bare, those azure eyes scanning my body with approval. Then, in one fluid movement, I was cradled in his arms and carried to the tub, where he gently set me inside. It was large enough to fit at least two bodies.

"Enjoy your bath," he leaned down and whispered.

I grabbed his collar and pulled his lips back to mine. "I won't enjoy this bath, unless you're in here with me," I growled against his mouth.

A sinful grin rose on those perfect lips. "If that is what you wish."

"It is."

Those darkened eyes, filled with passion, locked onto mine, lips curling upward. In moments Trystan was bare, his perfect, rock-hard sculpted body sank into the water.

His hands slowly slid up my thighs, his eyes never leaving mine.

"Tell me you want me, my flame."

"Every part of you, my prince." I could barely speak, my heart racing. Inside my core, an inferno raged.

My reply caused him to growl. And then, Trystan slowly slid up my body. Holding onto the sides of the tub, Trystan took me to heaven and back.

Catching our breath, with his arms still around me and my head resting against his chest, there was a loud knock at the door.

Trystan sighed, giving me a quick kiss on the lips before he exited the tub. Wrapping a towel around his midsection, he strode out of the bathing room, closing the door behind him. My heart fluttered, noticing how incredibly sexy he was.

The voice on the other side of the door was muffled, but I knew it was Kylan. I strained to listen to their conversation. But even with my vampire hearing, I couldn't make out what they were saying.

After a few minutes, Trystan came back into the bathing room. A sudden wave of anxiety rose as I gazed into his now hollow eyes. His expression told me that whatever Kylan had said to him wasn't good.

I stood from the tub. "What is it?"

Those hollow eyes turned to me. "We need to return to Carpathia."

"Why? Is there trouble?"

"I'm not sure until I return and confirm what was said." He was being very discreet.

"Trystan. What's going on?" I wondered if Princess Ivy had found out about us.

Trystan paused, uncertainty and sadness were swimming in his eyes.

My bare feet padded over to him. "Trystan. What is it?"

Trystan took the towel from his waist and wrapped it around my shoulders. "While Kylan was topside, Nyx visited him. There was a message attached to her from one of the guards in Carpathia." He paused again. "There were men, posing as guards, who lured Sabine and Brynna out from the castle walls." I froze, taking in his words.

Trystan looked away, broken. "I'm sorry, Calla. They're missing."

The world crumbled from beneath my feet, my heart shattered into thousands of tiny pieces.

We'd sent them away in hopes that they would be safe from what was to come. But now, they were in even more danger.

Pain shot through my chest, knowing how terrified they must have been.

I couldn't bear to think of what Roehl was doing to them. That they were locked up in one of those dark, dank cells in Morbeth. Sabine had helped me escape from that wretched place, and I knew Roehl would punish her for it. Not to mention Brynna, who had also escaped.

My legs gave, and I collapsed to the ground. I couldn't breathe. Dread and despair gripped me tightly.

Roehl now had my two best friends, and the upper hand. He knew with them in his custody I would do anything to save them. *Give* anything to save them.

Goddess. What were we going to do now?

Trystan wrapped me in his arms. "I need to return to Carpathia to confirm if what Kylan said is true. Will you come with me?" The lines in his brow deepened. "I know my father made you feel unwelcome, but I want him and the rest of my kingdom to know I have chosen my mate."

I closed my eyes, remembering the look on his father's face when he told me to leave. He even had a ship waiting for my departure because he wanted me to disappear from his son's life.

"Yes, I'll come," I said, with huge reservations.

I'm sure there wasn't anyone who liked being dismissed or disliked by their future in-laws. Especially one who held so much sway over an entire kingdom. What would Trystan's father do when he saw me back in Carpathia?

I could only imagine. But there was nothing he could do. Trystan and I were bound. Forever.

Trystan pressed his lips to my forehead. His touch and closeness always made me feel safe and secure. Made me feel stronger. He was the glue that held the broken pieces of me together. With him, I felt I could overcome anything.

"Get dressed," he said softly. "We need to tell the others." He walked out of the bathing room and poured me a glass of ruby wine that Kylan must have delivered.

"Drink, my flame. You will need your strength."

He was right. I would need every ounce of strength I had to return to Carpathia and the king.

Back downstairs, everyone had already gathered. The vampires were holding glasses of ruby wine while Kylan was letting the others know of the message that was delivered to him by Nyx.

Markus, standing next to him, went rigid. I watched his jaw tense, and heard his breath quicken.

"What do you mean they're gone?" he growled. "They were placed under your care!"

I could see the fear in his eyes and hear it in his voice. Markus knew better than anyone what Roehl was capable of, and I could tell he was terrified for Sabine.

Thalia came and stood beside him, trying to comfort him.

I made my way over to Markus and when his eyes met mine, I saw tears pooling within them. Placing a gentle hand on his shoulder, I tried to assure him. "We'll find them, Markus. I promise."

Markus shook his head. "I know we will find them. I'm worried what condition we will find them in." His chest heaved. "Do you think Roehl will let them live? He wants you to suffer, more than anyone else, and he knows that your friends are your weakness. Right now, they are pawns in his wicked game. And Roehl will sacrifice every pawn in his possession to win." He shook his head. "I should have gone with them. I was supposed to protect them."

I stood in front of him, grabbing both of his wrists. "Do not blame yourself for this, Markus. If that is the case, then I should have been there too. Or never should have let them leave.

"Roehl is playing a very dangerous game. He is playing with fire, and I assure you Markus, that he will burn for what he's done. We will rescue Sabine and Brynna, and Roehl *will* die. But first we must return to Carpathia to find out exactly what happened."

Markus closed his eyes and took in a few deep breaths, and when he opened them again, he nodded. I knew he wanted to say more. His body was still tense, his hands fisted at his sides. He was angry and frustrated that he couldn't run off and save them. But I knew Markus wouldn't make any fatal moves. He was smart. He had to have been, being the Captain of the King's Guard.

Kai gave his guards orders to return to Aquaria and alert his father as to what had happened.

"When are we leaving," Kai asked.

"We?" I questioned. "Are you coming with us?"

He sighed and shook his head, crossing his arms over his broad chest. "Did you think I would leave and miss all the action?"

"What? Meetings with the royals aren't enough action for you?" Trystan teased.

"Hell no. The most action I had was when my father almost beat me to death for falling asleep during those meetings."

I chuckled, glad Kai was coming. He had a way of turning a dreadful situation into something . . . a little less dreadful.

"How are you feeling?" I asked Nicolae. He looked like he'd had some rest, and I was happy to see he had a glass of ruby wine.

He raised his glass to me. "Much better. Thank you."

"Are you strong enough to help me transport everyone to Carpathia?"

"I am. Are you?"

I nodded, feeling more energetic after my glass of ruby wine.

Everyone gathered in a circle. Taking hold of each other's hands, Nicolae and I transported the entire group . . . hopefully to Carpathia.

CHAPTER
TWENTY-ONE

We arrived on the docks, right outside of Carpathia's mortal town, sporadically lit by small lamp posts. Night had fallen, and tiny snowflakes danced and twirled as they slowly drifted to the snow-covered ground.

It must have been late because the town was quiet.

Kylan, Andrés, and Feng quickly left the group, heading toward the outskirts of the town, and after a short while, returned with horses.

Grabbing my waist, Trystan helped me mount onto a large black stallion and then mounted the same horse, sitting behind me. I leaned back into him, loving the feeling of having him close. He wrapped an arm around my waist, while the other held the reins.

As the others mounted their horses, Thalia was left without one.

"Thalia, would you like to ride with me?" Kai asked, extending his hand to her.

She paused, her wide green and blue eyes glancing at me. I nodded and smiled.

Her face blushed as she turned and took Kai's hand. He pulled her up, settling her in front of him. I was glad she would be riding with him. Kai would make sure she was safe if anything happened along the way.

With everyone ready, Trystan made a clicking sound and our horse took off, taking the empty side streets that led to Carpathia's hidden vampire castle. Riding through the large black iron gate and up the cobbled path, my heart was raging inside my chest as we neared the castle and guards standing out front.

Trystan's breath feathered against my cheek as he leaned forward. "Don't worry, my flame. You are more than welcome here. This is our home too."

Could he read my mind? Everyone here must have known I was anxious about returning. I also realized Trystan had probably heard my quickened heartbeat. My heart was loud and treacherous and would always give me away, but it was a precious gift I would always cherish.

Dismounting the horses, three guards greeted Trystan.

"Your Highness," they said, bowing their heads, pounding fists over their chests.

Trystan inclined his head. "I need to speak to Frederik. Where is he?"

Two of the guards slid their dark eyes to me, their brows furrowing in confusion. I couldn't help but wonder if they were part of the farewell group that had led us down to the docks after I was banished.

The guard standing in front of Trystan spoke. "Frederik is making his rounds. I can send someone to retrieve him if you like."

"Yes," Trystan said. "And make sure the one you send covers his rounds."

"Yes, Your Highness." The guard bowed even lower at his waist, then they all stood and walked away.

A few servants, a man, and a woman, came out to greet us, bowing in front of Trystan.

"Please make sure my guests are well fed, and make sure you give them whatever they need," Trystan ordered.

"Yes, Your Highness," they replied. They stepped back and waited until the rest of our group dismounted.

"Kylan. Brone. Come with me," Trystan said. "Feng. Andrés. Please take everyone to the meeting room upstairs."

"Yes, prince," they responded, fisting their hands over their chest.

I loved seeing this side of him. The authoritative side. And I could tell his people respected and honored him. Trystan would make a great king because he was already a great leader as a prince.

He turned to me, pulling me into his arms. "Wait for me inside. Frederik is the head guard here and should know everything. I'll bring him up to the meeting room when he arrives."

"Okay," I breathed. I was nervous knowing I'd be back inside the castle without him. Right now, I would give anything to be invisible.

Trystan hooked a finger under my chin, raising my head just enough so his lips could meet mine with a passionate kiss that took my breath away.

Someone gasped, and when Trystan pulled away, I saw one of the servant girls with a hand over her mouth, her face blushing bright red.

Kai walked past and slapped Trystan on the shoulder. "Damn showoff," he chuckled.

Andrés passed us, fanning himself. "You two will turn our winter to spring if you keep that up."

I blushed, but Trystan's eyes remained fixed on mine. "I'll see you soon."

I nodded, my heart thumped loudly inside my chest.

As he walked away, Nicolae and Thalia came on either side of me.

"Are you sure it's okay to be here?" Thalia whispered.

Nicolae wrapped a loving arm around my shoulder. "They can dismiss her, but they cannot dismiss the fact they are mated." My eyes jerked to his. Was he really accepting the fact we had sealed the mating bond? "I have watched the two of you together, and I have come to terms that you were meant to be. Never feel ashamed that you are mated to the prince. He wears his feelings for you on his sleeve. Everyone around can tell he is smitten by you."

Right now, I didn't care if the king accepted me or not. Because having Nicolae's approval, knowing he was here for me, was just as good a feeling.

We followed Feng and Andrés inside the castle, and they quickly led our group up the stairs into a spacious room. At the center was a large, round wooden table with chairs set around it. Along the walls were gold sconces and tapestries of landscapes.

"Have a seat," Feng spoke to the group. "Trystan will be here soon."

Everyone took a seat, except me. I was too anxious, wondering what had happened to Sabine and Brynna. Were they with Roehl? Or were they still in Carpathia?

I paced the room, trying to bide my time by looking at the tapestries.

"Calla, the servants have brought drinks," Feng said softly behind me. "Come. Sit."

"Thank you," I said, slipping into a seat next to Nicolae.

Everyone seemed distant, drinking from their goblets. We'd all been through so much together, and we still had to overcome our greatest obstacle. The time was drawing near. I could feel the coldness of it seeping deep into my bones.

Trystan walked in with a large, brawny man. He had raven colored hair that fell to his shoulders, deep-set onyx eyes, and his face was hard and weathered. He looked like someone who had been alive for a very long time.

Brone and Kylan took a seat, but Trystan and Frederik remained standing.

"Tell them what you told me," Trystan said to Frederik.

Frederik bowed his head. "One of our men saw two guards escorting both women from the castle. When he confronted them, he mentioned he had never seen these guards before.

"They told him they had just been hired and were given instructions to take them out to the gardens for some fresh air and to stretch their legs. That was the last time we saw them. The men with them are gone as well."

My worst fears were confirmed. "Have you searched everywhere?"

"Yes," Frederik replied. "We scoured the entire area and even went into the mortal town. There is no trace of them."

"Were they afraid?" I questioned, and Frederik's brow furrowed. "The two women. Did they look like they were scared?"

"No," he said. "In fact, the guard said they looked relieved, like they were looking forward to a walk in the gardens."

My heart fractured, hot tears fell down my face. They had no idea the men taking them out for a walk were their kidnappers.

I had to stop the whirlwind inside my mind because it was going to drive me insane. It was conjuring every negative scenario possible that could be happening to them.

"What do we do now?" I sobbed. I was on the verge of a breakdown, knowing they were gone. I quickly took my goblet and drank the blood inside. I had to pull myself together and be strong enough to rescue them. Because that was our next move.

"Come with me," Trystan said, taking my hand.

He led me down the stairs, and up another set of stairs that led to his wing. Walking down the hallway, he walked us past the room I had previously stayed in and stopped in front of his door.

My heart was racing as he turned the knob and opened it, pulling me inside.

"Trystan?" a voice snapped. We both froze, seeing an unwelcomed guest sitting on his bed.

CHAPTER TWENTY-TWO

Princess Ivy stood, wearing a revealing cream-colored gown, her silky raven hair fell in curls down her shoulders. Those crimson red lips pursed, and her onyx eyes turned ice cold as they trailed down to our joined hands.

"Why is she here?" she roared, her finger aimed at me like a dagger. "The king banished her!"

Trystan growled, his hand tightening around mine. "What are you doing here, Ivy?" His voice was calm with an icy bite to it. "You are not allowed in my room."

"I am your fiancé, Trystan. Why wouldn't I be here?"

"The engagement is off." Trystan said, pulling me back out of the room.

But as we started down the hall, I suddenly couldn't move. A coldness swept around my body, tightening around my chest. I knew it was Ivy. She'd used the same magic against me the last time I'd seen her.

I suddenly felt her behind me, her sharp nails pressing against my throat.

Ivy sniffed me. "Why do I smell you on her, Trystan?" Her nails dug into my flesh, and I felt warmth trickle down my neck.

Trystan turned, his eyes went pitch black, lips curling over elongated incisors. A hair-raising growl ripped from his chest. "If you cherish your life, Ivy, get your filthy, fucking hands off of my mate," he threatened, his voice cold as death.

"Trystan!" The king snapped, standing at the end of the hall with two guards standing behind him.

Behind me, Ivy choked on Trystan's words, her magic wrapping tighter around my chest and now coiling around my neck.

"Mate?" A growl exited her crimson lips, and I wondered if she was going to rip my neck to shreds with her perfectly manicured nails.

My body relaxed as I called to my power.

I didn't want to send a blast into her chest, although I was tempted to, because I knew the king favored her. Hurting her would only make him hate me more.

My power wrapped me in a protective cocoon. Then, I felt it attacking Ivy's spell, instantly incinerating it. Ivy suddenly let out a scream and hissed. I wanted to laugh, as her hand jerked away. Her power was no match for mine. She had no idea who she was messing with.

Opening my eyes, I watched her run to the king, bawling.

"She's a witch," she accused, pointing her red painted fingertip at me. "She's turned Trystan against me."

Trystan kept his back at them, taking my hands in his, his eyes scanning my neck. "Are you okay?"

"I'm fine."

He inhaled a deep breath and closed his eyes. When he exhaled, his eyes opened and were back to his normal color. Linking his fingers in mine, he turned and led me toward his father.

The king shot us a hostile glare, his face contorted with rage. "Trystan, what is the meaning of this?"

"There is nothing you or anyone else can do or say, father. I am blood bonded and have chosen Calla as my mate. We have already sealed the mating bond."

Oh gods. He wasn't holding anything back.

"We were supposed to be married!" Ivy wailed, seeming more like a spoiled child who didn't get her way.

I could tell Trystan was trying to hold his composure. His hand gripped mine tighter.

"I only agreed to the engagement because I was under the Lethe curse. I would never have made the arrangement if I was in my right mind."

"You insolent son!" the king shouted. "You have been bewitched by her!" The king's eyes fastened on my chest, and before I could move, he reached over, grabbed the amulet, and ripped it off my neck. He was seething, his nostrils flaring as he held the amulet out in front of Trystan. "How dare you offer her your mother's necklace!"

Trystan's muscles tensed. "Calla's friend found the amulet in an old shop in Sartha. She bought it and gave it to Calla as a birthday gift. Yes, it was Mother's, but I know she would have been happy to know that Calla is in possession of it now."

"How can you say such a thing?" the king spat. "You know nothing of what your mother would want."

"No father," Trystan bit back. "*You* know nothing about her. You hid my mother away when she was ill and left her to herself when she needed you most. *I* was with her. *I* bore witness to her pain and suffering while you chose to run from it, burying yourself in work and your royal duties.

"Meanwhile, all she wanted . . . all she ever cared about was your love. You denied her that, father. Without your love, she was hollow. And because of that, she felt she had no other recourse than to seek out the mage who ended her life." Trystan was trembling, his jaw clenched. "And now . . . now, you've buried every single memory right along with her."

"How dare you," the king seethed.

"No father. How dare you!" Trystan's voice grew louder, braver. "How dare you set up an arrangement with a woman I despise? A woman I know for certain would ruin my life forever."

Ivy gasped, her eyes and mouth widening.

"And how dare you exile the only woman I have ever truly loved? Calla means more to me than this kingdom. More than its wealth or riches. And in the future, if I should become king, there is no one else I would want to rule by my side."

I kept my head down, tears falling down my face. I felt Trystan's unwavering love. It flowed from his words, pulsed through our connected palms, and hugged my soul.

Trystan turned to me, his eyes filled with hurt and sorrow. "Come, my flame."

He walked forward, leading me past the king and his guards. Past Princess Ivy whose eyes were shooting daggers at me.

"Trystan, stop!" the king roared. "How dare you walk away from me!"

But Trystan didn't stop, and he didn't reply. He kept moving, pulling me with him, down the hallway, the stairs, and out of the castle.

"Trystan," I breathed once we made it outside.

He paused and turned back to face me, enclosing me in his strong arms. I felt so safe and so secure there, like nothing else mattered. Nothing, except rescuing my friends and killing Roehl.

"I don't care what my father thinks, and you shouldn't either. He has no other heir to take my place. And should he disagree with our union, then he will have to live forever and rule this kingdom alone." He pressed his lips to my forehead. "My love. My flame. I will always walk beside you, even if the rest of the world walks away."

My heart was so full it was about to burst. I gazed into his beautiful eyes, swirling with so much love and emotion. "You are my life. The very air I breathe. I wouldn't want to live or survive in this world unless it was with you, my prince."

Trystan's lips crashed against mine, his kiss carrying me to a place far, far away.

CHAPTER TWENTY-THREE

EVERYONE CAME TO MEET us outside after Trystan sent a guard to let them know where we were.

"What happened?" Kylan asked as soon as he saw us.

"My father and Ivy know we have sealed the mating bond."

"Good gods." Kylan raked his fingers through his thick hair. "I don't know if I want to know how that went. I'm assuming not well since you're both standing outside."

Trystan and I looked at each other and chuckled.

Feng ambled over to us with a smirk. "I'm glad you told the king. He will have to chew, and possibly choke, on the information he was given, but I believe he will eventually come around."

Brone also came to stand in front of us. "If we came around, sooner or later, he will have to, too."

I knew Trystan's cadre didn't approve of me at first. They questioned Trystan's motives and wondered why they were sent to protect me, a mortal girl with no significance.

But they stayed with me, fought for me, and even when I was taken, they followed Trystan into Morbeth to save me.

"How could he not accept our queen?" Everett questioned. Callum nodded in agreement. "I would think any royal would kill to have her as their mate."

"To kill, or not to kill. That is the question," Kai said laughing, coming up from behind them. "I have given up all hope. Especially now that you two are mated." He patted Trystan's shoulder. "Take care of her my friend. Because it appears everyone will be watching."

That was a lot of pressure. The entire vampire world would be watching us. But I didn't care. As long as Trystan was by my side, my world was complete.

"Are we going straight to Morbeth from here?" Markus asked.

I sighed, knowing what Markus was feeling. I knew his mind was set on saving Sabine. He'd had a difficult time showing his emotions to her from the time we left Morbeth, but I knew he cared deeply for her. Being Captain of the King's guard had hardened him. I never saw him smile as much as I did when she was around him. She pulled out a side he had hidden away.

The softer, gentler side that could laugh and smile and open up.

What was our next move?

Glancing around, I didn't see my grandfather. "Where is Nicolae?" I asked.

All eyes swept the area. "He was right behind us," Kylan said.

Panic shot through me, wondering if something bad had happened to him. I left Trystan and ran back inside the castle, skidding to a stop to find Nicolae standing with the king at the bottom of the stairwell. They appeared to be having a serious conversation.

Turning their attention to me, the king's brows knitted together. His expression was hard, still twisted with anger, but Nicolae gave me a warm smile and a slight nod.

I bowed my head and backed away, leaving them to whatever they were discussing. Nicolae was level headed, and I hoped he could diffuse the king's flaring hatred for me.

Back outside, I let out a loud breath and let everyone know where Nicolae was. Trystan seemed unaffected, but I know it must have been hard for him. In front of his father, he chose me over his kingdom. That must have been an incredibly painful pill for the king to swallow. I could only imagine the thoughts running through his mind. How much more he hated me right now.

After countless grueling minutes, Nicolae exited the castle and strode toward me. "The king would like to speak with you, Calla. Alone."

I swallowed the huge lump in my throat, frozen with fear, my heart beating furiously against my chest.

"I will go speak to him," Trystan snarled, heading back inside.

"No," I said, grabbing his arm, stopping him. "This is something I need to do."

"I will go with you, then." He was genuinely concerned, and that alone made my anxiety rise.

I shook my head and steeled myself. "This is something I need to do alone. To prove that I can stand on my own."

Trystan sighed, giving me a sad smile. "My flame, don't be afraid. My father is a man, like any other."

Nicolae stepped in front of me and took my hand. "I have faith in you, Calla. And as Trystan said, don't be afraid. He only wants what is best for his son and for his kingdom."

I knew this day would have come sooner or later. Especially now that we were mated. I just wasn't sure if I was ready, especially after what had happened upstairs.

Tiptoeing, I pressed my lips against Trystan's. "I'll be back soon. If not, check the dungeons."

Trystan laughed. "You're so dramatic. Let me know if you need rescuing," he said pointing to his palm. "I'll rush in like the wind."

I couldn't help but smile, knowing he would do just that.

"Be brave," he whispered.

Heading in, I glanced at all the long faces of my friends. They were trying to be optimistic for me, but I could tell they were just as nervous. I gave them all a nod and painted on a smile as I made my way inside, trying to hide the fact I was trembling from the inside out.

A servant now stood where the king and Nicolae had been. He bowed at the waist when he saw me. "Please, follow me."

Goddess help me. I was being led further away from the group.

I followed the servant down a long hallway I had never been before. It was lit with golden sconces. Beautiful tapestries and paintings adorned the walls, and the ceiling above was hand painted to look like the sky.

My hands twisted nervously around each other as we finally stopped at the last door. The servant looked at me and bowed, his hands ushering me to enter.

I tried to slow my breathing, afraid I would pass out, then stepped toward the door and opened it.

Inside was a glorious room. A workspace fit for a king.

The king was sitting behind a large desk made of expensive wood. Behind him were rows of shelves, neatly stacked with hundreds of books. Above him a large chandelier hung, while candles burned around the room. To the left, was a small sitting area with a couch and two armchairs.

"Your Highness." I bowed my head and curtsied.

His head inclined to the couch. "Have a seat."

Trying my best not to look too afraid, I made my way over to the sitting area and plopped down on the couch. A servant inside the room immediately came forward with a tray.

"Would you like some tea?" he asked.

I smiled and reached for the delicate cup, glad the servant was here to witness any forthcoming murder. I sipped, trying to calm my fraying nerves, letting the hot tea slide down my throat.

The king stood from his chair, coming over and sitting in the large, plush armchair directly across from me. He said nothing, his face emotionless. I felt uncomfortable under the weight of his stare, like he was assessing me.

I took another sip of the tea, then set it on the table to my side. Sitting up straight, I crossed a leg over the other and placed my hands on my lap.

"Your Majesty," I said, my voice shaky. "I apologize for what happened earlier."

The king leaned back, crossing his arms over his chest.

I remembered the story Trystan had told me. About how much his father and mother loved each other. The king must have been broken. The illness and death of his beloved wife, hardening his heart.

"Are you apologizing for making my son defy me? For raising his voice to his king, choosing you over his duty to his kingdom and crown?"

My pulse was racing, but I calmly replied, "Your Majesty, I cannot and will not apologize for Trystan. What I do apologize for, is deceiving you the last time I was here. I should have let you know who I was, right from the start." I inhaled a deep breath and straightened my back. "I did not grow up as a royal. I lived a simple life in Sartha with my parents. Up until a few months ago, I was mortal. I knew nothing of your world, of kingdoms and crowns, or of the hidden wonders and dangers that live within it.

"At my eighteenth birthday party, Trystan appeared. He bit me, turning me into a vampire. I'm sure you've heard the story behind Princess Leora and King Romulus?"

The king nodded, his expression still hard as stone. "I have heard the stories."

"Then you know that Roehl sent out the death decree because Nicolae was a threat to Morbeth's throne, and he wanted everyone in his bloodline to die because of it."

I wanted the king to know why Trystan and I were close. Why I loved him so much, and how much he had given to keep me safe.

"Why has my son become so enamored with you that he would disregard his duties?"

He was asking the hard questions. But I would answer them as truthfully as possible. "Trystan came to Sartha the night of my birthday party. It was the first time I'd seen him. The first time I'd met him. He didn't tell me who he was, and all he said was that he felt a connection to me. That he had to come to Sartha to try and save me."

"Save you? Why?"

"He said when the death decree came, it came with a portrait of my family. When he saw me, he felt a connection between us. He couldn't explain it. He just knew he had to follow his heart."

The king's eyes went distant, so I continued.

"The night I met Trystan, he bit me against my will. My parents were already on a ship to Hale to trade at Merchant Port, so I was alone during the transformation. Trystan knew this and had followed me home to help me through it. When I woke, I found he had left me a note and a flask of his blood. It stated that he had claimed me, in order to save me, and if I were to drink his blood, it would seal our blood bond and Roehl wouldn't be able to touch me. However, if I didn't drink it, he would send someone to meet me at a tavern. Someone who would keep me safe."

The king straightened in his chair, his eyes wary and scrutinizing.

"I didn't drink from the flask Trystan left me. I couldn't be bound to someone I didn't know. So, I chose to run.

"My first encounter was with Kylan, who I met at the tavern. He saved me from some terrible men and took me to a cave where I was introduced to the rest of the cadre.

"During that time, Roehl had found my parents ship and murdered everyone onboard, including my mother and my best friend's parents. My father somehow got away, but he was being hunted.

"We were in the Whisper Woods when a Wanderer sent by Roehl, broke through our witch's wards, and captured me. I was taken to Morbeth and thrown into a cell where I was starved and tortured. If Trystan hadn't changed me, I would've died. I barely clung to life, but while I was there, a servant girl helped me. She secretly fed me her blood so I could live and endure the torture.

"During the Shadow Fest, that same girl found a witch who helped me cross over the veil. I met Princess Leora of Incendia in the In-Between. She told me she was my great-grandmother, and that she had bound my magic and powers so I wouldn't be a target.

"While I was with her, she released the spell and imparted her gifts to me." I held out my hands and showed the king my tattoos. This time he was close enough to see them fully. "Roehl found out about my powers, but before he could do anything, Markus and Sabine helped me escape.

"Not long ago, Roehl found my father. Trystan went to save him, but he was captured, and they were both tortured. The bastard made me watch as he lashed them, and then, I watched my father die." I paused, gathering myself, wiping the tears that had fallen. "I thought he was going to kill Trystan too, but instead, he gave him the Lethe potion. He cursed him and told me that Trystan would forget me. That when he woke, I would be his enemy. That he would hate me, and I would become the bane of his existence."

The king shook his head. "How did you break the Lethe curse? There is no cure, except for the one who conjured it."

How did he know?

The king noted my hesitation and unfolded his arms. He stood, slowly pacing back to his desk. "My wife. She—" he paused, his eyes pinching shut. "I thought her illness was due to a curse. No. I know it was a curse, so I had every witch, mage, and doctor of any great importance come to Carpathia to try to heal her. They went over every curse, including the Lethe spell. I have learned a great deal of curses and cures from her illness. But none could heal my wife." He faced me, his eyes narrowed. "We still don't know who would put a curse on my wife. She was kind to everyone. But I would like to know how you managed to cure Trystan's curse?"

I looked down at my hands that twisted nervously around each other. "A few days ago, we were put in another dangerous situation. We were attacked by an air elemental, presumably sent by Roehl. The man was going to kill me, but Trystan showed up and saved me, even while under the Lethe curse.

"Thinking he could cure the curse himself by claiming me, he tried. But instead of it curing him, it almost killed him. It was then I heard the voice of Princess Leora in my head. She told me the only way to break the curse was to seal the blood bond with Trystan."

"And?" The king's eyes were pinned on me.

"I would have done anything to save him, so I sealed the blood bond and . . . it cured him."

The king let out a deep sigh. He ambled back toward me, resting his hands on the back of the armchair, looking as if he was leaning on my words. "Do you truly love my son, Miss Caldwell?"

It was a simple question that required a heartfelt and truthful answer. An answer that could either make or break my visit here.

I peered at the king through tear-filled eyes and smiled. "I never experienced love. Never knew it personally until I met Trystan. He showed me firsthand what love was. He was there, time and time again, validating love to me in every way possible. Even when I denied him, he remained unwavering. Trystan is honest, just, and faithful. He is the kindest and bravest man I know.

"So, the answer to your question, Your Majesty, is . . . yes. Yes, I love your son. Not only with my entire heart, but with every part of me. When I am with him, he steals my breath away, and yet, he is the very air I breathe. He is the solid and steady ground my wavering feet walk on. And just when I think my world will fall apart, he is there, holding it all together. Holding me together.

"Trystan is everything good in my life. During these past months, I have learned that there is no one else in this entire world that I would want by my side. And if I am ever put in a position, or given a choice, I would gladly and willingly sacrifice my life to save his."

The king stood still, his expression unreadable. Then, I swear I saw his eyes glass over. A smile crept onto the corners of his mouth as he strode toward me holding out his hands. I paused, taken aback by this unexpected move, but placed my quivering hands in his.

The king helped me to my feet, his hazel eyes now soft and filled with warmth. "I was expecting a simple yes or no to that question, but you gave me what was in your heart. I am sorry, Calla. I was rash and unfair to you and your company."

My eyes widened, my heart palpitating. Was the king apologizing to me?

"You don't have to apologize," I said, shaking my head. "I understand your position."

"No. It was wrong of me." He closed his eyes, a single tear rolling down his cheek. "My wife was my entire life. She was also the air I breathed, and when she became ill and passed, I felt as if I was suffocating. She was the bright light in my dark world, and when she left me, my world fell apart. You see, I know how you feel about my son, because that is exactly how I felt about my wife." His lips quivered as tears fell. "I am so happy my son has found someone with a love like yours. It is rare for an immortal to find their true mate. The one that will love and cherish them. That will make them happy for the rest of their long lifetime. I see now, what Trystan sees in you. You are his perfect match." He gently squeezed my hands.

"I only wanted what was best for my kingdom, but I was also selfish and made poor decisions. Instead of forcing an arranged marriage I knew my son disapproved of, I should have talked to him. I've always trusted Trystan, but ever since my wife died, I have distanced myself from him. I know he resents me for it, but it was the only way I could survive.

"I couldn't watch my mate suffer and waste away. It shredded every part of me. When Trystan ran away, chasing you and neglecting his duties, I thought he was doing it to spite me."

"Trystan respects you, Your Majesty, and he would never spite you. I know that for a fact."

The king nodded. "My eyes and heart have been opened. I can see how much my son cares for you. Enough to stand up to me. I have never seen him so passionate about anything or anyone, and because of that, he made me question my own motives. That is the reason why I called you here."

The king released one of my hands, sliding his own into his pocket. When he pulled it out, the amulet was in his palm. "I am ashamed for taking this from you. Fate, it seems, wanted you to have this. To show that you indeed, belong to this family. Trystan was right. I know my wife would be honored that the amulet chose you." He held the two ends of the necklace up. "Would you allow me the honor to place this back around your neck?"

Hot tears burned my eyes. "Of course."

Giving the king my back, I lifted my hair as he placed the amulet around my neck. When I faced him again, he had a warm smile on his face.

"It suits you," he said. "And I am truly sorry for all you've been through, especially the loss of your parents. I'm proud that my son was there for you." He placed his hands on my shoulders. "You are family now, Calla. And from now on, you will have the full protection of Carpathia."

A sob of happiness burst from my chest. "I don't know what to say."

"Say you'll forgive me for being an ignorant fool. If you don't, my son will never forgive me."

I laughed, tears rolling down my face. "I have already forgiven you, Your Majesty."

"Good then." The king smiled and slapped his hands together. "Is there anything you require of me?"

I wiped my tear-stained face. "Roehl has kidnapped my best friends. I fear they are in Morbeth, so I have to save them. But I also must save the witches and guards that served under my great-grandfather. Roehl has given Nicolae and I an ultimatum. If we do not return to Morbeth, he will execute them all."

The king shook his head. "If you enter Morbeth, he will execute you as well. I've heard rumors that the Queen of Incendia has aligned herself with Morbeth."

I let out a deep sigh. "Yes, the rumors are true, and I will make sure she pays for it."

"Will you rule Incendia when she is gone?"

In front of this king who had ruled for centuries, I suddenly felt like I wasn't qualified. "I will become queen, but I will ask my cousin to act as regent while I am away. She knows the people, and I know she will do the kingdom justice."

"And what of Nicolae?"

That was a subject we had yet to discuss. "My hope is that when Roehl is gone, Nicolae will accept his rightful place as King of Morbeth. Nicolae hasn't spoken about it, but I know, if he truly follows his heart, he will accept his given path. And so will I."

"It's good to have a plan, even if it doesn't work out. At least you have a goal to work toward." The king walked back over to his desk and took a seat. "I will speak to Trystan. Please stay at least a night as my honored guests. I would like to be a part of discussing your next move."

This felt like a dream. Like I would wake up and find myself being banished from Carpathia all over again.

"Thank you, Your Majesty." I bowed my head and turned to walk away.

"Princess Calla," he spoke, coming toward me. "Don't worry about Ivy. I have sent two guards to escort her to the port where a ship will be waiting to return her to Northfall."

"What about the royals of Northfall?"

He smirked. "Excuse my language, but I don't give a fuck what they think. They are selfish, pompous assholes who raised a self-absorbed daughter. When I met her for the first time, I knew she was wrong for Trystan, but I'd already signed the contract."

"What will happen now?"

"Since you have sealed the blood and mating bond with my son, the contract is void." His smile warmed my heart. "I know you will be a great queen, just as my wife was."

There were so many emotions running through my mind, and it was all too much to process. "Thank you, Your Majesty."

The king folded his hands behind his back. "You may call me *father*."

My face flushed with heat. I wanted to pinch myself. "Thank you . . . *father*," I said, bowing my head.

His smile spread like rays of sunshine across a brilliant sky, while my mind was trying to process the entire conversation. In one moment, this man hated me. And the next, he was telling me to call him father.

I walked away feeling like I was walking on clouds.

Miracles did in fact happen, and I couldn't wait to tell Trystan.

CHAPTER TWENTY-FOUR

HEADING BACK TO THE others, I found them gathered inside the foyer.

I kept my face serious as Trystan rushed to meet me, his eyes searching my face. "How did it go?"

I paused, then Trystan shook his head. His expression turned furious. "Where is he?"

He began to stomp away, but I grabbed hold of his wrist and whispered, "*Father* would like to speak with you."

He paused and turned to me with a confused expression on his face. "Father?"

I nodded, a smile unfurled on my lips as I slipped the amulet from under my tunic. "Yes. He accepts me, Trystan. He accepts us." I fell into his strong arms which enveloped me, hugging me tightly. "He even asked me to call him father."

Trystan let out a breathy laugh. "Are you sure you are talking about *my* father?"

"Of course, I am." I smiled against his chest. "He wants us to stay here for the night. I think we should because we need to figure out what our next move is." I glanced up at him. "He really does love you. He was in so much pain when your mother was sick. When she died, he became lost and pulled away. He wants to talk to you. Please go to him."

Trystan kissed my forehead. "I'll go." He then leaned down, whispering into my ear. "Tonight, you will be staying in my bedchamber."

Heat ignited in my core as he walked away.

I met the others and gave them a quick summary of my encounter with the king, leaving out the more personal details. Details he might not have wanted to make public.

They were relieved and thrilled to know I was finally welcome in Carpathia and into the Vladu family.

"So, he finally came to his senses," Kai said, shaking his head. "I can't believe it took him this long,"

I gave him a sad smile. "I feel sorry for him. His wife was his entire world, and when she died, his world fell apart."

There was a commotion outside.

Guards ran into the castle, their eyes scanning the area.

"What's wrong?" Kylan asked, heading toward them.

One of the guards stopped in front of him and bowed his head. "Princess Ivy disappeared. We took her to the dock, but she vanished right before our eyes. We can't find her."

Kylan's worried eyes shot to me. All the men, including Everett and Callum, positioned themselves around me.

"Calla," Feng said. "I think we should take you upstairs. It will be safer to protect you there. It's too open down here."

I nodded but sighed, wondering when this would end. I wasn't afraid of Ivy, but they were looking out for my safety, and I wasn't going to go against them.

"Andrés, come with me," Kylan ordered. "Markus, would you like to come? To look for an invisible *snake*?"

"Of course," Markus said, with a grin.

"We will join you as well," Everett said, with Callum at his side.

"She needs to be found immediately, so I'll also go," Kai added. His luminous eyes met mine. "Will you be okay?"

"I have Brone, Feng, and Nicolae. Not to mention, Thalia." I pulled Thalia to my side, and she smiled.

"She will be fine," Thalia replied.

"Good, then." Kai gave her a wink. "Stay safe, ladies."

As Kylan, Andrés, Markus, Kai, Everett, and Callum exited the castle, the rest of us made our way to the staircase.

And then, it happened so fast. Too fast.

My body was slammed from the side, and I fell to the ground, rolling onto my back. Immediate pressure was on my waist, pinning me down. And then, a sharp pain pierced my chest.

I screamed in pain, everyone around me in shock, wondering what the hell had just happened.

"Calla!" Thalia cried. "She's bleeding." Her finger aimed at my chest.

Nicolae waved his hand and Princess Ivy became visible. She was straddling me, holding a bloody knife in her hands. Her hair was wild, face twisted with rage, tears and black kohl were running down her pale face. She looked like a monster.

"You whore! You stole him from me," she screamed. "Trystan was mine."

Ivy raised the dagger, ready to plunge it back into my chest when branches from a nearby plant shot forward and wrapped tightly around her wrists, yanking her off me. Another branch wrapped around Ivy's neck, and another around her midsection and legs, squeezing until she was choking, and her eyes rolled back.

Thalia had called them, her eyes focused, hands stretched out toward Ivy.

Feng and Brone rushed forward, seizing Ivy's arms. She couldn't breathe. Her face turned bright red as the plants coiled tightly around her neck. Thalia was killing her.

"Thalia, stop," I exhaled, reaching for her outstretched hand. Blood poured from the wound in my chest. "Don't kill her."

Thalia's eyes jerked to mine. "Why shouldn't I kill her? She should die for what she's done. She tried to kill you!"

Kylan and the others charged back inside, their eyes trying to piece together the ghastly scene. Kai, Everett, and Callum raced over.

Nicolae was at my side, pressing his palm against the wound, attempting to stop the bleeding. Worry swam in his golden eyes.

Struggling to raise my arm, I realized —

"I can't move," I moaned, the pain in my chest throbbing.

"Someone call a healer!" Kai urged.

Servants dashed off, and Ivy went limp. She was gurgling, her face turning purple.

"Thalia," I breathed. "I order you to release her."

Thalia grunted her disapproval, then dropped her hands. Everett and Callum moved to her side. The branches instantly relaxed from around Ivy and slid to the ground. Brone and Feng grabbed her.

Trystan and his father, along with two guards, came rushing toward us from the back.

"Calla!" Trystan shouted. He was clutching his chest like he was in pain but sprinted and collapsed at my side. His hand gripped mine. Wide, terrified eyes shifting to see Nicolae's hand pushed against my bloodied chest.

"What happened?" he growled, his eyes darkening.

Thalia stood above me, her eyes hurling daggers at Ivy. "Princess Ivy stabbed her! She tried to kill her!"

Trystan let out a growl. "And no one stopped her?"

"She was invisible," Nicolae said. "No one realized what was taking place until after it happened."

Trystan watched the blood flowing from my wound. "She's not healing. Why isn't her wound healing?"

Nicolae took Trystan's hand and held it against my wound, replacing his. He then stood and moved to the dagger, snatching it off the ground. Holding it to his nose, Nicolae sniffed it before muttering a spell. Yellow and violet dust shone on the dagger and its handle. Concern swelled in his eyes. "This blade has been tipped with poison. Juniper and Wolfsbane."

"What does that mean?" Thalia questioned, glancing at my chest and then back at Nicolae.

"Juniper induces temporary paralysis. It could last days," Nicolae explained. "But Wolfsbane is fatal. It's meant to kill."

Ivy had come to, letting out a cackling, vicious laugh. "You chose her over me, Trystan. Now, you will watch her die."

"You will pay greatly for what you have done," the king thundered. He turned to his guards. "Get her out of here!"

Brone and Feng dragged Ivy out, kicking and screaming. At least a dozen guards circled them, following them out.

Nicolae closed his eyes and ran his palm over me. "The blade missed her heart," Nicolae finally said. "But it came close. We need a healer to withdraw the poison."

I was teetering on consciousness. There were too many people around asking too many questions. All I wanted to do was close my eyes. They were heavy. So heavy.

"Calla," Trystan pleaded. "Stay with me. Please."

"Where is the healer?" the king shouted. "Bring me the gods' damned healer!"

"She's fading," Trystan exhaled.

Through blurred eyes, I watched Trystan bite his wrist. He then pressed it to my mouth. I drank from him, letting his powerful blood pour down my throat.

When his wrist pulled away, I felt no pain, but all I wanted to do was close my eyes. I looked down at my chest, blood still oozing from the wound.

The poison must have slowed the healing process, even with Trystan's powerful blood.

"Trystan," I breathed, my eyes heavy, unable to stay open.

He leaned over, his face inches from mine. "Yes, my flame."

"I love you."

He smiled as a tear trickled down his face. "I love you, too."

My eyes felt like sandpaper when they opened.

"She's awake," the king announced. His worried face was the first to come into view. A tense and concerned smile was painted on his lips.

"Calla," Trystan breathed, his hand grasping mine.

I tried to raise my arm, but it was still frozen. "I can't move." My anxiety rose and my breath quickened.

Nicolae's face appeared in front of me. "It's temporary, Calla. You've only been asleep for a few hours." He popped open a small vial of clear liquid. "The healer left this. It will put you back to sleep, and hopefully, the next time you wake, the effects of the Juniper will have worn off."

Tears of frustration rolled down the sides of my face, but Trystan was there to wipe them with a damp cloth. "I'll be right here when you wake," he reassured, slipping a hand under the back of my neck. With Trystan gently raising my head, Nicolae poured the contents of the vial down my throat.

It was bitter, but I welcomed its effects.

The next time I woke, I immediately raised my arm, exhaling in relief. The effects of the Juniper had finally worn off. Glancing around, I realized I was in Trystan's bed chamber. It was empty, except for the shirtless prince lying next to me, sound asleep.

I lay still, admiring his handsome face, unkempt hair, and perfectly muscled body adorned with tattoos. I leaned over and pressed my lips against his, and those azure eyes popped open.

"My flame. How are you feeling?" I loved the sound of his husky, morning voice.

"I feel fine."

I sat up and peeked inside my white sleeping gown to find my entire chest was bandaged, the white gauze clean. No blood had seeped through. Twisting, I felt no pain at all. Trystan's blood must have healed me.

Trystan rolled to his side, resting on an elbow. "I'm glad." A wide smile grew, brightening his face. "I have never seen my father so concerned. He sat right next to you for thirty hours straight. Nicolae finally convinced him to leave and get some rest, but he demanded we let him know as soon as you wake."

I couldn't help but feel a buzz of warmth and happiness that the king cared so much.

"How long have I been asleep?"

"The magic in the potion put you to sleep for forty-eight hours."

"I've been asleep for two days?"

"Yes, and I have been right here, anxiously waiting for you to wake up and open those beautiful golden eyes."

He never failed to warm my heart. "How did you know I was injured?" I questioned. "Did the servants call you?"

Trystan grabbed hold of my hand. "No. I was talking to my father when a sharp pain shot through my chest. I suddenly couldn't breathe. I instantly knew something was wrong. That something had happened to you."

"You felt my pain?"

"I did. It must be the connection between us. The bond we share."

That was unexpected. The bond had sent him a warning, and I wondered if I would ever feel his pain if he was injured.

I prayed I'd never have to find out.

"My prince," I breathed, leaning over, and kissing him again. "Could you help me take the bandage off?"

A wicked grin rose on his lips. "It would be my pleasure." I raised my arms as he slipped the bedgown over my head. His fingers went to work, untying and unraveling the bandage, until my entire chest was bare to him. His eyes darkened as he ran his fingers over the small scar below my breast. "I can do much more if you want me to." His lips pressed against the scar, slowly moving upward, caressing my breast.

I moaned as Trystan pulled the sheet from his torso revealing his nakedness. *Gods above . . .*

"Do you feel any pain?" he breathed.

A sinister grin rose on my own lips. "I do. There is an ache between my legs that can only be cured by you."

Trystan reached over, his muscles tightening as he positioned himself above me.

I paused, placing a hand on his chest. "What about your father? You promised to let him know when I woke up."

His lips caressed my neck, jaw, lips, causing me to moan. His voice feathered against my ear. "My father can wait."

Trystan fell into my arms and ravished me entirely—heart, body, and soul.

CHAPTER
TWENTY-FIVE

"I'm relieved to see you well," the king spoke as I took a seat at the dining table. He must have been worried.

Brone took a seat across from me, his eyes narrowing. "This woman bears more battle scars than I do. She has been tortured, shot with arrows, and stabbed. Yet, a few days later, she is having breakfast with us."

"I know men who have met their demise with fewer wounds," Feng agreed.

Brone glanced at Trystan. "I think you should consider having armor fashioned for her. I have never known anyone sustain so much injury in such a short amount of time."

I couldn't help but chuckle, knowing it was true. "It doesn't help that a psychopath is hunting me. And I am able to sit here because of my mate's magical blood."

Trystan's hand gently squeezed my thigh. "What's mine is yours," he murmured close to my ear, making warmth bloom in my chest.

"I knew Ivy was evil, but I never expected she would try to kill Calla," Kylan hissed.

"How could you not expect anything less?" Kai let out a frustrated puff of air. "No other kingdom would accept that wench."

That made me wonder . . . "What happened to Ivy?"

The king placed his goblet on the table. "My mages have bound her magic. She is subdued, shackled, and on a ship to Northfall, where my guards will deliver her kingdom a decree from me. Because she attempted to kill my son's mate, and future queen of Carpathia, she is never to step foot on Carpathian soil again. If she does, she will be immediately executed." The king smiled at me. "You don't have to worry about her anymore."

I nodded, glad she was out of Carpathia. And with her magic bound, she wouldn't be able to cause any more problems. Hopefully.

"Now that I'm healed, we need to talk about rescuing Sabine and Brynna."

"Yes," Markus agreed. He had been quiet. Along with Thalia, Everett, and Callum who were seated on the opposite side of the dining table.

"You should still take a few more days to rest," Nicolae said. "You may have healed, but you also need to recover your strength. We need to be completely prepared when we enter Morbeth."

"I hope you all realize that when we leave here, we will be going to war," Kai noted, taking a bite of crispy bacon. He grinned, wiggling it in front of me.

"I know, you damned tease. Which is why we need a plan."

Kai let out a barking laugh. "It's good to know you still have your spunk."

"I will never change, no matter what position I take in the future. After this is over, I need to bring joy back into my life." I turned to Trystan. "I want to be happy. To live a life filled with adventure, laughter, and love."

Trystan leaned over and kissed my nose. "I look forward to that life with you."

I noticed the king was silent, then watched him dab his eyes with a napkin.

"Are you alright, father?" Trystan asked.

"Yes," he replied. "I was just thinking of your mother. Calla reminds me so much of her in her younger years."

My heart both swelled and broke inside. Maybe I could bring some sunshine back into the king's dark and desolate world here in Carpathia.

"We really should be discussing your next move," the king said, straightening in his chair.

Kai placed his fork down. He was sitting next to Thalia, and they looked so good together. Like a normal couple enjoying a normal breakfast. "You have the armies of Aquaria, Sartha, Aquaris, Hale, Baelfast, and Carpathia behind you," Kai stated. "You just need to let us know when and where to assemble. My father is waiting for my update."

"I don't know if we need the armies. Roehl only wants me and Nicolae to enter Morbeth in order to save King Romulus's people."

"You can't enter Morbeth alone. If you do, he will kill you," Kai said. "He had no problem killing your father and torturing Trystan."

"I understand how great the risk is. But it is a risk we must take. Hundreds of lives are at stake and counting on us. And now, my best friends are there. I promised I would keep them safe."

Nicolae set his elbows on the table. "I think having the armies stationed outside the Red Wall might be all it takes to show Roehl that most of the kingdoms in Talbrinth are willing to fight against him. Even if a battle doesn't happen, it will have a great impact and send him a strong message."

"I agree," the king said. "And if war does come, we will fight alongside you."

A thought popped into my mind. A possible plan that could work if all the pieces were in place. But it could also backfire and go very wrong.

However, weighing the options we had, I was willing to take that risk. My entire life, since I'd turned eighteen, was one giant risk.

I shared the idea with the group, but there were many concerns, especially from Trystan. He said the only way he would agree with the plan is if he went with me. But Trystan was now a target. He had defied Roehl's Lethe curse, breaking free from it. I knew that fact alone would put him at an even greater risk than me.

"We still need time to practice and hone your gifts," Nicolae said. "We need every advantage we can get."

"The only element I really need to work on is air." I glanced over at Trystan and gave him a wink.

He gave me an adorable lopsided grin. "Then today, that's what we'll work on."

Andrés leaned forward on his elbows. "Can you wait until the sun sets so we can watch?"

Trystan shook his head. "Andrés, when night falls, she can give you a firsthand demonstration."

"Oh, I will not miss the chance to see that," Brone laughed. "How about spinning Andrés in a mini tornado? That would be fun."

I grinned. "I'll let you all test out my new ability tonight and see if it is worthy enough to go against Morbeth."

"Sounds fair," Brone said. "But be ready, princess. We won't hold back."

I finished the last of my ruby wine. "I don't expect you to." Grabbing hold of Trystan's hand, I stood. "Let's get started."

Trystan had more clothes for me delivered to his bedchamber, so I dressed in black pants with a crimson tunic, throwing the cloak Sabine had given me over my shoulders. I decided to wear my hair in a single braid over my right shoulder.

Trystan was in all black — his signature color — with a black cloak over his shoulders. We walked to the stables, where Trystan mounted his black stallion, and I mounted Shadow.

"What a handsome couple you make," the stable hand muttered while brushing a mare in an adjoining stall. He was an older gentleman, with kind eyes.

"Thank you," Trystan said, tipping his head. "This is Princess Calla, my mate and future Queen of Carpathia."

The man's eyes widened. He dropped the brush in his hand and stood, bowing at the waist. "It is a great honor to meet you, Your Highness."

Trystan glanced at me with a grin, inclining his head.

"Oh!" I didn't realize he was talking to me. "Thank you. I am so grateful you have taken care of my horse."

His brown eyes met mine. "It is our pleasure, Your Highness. Safe travels, wherever you may go."

I bowed my head and gently heeled Shadow, following Trystan out of the stable.

"Where are we going?" I asked, trotting next to him.

"To the arena. I missed your practice last time we were here, but this time we will have the entire place to ourselves."

I liked the sound of that. Remembering the trail that led up to the arena, I gave Shadow a clicking noise, and he took off in a gallop.

"Keep up, my prince," I hollered back.

Trystan's laugh echoed behind me as he kicked his horse and galloped after me on the snow-covered trail.

At the arena, we dismounted and let our horse's roam. I knew Shadow wouldn't go far. He always stayed nearby.

Entering the arena, I quickly lit the torches with my power, illuminating the inside.

"That was badass," Trystan said, coming up behind me, wrapping his arms around my waist.

"My prince, we are not here to roll in the hay, although it is tempting." I turned and kissed him on the lips. "We have to focus, and I need to learn everything I can from you."

He stepped back, folding his hands behind his back. "Alright then, what would you like to learn first?"

"I want to learn how to move like you do. Like the wind."

"There is really nothing to it," he said. "I suppose it's a lot like transporting. Your eyes choose your location, but your gift takes you there." I felt a rush of air, and suddenly Trystan was standing on the opposite side of the arena.

Gods, he was fast.

"Come to me, my flame," he said through our bond.

My heart pattered as I concentrated on where he was. "Take me to him," I whispered to my power.

Before I could take a breath, Trystan wrapped me in his arms.

"I did it!" I exhaled, throwing my arms around his neck.

"Actually, you transported yourself instead of using air," he chuckled.

My smile turned into a frown. "What?"

"If you used air, you would see your entire movement — from there to here — like you were in slow motion. Did you experience that?"

"No," I sighed.

"Hey." He lifted my chin. "It doesn't matter if you move by air, or you transport. The main thing is you did it."

"I suppose. But I'd like to move like the wind."

Trystan turned me around, my back pressed against his front, his hands grasping mine. I could feel the power pulsing between our touching palms, buzzing through my entire body. Then I gasped as we moved. He was right. Everything ahead of us was like a blur, but there was one spot, one unblurred spot that we were heading straight to.

Suddenly, we were stopped, and the world seemed to shift beneath my feet. Feeling off balance, Trystan steadied me.

"How was your first time?" His breath caressed my ear.

"Magical."

"You tend to be a little off-balance the first few tries, but the more you use it, the sturdier you will become." He stepped back and crossed his arms over his chest. "It's your turn."

I batted puppy dog eyes at him. "On my own?"

"Never." He grinned, a dimple adorning his cheek. "I'll be right here, watching."

"Fine," I said, bending side to side.

Trystan's nose crumpled. "What are you doing?"

"Stretching."

"Why?"

"Because I want to be limber while I travel."

He shrugged, and I sucked in a deep breath and concentrated on a spot across the arena.

I called the air and asked it to take me there.

My body tingled, and then I was thrust forward. Thrown off kilter, my focus faltered, and the air shifted to carry me to the new spot. As soon as I stopped, my body continued moving. I tucked and rolled, then stood up on my feet. Trystan was suddenly beside me.

"Did you look away?" he sighed, holding me steady.

"How did you know?"

"You were headed in one direction and suddenly shifted."

"That's exactly what happened." I dusted the debris off my pants. "I really need to work on my landings."

"That tuck and roll was pretty awesome." He stepped back, away from me, arms crossed. "Do it again." Trystan moved like a blur back to the other side of the arena, arms still crossed, standing still like he hadn't moved.

I growled and he must have heard because he let out a boisterous laugh.

"You asked for my help, and I am a bit of a perfectionist, my flame. You will master the air by the end of this day."

Gods. I would need to soak in a hot bath and drink an entire bottle of ruby wine when we were done.

I steadied myself, and this time Trystan was my goal. It would be easy to keep my eyes focused on him. Whatever I did last time worked, so I sucked in a deep breath and relaxed. *Light as a feather and sturdy as a tree. Come to me, air, and carry me.*

My blood tingled, my focus remaining on Trystan. I was thrust forward, everything moving like I was in slow motion, and then I was back in his arms.

"I did it!" I exclaimed.

"Yes, you did." Trystan pressed his lips to mine. "I'm proud of you."

"Will I get a kiss every time I complete a task?"

"Maybe. But if you master air today, I will make sure you are thoroughly rewarded tonight."

Goddess. I would do my freaking best.

For the next hour, my air gift transported me back and forth in the arena until it was second nature. Moving without reciting my air mantra, I just called to the air, and it answered.

After I'd mastered movement, I spent the next hour using air as a shield and as a weapon. Trystan made sure my shield was strong and impenetrable before he moved on.

Next, he showed me how to send air as a weapon, much like how Kai taught me how to make water daggers. This would be helpful if there wasn't water around.

One after the other, I threw air and blocked his weapons until my arms and back were screaming.

I took a seat on a haystack, trying to catch my breath. Trystan ambled over to me, looking fresh and lively.

"You need to feed," he said, sitting next to me.

I glanced up at him. "I want you to show me how to travel in an air funnel."

"After you feed," he said, biting his wrist.

"I can't keep feeding from you."

"Why not? You're my mate, and I offer it freely."

"Won't it make you weak?"

"No," he laughed. "What weakens me is when I see you weak. Drink, and then we will go outside, and I will demonstrate."

I took his wrist and held it to my lips. This time, without injury, as soon as his blood touched my tongue, I let out a moan, feeling its incredible power.

His blood was an addiction, and I was the addict. It was the sweetest yet most savory thing I had ever tasted. Trystan closed his eyes as I drank from him, this precious act between a pureblood and his mate.

This time, the feeding felt different. I felt his love flowing through it, touching, and healing every part of me. Like a warm hug, caressing every molecule. It was passionate. Bordering on erotic. It tingled through my limbs, warming my core, bringing life back to my weary body.

I pulled away, wiping my mouth, then turned to face him.

"Thank you," I breathed.

"Until we leave for Morbeth, you will feed from my blood. It will ensure that you will be strong enough for what is to come."

I nodded. I wouldn't say no to that. I craved his blood. I needed it. And so did my body.

"I've been thinking about the gift the Fire Goddess gave us. Wondering what it can do. Do you think we should test it?" I held out my palms, face up. "When we hold hands, I feel the power between us, but not like how it was in the Celestial Realm."

Trystan held out his palms in front of him. I smiled, seeing the twin tattoo of mine—the one with the fire in the center—embedded in his left palm. His own air element was marked on his right.

"I've noticed that too."

"Maybe we have to activate it?" I really wasn't sure. Helia had told me that there was no training manual for my powers. I would know how to use them. But this was different. This was a gift she gave to both of us. That we had to be together to use it.

"I'm game," Trystan said, standing. He held out his hands to me.

"Should we take this outside?" I asked. "After what Helia said, I'm afraid we might destroy this arena."

He shrugged his broad shoulders. "This arena could use an update, but I don't think the guards would appreciate it. It's the only covered place they can practice." I took his hand, and he led me outside.

As we exited the arena, snow crunched under our feet. The frigid air felt enlivening, and I welcomed its bite on my heated face.

"I think we should move away from our horses," Trystan said, grabbing my waist. In a split second we were up on the ridge above the arena. Behind us was a large open area. Perfect for practicing.

"Shall we?" Trystan held his hands up in front of him, palms facing me.

I smiled and laid my palms on top of his and closed my eyes.

"Connect our power," I whispered.

I gasped, steadying my legs as a surge of power coursed through our connected hands. It was so powerful it nearly knocked the air from my lungs. Opening my eyes, Trystan's intense gaze was fixed on me.

"Guide us, my flame," Trystan breathed. "I'll follow your lead."

I nodded and with a single thought, our bodies encased in flame.

Letting my right hand slip from his, I held it out in front of me. A large ball of fire grew, pulsing with blue, red, and gold. Trystan did the same with his left hand, and a twin ball of flame appeared, pulsing in rhythm with mine.

I slowly brought my hand closer to his until the two orbs were touching, absorbing into each other, becoming one large ball of energy. It was hard to catch my breath. The power coursing between us was overwhelming.

Above us thunder rumbled, and lightning cracked. The ground shook and trees swayed. A wind funnel spun around us, turning the glittering snow to ice crystals as it combined with the flames. Every element was within our grasp.

Fire, water, earth, and air were critical to sustaining life. It was the beginning and end of all things.

My fingers tingled, and my body hummed with incredible power. I knew we had created something beyond what I had ever imagined. A combination of me and Trystan.

I paused, letting the raw, unmitigated power course through me. Letting my body and mind welcome it so it would be as familiar as the rest of my gifts.

"What do you think would happen if we released this?"

Trystan gave me a grin. *"I think it would rattle all of Carpathia."*

He was right. I didn't want to send this power out, not knowing what it could do.

Facing Trystan, I held my palm up, and he did the same, the fiery orb throbbing with power between us. We pushed our palms through the orb until they touched. The power withdrew, seeping back into our connected hands, absorbing back into us.

I gasped, falling forward into Trystan's sturdy arms. Both of us left breathless.

"I've never felt anything like it before," I rasped.

"Neither have I," he admitted, shaking his head. "It was incredible."

"The key, when the time comes, is to stay together," he said. "The Fire Goddess made sure it was that way for a reason. We can end this, as long as we are together."

"Do you think that kind of power could destroy Roehl?"

"I think it could destroy an entire kingdom."

He was right. It was an untapped, untethered power. A personal gift from the Fire Goddess that could end this war.

It was a game changer.

CHAPTER TWENTY-SIX

"WHAT DO YOU WANT to do next?"

I tapped a finger against his chest. "I want you to take me somewhere in your air funnel."

"Are you sure?" Trystan laughed, and I welcomed the sound. I craved everything about him, particularly his laughter. Especially after watching him lack any kind of happiness while being cursed and tortured.

"I am absolutely sure." I folded my arms around his neck.

This time, Trystan's eyes turned midnight blue as he gazed up into the sky. The wind picked up around us, whipping stray hairs that had fallen from my braid. With one hand, Trystan pressed me tightly against his body. The other, he used to control the air.

Faster and faster the funnel twisted around us, and then, our feet lifted off the ground. I could faintly see what was on the other side of that great wall of wind as we raised into the sky.

"Where do you want to go?" Those midnight eyes landed on mine.

"Anywhere, as long as I'm in your arms."

His arm tightened around me, a smile pulling at the corners of his sinful lips. Trystan raised his hand and carried us above the trees, moving toward the opposite side of the island. As we neared the edge, he set us down on a cliff. The glorious sea framed the view before us, while below, the waves sounded like thunder as they crashed against the rocks.

Trystan's eyes went to a small piece of wood stuck into the ground with the symbol of Carpathia burned into it.

I thought back to the story he told of his mother, about the time she had gone missing. Trystan said she was going to end her life, but they found her just in time, standing on the edge of a cliff.

Trystan kneeled in front of the wood, kissed his fingers, and rubbed them against it.

"Is this where your mother is buried?" I whispered, coming up behind him.

His head twisted back, his eyes saddened. "Her ashes were scattered here. She loved this place." He stood back up. "Before I was conceived, she sprinkled wildflower seeds all over the ground here, so during the spring and summer months, the cliff is filled with them. A kaleidoscope of colors." His eyes brightened at the memory. "She would bring a blanket and sit for hours, listening to the wind and the birds, watching the water and the clouds above while I played. She said it was calming.

I smiled, picturing his mother in my mind, and Trystan running around as a child.

"You're smiling." He said endearingly.

"Back in Sartha, my cottage was also near a cliff. I used to sit outside on my porch, curled up in a blanket with a good book. Countless days and nights were spent watching the water and listening to the waves crash against the shore below. It was soothing, and I often wondered what else was beyond my small shore of Sartha. If I would ever travel beyond the Argent Sea."

"You have done much more than that, my flame." His eyes were filled with so much warmth. "My father was right. You are a lot like my mother. I wish she was here because I know she would have embraced you as a daughter."

I raised my face to the sky and closed my eyes. "I believe she is still around, watching over you and your father." Opening them again, I found Trystan a few feet away. "I feel she played a part in the amulet ending up in that small shop in Sartha, knowing Brynna would walk in and buy it for me."

Trystan's smile beamed like the sun above us. "I believe that, too. With my whole heart." He laced his fingers in mine. "Come, let's go back. You have mastered the tasks I gave you today."

"I have an incredible teacher."

"I suppose you do," he chuckled. "Would you like to transport us back?"

"Nope. I liked being in your arms while you use your gift. Besides, I purchased a round-trip ticket in my prince's twister."

"You did?" His eyes narrowed, brow crumpled. "I don't remember any payment being made."

I pressed my lips against his, giving him a passionate kiss. "The rest will be paid tonight."

Trystan wrapped an arm around me. "I look forward to your payment." He then lifted us into the sky.

That night, everyone gathered on a small patch of grass in front of the castle, where I demonstrated what Trystan had taught me.

Andrés came at me first, afraid to use his sword against me, but after I blocked his first three swings with my air shield, he loosened up. He was fast but having elemental gifts was a definite advantage.

Brone was next, and his hits were much harder. I felt his strength radiating through the air shield, echoing in my muscles. Trystan gave him a stern look, but he shrugged it off.

"She needs to know what a real hit feels like, so when it happens, she'll be prepared," Brone's deep voice said.

I agreed with him, waving him forward. "Bring it, big guy."

Every strike was blocked, but my shoulder and arm were throbbing from his monstrous hits. I wasn't sure if I could take another. Before Brone let his club fall one last time, I threw my hand forward. A blast of wind slammed into his chest, sending him flying about ten feet back. Brone landed on his backside, his legs flying into the air.

He growled and rolled to his knees before getting up. "Hey, I wasn't ready for that," he grumbled.

I shrugged, crossing my arms over my chest. "I wanted you to know what a real hit feels like. Maybe next time, you'll be prepared." I winked at him, and his face turned sour.

Everyone laughed, except for Markus who was off to the side, arms crossed over his chest. I could tell his mind was weighted with worry. Ever since Sabine and Brynna were taken, he kept mostly to himself. I know it was because I had given him the order to protect them, and he felt like he had failed. I would have to talk to him. To pull him on the side and let him know that it wasn't his fault, and it wasn't a simple task to burst into Morbeth to rescue them.

Markus turned and walked back into the castle. I sighed, deciding to deal with him later.

Everyone else cheered and clapped, proud of what I had accomplished in such a short time. Nicolae even came over and wrapped me in a hug.

"It seems you have a firm grip on your elemental power. Using them in synchronicity will help during a battle. You have a full arsenal in the palms of your hands."

"I do. Thanks to all of you."

Nicolae pulled me to the side. "I talked to the king. He will have his army gathered and ready to leave Carpathia for Baelfast in two days. Kai said he will leave tonight and return to Aquaria to let his father know. They will also have their armies ready. Within five days, they can be gathered outside of the Red Wall."

I nodded, my stomach twisting, knowing we had a timetable.

I pulled Nicolae further away from the group. "I need your help. I need to get into contact with someone."

"Who?"

"Erro," I whispered. "He is the only other person I know, besides us, that can transport."

"Why would we need him?"

"Roehl will not allow anyone but you and I to enter Morbeth. But I will need Trystan in order to defeat him." I then explained to Nicolae what had happened at the arena. I knew Roehl wouldn't allow Trystan into Morbeth without paying a high price. I had to find another way around it. A way to get Trystan to me when the time was right.

"I'll try to contact him, but it is nearly impossible to get in touch with a Wanderer. They are so heavily warded, and with Roehl's threats, I can imagine the kinds of magic they have in place to protect them against any outside forces."

"All I ask is that you try."

"I will." His golden eyes were filled with worry. "Do you think you have prepared enough? In five days, we must be ready."

I nodded, feeling good about my powers, and how much more connected I'd felt every time I used them. "I'll be ready."

"Good." He held out his hand to me. "We'll get through this together."

"Together." I said, taking hold of it. "I'm glad you're here."

"I am too," he said. "We'll finish this, one way or another. For now, I'll return to my room to see if I can contact Erro."

I nodded and gave him one last hug before he left, then I headed back over to the group.

Feng stepped in front of me and held out a small package in his hand. "For you, princess."

"Me?" I took the package and tore open the paper, which was neatly tied with string. Gasping, I held the most beautiful and intricate carving in my hand. It was a rider atop a horse.

A stallion. A crown was atop the rider's head, a cape flowing behind him.

I knew exactly what this was. It was a carving of Trystan.

Feng stepped in front of me. "That day when we went to the arena and our prince appeared on the ridge above us—still cursed—I saw the look on your face," he explained. "The longing. The love. The pain. I wanted to capture that moment as a reminder. That despite the circumstances, you overcame it."

I remembered the moment so vividly, and a rush of tears filled my eyes.

"Feng, this is beautiful beyond words, and there really are no words that can express how grateful I am. I will cherish this forever." I hugged the carving to my chest.

"You're very welcome." Feng smiled and bowed his head, then backed away.

"You're lucky," Brone huffed, coming up beside me. "I've been begging him for one of his carvings for years and received nothing but attitude."

"I'll carve something for you," I offered.

Brone's eyes lit up. "Princess, I didn't know you could carve."

I shook my head. "I don't, but I can learn."

The light in his eyes extinguished, his lips pulled downward. "Never mind."

I smacked his arm. "Look who has the attitude now."

Kylan called him, so he gave me a sinister grin and walked away.

Kai and Thalia strode over to me next.

"I heard you were going back to Aquaria tonight."

"I am," Kai replied. "I will make sure the royals are alerted and will have their armies in Baelfast in five days."

"Thank you so much," I said, throwing a hand over my heart. "Please be safe."

He paused and glanced over at Thalia, who was blushing at his side.

"Would it be okay if I took Thalia with me?" Kai asked, reaching over, and taking her hand.

My heart instantly warmed and a smile bloomed on my face.

Thalia stepped forward and grabbed my wrist. "I won't go if you need me here."

"No," I said, pulling her into a hug. "Go. We will meet you in Baelfast."

"Are you sure?"

"I'm positive." I looked at Kai. "Please take care of my cousin. I can't afford to have anyone else taken from me."

He grinned and placed a fist to his heart. "You have my word. Her safety will be my priority."

I nodded, my smile so big my cheeks ached.

I'm happy for you, I said to Kai through our connection.

"We're still getting to know each other, but after the few days I spent with her, I found we have a lot in common. One big plus . . . she can eat the same foods I do."

We both laughed and Thalia grinned pointing between us. "Are you two—?"

"Yes," I said. "I'm sorry. I was just making sure he takes care of you. You are important to me and to the future of Incendia."

Thalia bowed her head. "I know."

Trystan came up from behind me and wrapped his arms around my waist.

Kai held out his arm, and he and Trystan grabbed each other's wrists.

"We'll see you in five days, my friend," Kai said.

"See you in five days," Trystan replied.

CHAPTER
TWENTY-SEVEN

Nicolae tried to contact Erro, to no avail. We still had four days left, but I was worried that if we didn't get in touch with him, my plan wouldn't work. We were running out of time . . . and options.

The next day, Trystan and his father went to gather the Carpathian army. Everett and Callum insisted on sailing with the army in hopes of finding Incendia's ships in the port of Baelfast. I agreed, wishing them well, but had a gut feeling that the ships were most likely on their way to Crimson Cove, just outside of Morbeth.

From Trystan's balcony, I watched an army of at least five thousand men gather on a large field below. They were standing at attention in perfect lines, dressed in black fighting leathers with silver vambraces, shields, and swords. Atop their heads were black helmets, and the crest of Carpathia on their chests. At the front of the army were men on horses, flying two flags of Carpathia. Two more riders carried white flags adorned with black dragons.

I'd never witnessed anything so incredible. It was a sight to see these brave men, honoring their king, ready to fight with a single order.

They were heading to Baelfast to fight for me and Nicolae.

My heart burst and tears of admiration flowed from my eyes as I continued to watch.

Facing the army were ten men on horseback. The two in the middle were obvious — Trystan and his father. They wore their royal garb of black with golden crowns atop their heads and long black capes flowing behind them. Trystan on his black stallion, and his father on a steed of white.

I watched the king raise his hand, then heard the blaring of trumpets. Like a well-oiled machine, the army of men marched forward, toward at least a dozen ships bearing Carpathia's flags, waiting in a large port a few miles adjacent to the mortal one.

The ships and port were hidden and warded from human eyes.

It had begun. The beginning of the end.

But to what end? I guess we would soon find out.

"Hold on, just a little while longer," I whispered to the wind, hoping it would find Sabine and Brynna, and carry them some comfort. *"We are coming for you. I promise."*

I watched Trystan ride back to the castle with his father and guards in tow. One day, he would rise and become king, and I would be his queen. Together we would rule this kingdom.

But first, we had to deal with Morbeth.

Trystan walked into the room, and as soon as I breathed in his scent, my anxiety melted away.

"My flame," he said, stripping his cloak off, setting his crown on the bed stand. "How are you feeling?"

"Much better now that you're here." I smiled, trying to hide the negative thoughts swirling through my mind, but he could read me like a book.

"What's wrong?"

I turned back to look out the window. "I'm worried about my friends, the witches, and guards being held prisoner, and the countless men that are being sent to Baelfast."

Trystan pulled me into his arms. "I cannot offer you anything but the knowledge that this will soon be over. And once it is, we will be free to live our lives in peace."

I sighed against his chest. "I long for that day."

"Me, too," he said, kissing the top of my head. "My father asked me to invite you and Nicolae to lunch. He has a few things he would like to discuss before we leave."

"What things?"

"I honestly don't know."

"Alright. When is lunch?"

He gave me a dimpled grin. "Right now."

The circular, private dining table was set festively with fragrant white roses, red winter berries, and greenery. In front of us, ornate golden goblets were placed.

Nicolae showed up, and we all took a seat. It felt intimate with just the four of us, especially now that the king and I had made amends.

Servants came and filled the goblets with ruby wine, but after drinking Trystan's blood, all other blood tasted stale and bland. He'd ruined the taste of all other mortal blood for me.

"Thank you for coming," the king said to me and Nicolae. He then cleared his throat. "I know you are on the verge of battle, but in hopes that it will end swiftly and justly, I would like to propose an upcoming event."

I sat up in my chair and nodded, wondering if it was the winter festival.

The king folded his hands on the table. "I would like to have someone brought in to start planning preparations for your royal wedding."

Royal wedding. My heart palpitated in my chest.

I, Calla Caldwell, the girl who had lived my entire mortal life in the shadows, would become a princess, marrying the man of my dreams. A prince. A real-life, devastatingly handsome prince.

"Calla?" Trystan spoke gently through our bond.

My mind snapped back to reality. "I'm sorry," I breathed. "I was just thinking about how this all seems too good to be true."

The king gave a hearty laugh. "Well, I can only imagine. I know we started off on a very rough note, but the night of Ivy's dinner, the moment you stood up to me with a fire in your eyes, and said, *'Your son is a great prince, and I have* no doubt *he will be an even greater king.'* I knew right then and there that you were special, and that you cared deeply for my son."

"I don't remember that. When did it happen?" Trystan asked.

"It was after you stormed out of the room," the king replied. "You were clearly upset that Ivy had used magic against Calla."

Trystan gave me a look that melted me. *"Just when I think I can't love you more, you surprise me."*

"My prince. I am only here because you *saved me."*

"How about a spring wedding?" the king suggested.

I smiled brightly because spring was my mother's favorite season. It was the season she married my father, out in a meadow, under a gazebo filled with red and cream-colored roses. "I think a spring wedding would be magical."

"Then spring it shall be." The king clapped his hands together. His hazel eyes turned to Trystan. "My son, I have also given a lot of consideration to what I am going to say next. It is not something I take lightly, but something that I believe will be best for me and for the kingdom."

"What is it, father?" Trystan asked, his brow furrowed with concern.

The king leaned forward. "After your wedding, I am going to step down as king. I want you to take my place."

My eyes snapped to Nicolae, whose eyes were wide.

Trystan shook his head. "Father, why? You still have many years left."

The king leaned back in his chair. "I do, but I'm tired. So very tired. After losing your mother, I lost the will to do anything at all. You have no idea how much she helped me keep this kingdom running smoothly. The people loved her more than they did me." A sad smile rose on his lips, his eyes distant. "After she died, I barely pulled myself together to make sure Carpathia didn't fall apart. Nothing of value mattered anymore. Ever since that day, there has been an ache in my chest that won't go away."

"Then why did you bury every memory of her?" Trystan's eyes held so much pain. He loved his mother and didn't understand why his father erased everything of her from the kingdom after she passed.

"It was because I was angry. Angry, I couldn't help her find a cure. Angry that instead of coming to me, she chose to secretly seek out a mage to end her life." A tear trickled down the king's cheek. "I know it was selfish of me. I know she was in pain. But she should have come to me. I wasn't prepared for her to leave and never return."

"You had pulled away from her long before she passed." Trystan was trying to hold his composure, but this was something he was passionate about.

Nicolae and I remained quiet. He kept his head down, sipping on his ruby wine. I just sat still, letting them work through this, knowing it needed to happen for them to move on.

"I pulled away because I couldn't bear to see her in pain. It killed me, Trystan. To watch the woman I was supposed to spend the rest of my immortal life with, lose her mind. The woman I had given my entire heart to."

"Then what happened?" Trystan's hands were fisted on the table.

"She forgot me," the king sighed. "I came to her one day and wrapped my arms around her and gave her a kiss. She screamed and pushed me away and told me to leave and never come back. Her eyes . . . in her eyes, there was no recollection of me. It was as if all the years we spent together had vanished, and I was a stranger to her. That's why I left. Not because I wanted to. But because she told me never to return."

"Wait," I exhaled, my chest tightening. "You have just explained what I went through with Trystan. Your wife was cursed with the Lethe potion."

"It sounds similar, but we had no affiliation with Morbeth, or with Roehl. There was no reason for them to curse my wife."

I nodded, knowing I would have to talk to Markus after this.

The king continued. "Trystan, these past years, you have proven to me that you can rule. And now that you will have your queen by your side, I know Carpathia's future will see its greatest days.

"I want to travel. I want to visit the places your mother loved so dearly." He reached over and took Trystan's hand. "I know ruling a kingdom is tasking, but I trust you. Calla is right. You are a great prince. The people of Carpathia respect and honor you, and when you rise, I have no doubt you will be an even greater king than I was. Especially with Calla at your side."

"No, father," Trystan said. "I can only hope to be as great as you one day."

The king patted Trystan's hand. "Then it is set. A spring wedding and a coronation."

My stomach danced with butterflies. It was a lot to take in, but if Trystan had to rise, so did I. Our lives were laid out before us. We just had to accept the roles and let fate guide us.

Heading back to the room, I stopped Trystan.

"I need to talk to Markus," I said. "Please excuse me for just a moment. I'll meet you in the room."

"Do you want me to come?" Trystan asked.

"No. I need to talk to him alone. He needs to know he is not responsible for Sabine and Brynna's kidnapping."

Trystan nodded and kissed my cheek. "Go then. I'll see you soon."

"I won't be long."

I thought of Markus and asked my power to take me to him. In a second, I was standing outside of a door. Knocking three times loudly, I waited.

Footsteps pounded against the floor inside and then, the door swung open.

Markus stood there, hair in disarray, eyes heavy like I'd woken him up. "Calla? What is it?"

"I need to ask you something."

"Of course. Come in."

Markus stepped to the side, allowing me to enter his room. It was dark, the curtains drawn shut, but a lantern was lit on the bed stand.

"Sit," he said, pulling an armchair up. He sat on the side of his bed.

"Did you know Roehl's mother?" I asked.

"I did. She was quiet but cunning. A snake wearing a crown."

"Did you ever see her use the Lethe potion?"

Markus's eyes narrowed, brow crumpled. "Why?"

"Because I believe Trystan's mother was cursed by it."

Markus sighed and raked his fingers through his dark hair. "Yes. The mages created it and gave it to her. She is the one who taught Roehl how to combine a spell with the potion to bind it."

Goddess above.

"Did the king and queen of Carpathia ever visit Morbeth?"

"Aside from them attending a few balls, not many royals came to Morbeth."

"So, you don't remember the royals of Morbeth and Carpathia getting together?"

Markus pressed his thumb and finger against the bridge of his nose. "Wait. There was one time when they did come to Morbeth alone, to discuss trade. I noticed that the queen did try to flirt with Carpathia's king, but he ignored her and stuck close to his wife."

"How long ago was that?"

"I don't know. Years ago."

"At least ten?"

"Yes."

"Now that I think back, I do remember something I thought was quite odd."

"What?"

"I remember the queen had gone to the kitchen to get a bottle of wine. She had never gone to the kitchen before. When I followed her, she snapped at me and told me to leave." He leaned forward on his elbows. "Do you think she poisoned the queen?"

I nodded. "I do. It's the only rational explanation."

"The queen ended her life not long after that," Markus said. "Maybe she knew they would eventually find out."

"The cure to the curse died with her," I whispered.

That night I called a meeting with Trystan and his father, bringing Markus with me. I told them what my gut told me, and how it had been confirmed with Markus.

Rage filled the king's eyes. "The Queen of Morbeth? Why? We only went into Morbeth once on a private invitation and were only there for a few hours to discuss trade. Nothing out of the ordinary happened. We left on good terms." The king shook his head. "Besides, my wife didn't show signs of the curse until months later."

Markus bowed his head. "She didn't show signs because the queen had probably woven a time spell into the potion, to remove any suspicion. I've watched Roehl do the same thing. As punishment, he once gave a man the Lethe potion and sent him home. The spell was released on the third day, like Roehl had intended."

The king's bloodshot eyes were distant, his hands fisted tight. "My fight with Morbeth has now become personal. Their queen cursed my wife, and now, the prince dared to use that same curse on my son?" He slammed his fists against his desk, his eyes shooting to one of his guards. "Prepare a ship. I will leave for Hale immediately."

"Father, why are you going to Hale? We leave for Morbeth in four days."

The king stood and walked over to Trystan, resting his hands on his shoulders. "Don't worry about me. I have some business to take care of, and rest assured, I will meet you in Morbeth."

The king stood and walked out of the room.

Markus bowed. "I'll take my leave," he said, walking out and leaving me and Trystan alone.

Trystan immediately wrapped me in his arms. "I'm glad we finally know what happened to my mother. It will finally give us the closure we desperately needed."

"I'm sorry she had to suffer," I said. "But I'm glad you were there for her."

"I do know a bit of what she went through. And now, I do feel for my father. The Lethe curse is the cruelest spell, especially when used against mates."

I looked up into his gorgeous eyes. "We beat it."

"We did. And now, we have to defeat the one who gave me the spell."

I hugged him tightly. "We will."

We had to. There was no other choice.

CHAPTER
TWENTY-EIGHT

THE NEXT FEW DAYS were very busy. While the king was gone, Trystan tended to the duties of their kingdom, and I continued to practice with Nicolae, Markus, and Trystan's cadre.

Markus was in a much better mood, knowing that we were only one day away from joining the armies of Talbrinth just outside of Morbeth to rescue Sabine, Brynna, and the others held under Roehl's wicked thumb.

My practice sessions were brutal, but every time I used my power, the more connected I was with them. Helia was right. I didn't need a manual. What I needed was already inside of me. With a simple thought and intention, my powers responded, and with Trystan's blood fueling me, I didn't tire as I usually did. His blood kept me strong, giving me a deeper connection to my gifts.

Nicolae made sure I was adept at using the basics of all my gifts so they would become second nature. Markus and

Trystan's cadre came at me without holding back, making sure I called each gift swiftly and used it correctly, repeatedly. Fire, water, earth, air. I even found that by using combinations of both, I could create something new.

Fire combined with earth created magma. Brone caught the brunt of that one. He'd sunk ankle deep into a puddle of magma, literally melting his boot off, and severely burning his skin. After some blood, he was fine, but his hits seemed even harder.

Fire and water also created steam, and when aimed for the face, caused temporary blindness, which poor Andrés witnessed firsthand.

By the time our sessions ended, I could barely move. But every night, Trystan would have a hot bath with healing salts ready for me. After that, he made sure I fed from him. It was such an incredibly intimate and powerful act that gave me everything I needed to heal and be ready for the next day.

After multiple attempts at trying to make contact, there was still no word from Erro, and I was getting worried. He was vital to the success of the upcoming battle. Without him transporting Trystan inside Morbeth, Nicolae and I would be on our own, and I wasn't sure if our powers alone could protect us against Roehl and the archaic, dark magic of his mages.

Nicolae and I knew Roehl would stifle our powers. He'd done it every single time in the past. This last time, in Dead Man's Land, I'd only survived with Flint's help, and I knew he would also be vital to me when we returned to Morbeth.

Getting out of a hot bath, I slipped on a robe.

"Calla, are you there?" Kai asked through our bond, making me jump.

"I'm here."

"The royals want to meet with you and Nicolae."

I was still trying to catch my breath and that one statement made it race again. *"What? When?"*

"Can you transport to Havendale in an hour? Their king is preparing a banquet."

"Is everyone already in Baelfast?"

"Mostly. Sartha and Aquaria's armies should be arriving at the docks by nightfall, but the kings have gathered here. They all want to meet the lost Incendian royals in person before they march on Morbeth."

"I'll talk to Nicolae and Trystan."

"He can tag along, too." He chuckled. *"Get ready and transport to the castle. It's important you both come."*

"We'll be there."

Trystan had just walked in with a glass of liquid amber in his hand.

"I just got word from Kai. Royals from the other kingdoms want to meet me and Nicolae tonight. The King of Baelfast is having a banquet."

"When?"

I shot him a worried look. "In an hour."

"An hour?" He paused, gulped down whatever was left in his glass, and looked back at me. "Okay. That's doable."

"What does someone like me wear to a banquet filled with royals? I have nothing to wear but training clothes."

"Wait right here," Trystan said.

While he was gone, I pulled the water from my hair and slipped on some pants and a tunic.

Trystan returned ten minutes later, followed by two women. The same women who had been here before to get me ready for the dinner they'd had for Ivy.

The blonde woman was carrying a basket filled with brushes and things to get me ready. The brunette carried three long gowns into the bathing room and hung them up.

Trystan came up behind me. "I'll leave you to get ready." He gave me a quick kiss and started back for the door.

"Where are you going?"

"I'm going to pay Nicolae a visit."

"Where did you get the gowns on such short notice?"

He gave me a warm smile and replied, "They were my mother's."

I didn't know what to say, but he pointed at the two women. "They assured me the gowns are your size."

The women smiled and bowed their heads.

"Thank you," I said.

Trystan winked and headed out the door, while I sat in a chair and the women began readying me for the banquet.

"What are your names?" This was the second time I'd met them, and I thought it was rude not to ask.

"I am Jewel," the brunette answered. She was applying makeup to my face. "And she is Maia."

Maia paused from working on my hair and bowed her head.

"It's nice to see you again," I said.

"You as well," Jewel replied, focused on her work.

From our last encounter, I knew they didn't say much, but they were quick and amazing at what they did.

A knock at the door sent Maia to open it. She returned with a medium-sized box in her hands. After placing it on a table, she went right back to work, finishing my hair.

I didn't want to ask what was inside. I figured if she wanted me to know, she would have told me. Maybe it was supposed to be a surprise.

Work complete, Jewel and Maia moved into the bathing room.

"Come, Your Highness," Jewel said. "Choose a gown."

Maia stepped in front of the mirror as I walked over to the gowns. There were three. One was in dark blue, one in emerald, and one in crimson.

I didn't want to stand out, so I chose the simplest gown in crimson. It was not too formal, and not too casual. A sleeveless silhouette, V-neck, which was tied at the waist and flowed from the waistline to the floor.

Jewel helped me into the gown, while Maia went back out and retrieved the box.

Placing it on the counter, she lifted the lid. Inside was a beautiful golden crown on a silk pillow. It was enchanting, with diamonds and rubies set in a delicate filigree.

"Do I have to wear this?" I asked, thinking it might be a bit much.

"Of course, Your Highness," Maia said. "The prince will be wearing one, too. All royals wear crowns at events." She then asked me to bend so she could put it on my head, and Jewel helped her pin it in place.

"Come," Jewel said, leading me back out, to a full-length mirror set against one wall.

As soon as I looked in the mirror, I gasped. These two women were magical. I looked . . . like a royal. My hair was half up, half-down, with curls on the ends. The golden crown was pinned perfectly in place. The makeup, which made me look flawless, complimented the dress.

Jewel placed a pair of black and crimson heels on the floor, and I slipped into them. They were also a perfect fit. How they managed to pull this off in such a short amount of time baffled me.

They gathered their things as I spun in front of the mirror, in awe of the transformation.

"You are beautiful, Your Highness," Jewel said. "We will take our leave now." They both bowed and headed for the door.

"Thank you so much. From now on, I want you both to be my get-ready for any event girls." They both looked at each other and giggled.

"It will be our pleasure," Maia said. They bowed again and left the room.

A few minutes later, there was a soft knock and Trystan entered.

As soon as his eyes spotted me, he froze. His eyes widened and suddenly darkened.

I had to compose myself, because as soon as he entered, he took my breath away. Trystan was drop-dead gorgeous, dressed in his black royal garb, with a similar golden crown atop his head.

"Gods, you are a vision," he said, stalking toward me.

I held out a hand and pressed it against his chest. "My prince, I'm afraid if you come any closer, all the hard work the ladies did to put me together will be for nothing."

He gave me a devilish grin and took my hand, pressing it to his lips. "Then when the banquet is done, we shall return to my bedchamber, where I will destroy their handiwork."

He then reached into his pocket and pulled out the ring. "I don't think there will be a perfect time to propose. But I did get Nicolae's blessing." He slipped the ring back on my finger. "I want the royals to know that you are my mate. My chosen."

"Won't they already know? You said they can scent our mating bond."

His smile rose. "They will."

I wasn't going to question his motives. I loved the outward expression of the ring, knowing that he was my husband.

"Are you ready?" he asked, giving me his arm.

I nodded. "Is Nicolae ready?"

"He is. He's outside, waiting, giving you the extra time needed."

I smiled and took his arm, and he led me out to the hall.

Nicolae turned and smiled. He was handsome, also dressed in a black suit with a cape draped over his shoulders.

"You're beautiful, Calla," he said with a warm smile.

"Thank you." I couldn't help but smile back at him. "You look very handsome, grandfather. But . . . where is your crown?" He wasn't wearing one.

"Trystan brought me one, but I refused. I am not yet ready for a crown."

I nodded and gave him a smile.

"Shall we?" he asked, holding out his other arm. "To the castle of Baelfast, we go."

I took his arm and in moments, we appeared at the entrance of a glorious castle.

CHAPTER TWENTY-NINE

STARTLING THE GUARDS, THEY surrounded us, but when they noticed Trystan, they stepped back, placing fists on their chests, and bowed.

"Prince Trystan, are you here for the banquet?" one of the guards asked.

"I am," he replied.

The guard's eyes slid to me and widened. He bowed his head. "Princess."

I smiled and tipped my head.

Nicolae stood behind us, and without the crown, the guards weren't sure who he was. They greeted him with a bow only.

A servant exited the doors. "Prince. Princess. Please follow me."

He led us inside the castle, and I couldn't help but gawk and soak it all in. It wasn't as grand as Carpathia, but it was close. Baelfast's castle, hidden in the city of Havendale, was lavishly decorated with emerald greens and gold. Chandeliers, tapestries, floral arrangements, and luxurious furnishings adorned the entire inside. One grand staircase, in the center, led up to four floors of rooms.

The servant led us down a large hallway that opened to an entrance to the ballroom. Music was playing and voices were chattering. As soon as we stepped inside, everyone in the room turned and looked at us. I squeezed Trystan's arm, wanting to slide behind him.

"Don't be afraid, my flame. No one here is greater than you. Remember who you are. You are Incendian royalty and now a Princess of Carpathia. Raise your head and walk tall."

A tall, slender man, clean shaven, with long blond hair tied behind the nape of his neck, strode to us with a wide smile on his face. He looked middle aged, fitted in a black suit with gold embellishments. On his head was a golden crown filled with emerald gems.

"Ah, Prince Trystan," he chimed. "Where is your father?"

Trystan bowed at the waist. "He is in Hale on business, but he should arrive in Baelfast by morning."

"That's good to hear." His eyes shifted to me, and a grin pulled on his lips. "And is this our guest of honor?"

Trystan faced me and smiled. "This is King Demetrius of Baelfast."

I bowed my head. "Your Majesty."

"Let's drop the formalities, shall we? When royalty gathers, we never use them. Tonight, I am Demetrius." He bowed his head slightly at me, then turned his attention to Trystan. "So, who is this beauty on your arm?"

"She is Calla Caldwell. Incendian Royal and my mate."

The king raised his brow at Trystan, then took my hand and pressed his lips to it. "Calla Caldwell. Come, let me introduce you to the others."

"Wait, I would like you to meet my grandfather, Nicolae Corvus. He is a prince of Incendia and heir of Morbeth."

The king locked eyes with Nicolae, then held out his hand. "Ah, the elusive Nicolae Corvus. I've heard stories of you, Incendian prince. I am honored you are here. Come, let the others welcome you as well."

Trystan stayed right at my side, but he had no choice. I had his arm in a death grip.

As the king led us over, the rest of the men gathered in a small group, waiting for us. It appeared I was the only woman here, and that made my anxiety rise even more. Then Kai stepped forward from the back of the group with a glimmering smile.

A chuckle. *Breathe, Sea Star. You look like you're about to faint.*

"I'm trying. I feel like—"

"A princess?"

"No."

"Well, you are one, so suck it up and play your part. Like me," he said, raising a glass of amber liquid.

I rolled my eyes, and he laughed. Then I heard the men's whispers.

"Is that her?"

"She is a beauty."

"I didn't think she would be so young."

"Why is Prince Trystan with her?"

"Isn't he engaged to Princess Ivy?"

"Yes, he is. Where is Princess Ivy?"

They'd all probably received the letter of his engagement, and now I felt like I was a mate wrecker.

"Don't listen to their worthless banter, my flame. They are old and bored and thrive for any kind of gossip."

I nodded, but my gut still tightened into one big knot.

King Demetrius paused in front of the gathered men. Nicolae stepped to my other side and gave me a warm smile. "Royals of Talbrinth. I would like to introduce you all to the heirs of Incendia." He swept his hand to Nicolae. "This is Prince Nicolae Corvus, and his granddaughter, Princess Calla Caldwell."

There were murmurs, too many I couldn't make out.

It seemed that all the kings were handsome, in their own way. None looked older than forty.

"Trystan," one of the royals spoke. He was a brawny man, chocolate eyes with auburn hair and a full beard. "Have you claimed the Incendian heir as your concubine?"

Concubine? My insides heated with anger.

Trystan gently squeezed my arm and smiled warmly at the man. "No, Ambroz. Calla is my mate."

His brow furrowed. "What about Princess Ivy?"

Kai stepped in front of us and turned to the crowd. "You all know Ivy. Trystan never agreed to the engagement. The Royals of Northfall were persistent and begged Trystan's father to join them. But Trystan was already blood bonded and mated to Calla. So, the engagement is void."

"How do you know this, Kai?" another royal spoke. He was tall with short red hair and no facial hair. "Because, Louis . . ." Kai forced himself between me and Trystan, placing his arms around our shoulders. "They are my friends, and I am in the loop, which you all seem to be way outside of."

"Kai," a deep voice admonished. His father stepped around the red headed man and came to me, wrapping me in a hug. "Calla, how have you been? I've been worried since you left Aquaria."

"Your Highness, I am so sorry I left abruptly."

"Don't be sorry. Kai has been keeping us *in the loop*." He gave me a wink.

I chuckled. "I'm glad. How are Queen Adira and Hali?"

King Gerard smiled warmly. "They are fine. Hali is here with your cousin."

"Where?" I glanced around the room.

"She is not a royal," Kai whispered, "so Hali decided to stay with her in one of the rooms."

I nodded, glad she was here. I was looking forward to paying them a visit.

"If Calla is in fact an Incendian Royal, can she demonstrate her power for us to ease our minds?" The royal who spoke was a tall man with dark eyes and clean-cut raven hair.

"That's Lannister. King of Hale," Trystan said, and I nodded.

"Are you up to showing them a bit of your power?" Kai asked.

"Not really."

"Do it. Make their jaws drop."

"Kai."

"Sea Star, these men rule Talbrinth. Show them your power and step up beside them. Besides, that's why you're here. They have sent their armies to back you against Morbeth. They want to make sure you are an Incendian Royal."

"My flame." Trystan's voice was calming. *"You don't have to do anything that will make you feel uncomfortable."*

"Do you think I should do it?"

"Me? I would love to see the maids sweep their jaws from the floor after seeing how powerful my mate truly is."

I let out a deep sigh. *"You and Kai are so alike."*

"Are we?" His head snapped to me, azure eyes locked on mine, darkening.

I shook my head. *"Just in words. Nothing else."*

King Demetrius stepped in front of me. "Will you demonstrate for us?"

I turned to Nicolae, and he gave me a subtle nod. He was for it, too.

I took a step forward. Every eye in the room was fastened on me.

"Shine, my flame."

Straightening my back, I held out my right hand in front of me, palm up. A huge ball of flame appeared in it. But I knew they'd seen elemental powers before. This was no different from what any other Incendian could do.

Thrusting my left hand out to the table, toward glasses filled with water, I heard gasps as the water pulled from those glasses, coming to rest in a ball of water in my palm. Water and Fire were now in my grasp.

Around the room were large potted plants. Ferns, palms, and even flowers. I called to earth, and the roots of the plants crawled forward, creating a barrier around me, almost like a large bird cage. Then, I called to the air. A gust of wind swept through the ballroom, swirling through my hair, and around my dress. I let go, my body enveloping in flame. The wind, air, and fire swirled around me. The roots wrapped around my legs, keeping me secured to the floor.

"Her eyes," Ambroz—King of Sartha—muttered. His own eyes were fixed on mine.

King Gerard, Kai's father, had a smile and a look of pride on his face.

"She can call on every element," Louis—King of Aquaris—whispered to Demetrius.

"She is glorious," Demetrius replied. "Is she not, Lannister?" He nudged the King of Hale with his elbow.

"Indeed," Lannister answered.

"There is no doubt she is Leora's kin, and an Incendian Royal," Demetrius whispered to himself.

I relaxed. The air died, and the roots escaped back to their homes in the planters. The flame from my body died, as did the one in my palm. All that was left was the water.

"I taught her how to throw water daggers," Kai boasted loudly. "Show them, Calla."

Kai jogged to the other side of the room, grabbing a tray from one of the servants, holding it up in front of him.

"Do it!" Lassiter urged.

"Yes, do it," Ambroz added.

I grinned and created five water daggers that floated above my palm. Facing Kai, I gave him a grin and threw them. Spreading my fingers, the daggers separated, moving further from each other. Kai's eyes went wide, realizing his tray was too small.

"Calla. Don't kill me."

Right before the daggers hit Kai, I fisted my hand. The daggers turned into balls of water, smacking Kai in the face, shoulder, and legs. Laughter roared behind me. Kai was dripping wet from head to toe.

"That was the best demonstration yet," Demetrius hollered to Kai with a broad smile. "You taught her well."

Kai gave me a pointed look, pulling the water from himself. In seconds, he was dry.

"Fine. I deserved that."

I smiled at him. *"My demonstration was over, and you provoked me. I would like to remain out of the spotlight for the rest of the night."*

"That might be hard. The banquet was set up to meet you and Nicolae."

"Come, let's sit," Demetrius said, leading everyone over to the large table set for royalty. The plates and settings looked like they were made from gold. The goblets were inlaid with glittering jewels. The center of the table was decorated with the most beautiful bouquets of red roses and greenery, and large pitchers filled with Ruby Wine.

"Is there real food around here?" Gerard asked. "There are a few of us who do not live off of ruby wine."

"Ruby wine. That's a clever way of putting it, Gerard," Demetrius chimed. He turned to his servants. "Please bring a tray of mortal food for our friends." The servants bowed and left the room.

"Nicolae, you must be proud of your granddaughter," Ambroz said, taking a seat next to him.

"I am very proud of her." Nicolae's eyes slid to me. "She never ceases to amaze me."

"We heard the news about King Romulus," Lannister said, sitting across from Nicolae. "I offer you my deepest condolences."

"As do we," Demetrius added, and Nicolae bowed his head. "Roehl has become murderous and unruly. He is a danger to all of Talbrinth and needs to be dealt with. Which is why we have joined forces with you." He slapped a hand on Gerard's shoulder. "Not to mention Gerard and Kai's persistence. Also, Baelfast shares a border with Morbeth. We cannot afford another war, or have Roehl think he is powerful enough to overthrow any one of us."

Everyone at the table agreed.

King Demetrius took a sip of his ruby wine. "I also hear the Incendian queen has betrayed her people and is sleeping with the enemy."

"This is true," Nicolae said. "She will be dealt with soon enough."

Demetrius seemed pleased with his answer.

For the next thirty minutes, Nicolae answered most of the questions the royals had about what had happened to him. The truth behind Roehl's death decree. And how we ended up here.

"So, about tomorrow, what is your plan?" Ambroz asked.

There wasn't really a plan. No one would be able to enter Morbeth except me and Nicolae. So, the armies would gather on Dead Man's Land, far enough away from the deadly arrows of Morbeth's army.

Then, it was a waiting game. A wait to see who was stronger. Who would survive?

"You look tired," Trystan whispered, taking my hand.

"A bit. Today's practice was brutal."

Trystan stood from his seat and bowed at the waist. "I'm sorry, gentlemen. I am going to take Calla back to Carpathia to rest. She will need every ounce of strength to defeat Roehl tomorrow."

Lannister's onyx eyes fastened on mine. "Do you believe you can defeat him?"

That was the ultimate question. The one every royal in this room wanted to know.

I stood tall and looked him directly in the eye. Confident in myself and in my gifts, I replied, "I do."

Lannister smiled and tipped his head. "Good then. Rest up, Calla. We wish you the best of luck tomorrow."

Nicolae also stood from his seat. "I'm afraid I will need to leave as well. I would like to see them home safely." He bowed to the royals at the table. "It was a pleasure to meet all of you."

"The pleasure was ours." Demetrius rose to his feet. "If Roehl is defeated tomorrow, since you are the rightful heir, will you assume the throne, Nicolae?"

Nicolae paused. "I am considering it."

"Don't wait too long. The people will need a ruler to rise. They expect it, or else they become unruly." Demetrius grinned and held out a hand across the table, and Nicolae shook it. "If you do assume the throne, Nicolae Corvus, I look forward to doing business with you in the future. Since we will be neighbors." He bowed his head to me and Trystan. "The people of Morbeth have needed rescuing for quite some time now, ever since Roehl has taken over. I am looking forward to his defeat and brighter days for their country."

"As do we," Trystan said.

We said our goodbyes to everyone at the table and excused ourselves.

Kai followed us out. "Do you want to stop in and say hello to Thalia and Hali before you leave?"

I nodded. "I would love to."

"If you don't mind, I'm going to head back," Nicolae said. "Unless you need me to stay?"

"No. I can easily transport us back to Carpathia," I said. "And Trystan will be with me."

He leaned over and kissed me on the forehead. "You did well tonight. Rest up and I'll see you in the morning."

"Bright and early," I breathed.

As Nicolae vanished, Kai led us up the stairs to the second floor. Down the hall, he stopped at a door and knocked. I heard the pattering of feet, then the door swung wide open.

Hali's ice-blue eyes widened. "Princess Calla!" she exclaimed, running over and throwing her arms around my waist. "It's good to see you."

"It's good to see you too, Hali," I said, hugging her back. "How have you been?"

"Busy," she huffed. "I'm playing cards with Thalia, and she's impossible to beat."

Thalia came to the door with wide eyes and cards fanned out in her hand. "Calla. Prince Trystan. It's good to see you both."

"I hear you aren't giving Hali any chances." I chuckled. Thalia shrugged and gave me a sly grin.

Kai exhaled and placed a hand on his sister's shoulder. "Hali, what did I tell you about swinging the door open before asking who it is?" he scolded.

Hali threw her arms over her chest. "We are in a hidden castle in Baelfast that is heavily guarded. No one knows or cares we are here."

Kai rolled his eyes, and Trystan placed a hand on the top of Hali's head. "Listen to your brother, Hali. He only wants to keep you safe."

Hali let out a deep sigh. "Fine. Next time I'll ask."

Kai shook his head. "Oh, but she'll listen to you?"

Trystan shrugged and I couldn't help but laugh.

"You look beautiful, Calla," Thalia said. "How did the banquet go?"

"It went well, but I'd rather be home in bed."

Thalia glanced over to Trystan, then back at me. "Yes, I'm sure you would."

I felt my cheeks warm. "Well, we better be off. Give the girl a chance, cousin."

Thalia snickered. "She's more than capable of beating me. If she wins, it will be on her merit and not because I let her. That way, her victory will be much sweeter."

"Yes, I told her not to let me win," Hali chimed. "Kai always lets me win, and it's so boring."

"What?" Kai snapped. "Oh, no more chances for you in the future."

"I won't need them," Hali sneered.

I laughed and grabbed Trystan's hand. "I'll see you guys tomorrow. It's going to be a big day." We all tried to keep the situation as light as possible, but we all knew how dangerous tomorrow would be.

"Sleep well," Kai said.

"You, as well," Trystan replied.

I closed my eyes and thought of Carpathia and Trystan's bedchamber. Our bedchamber.

In seconds, we were back.

CHAPTER THIRTY

I COULDN'T SLEEP. EVEN wrapped tightly in Trystan's arms my mind felt like it was caught in a whirlwind, and so was my stomach.

In a few hours I'd be coming face to face with Roehl. It wasn't as simple as walking into Morbeth, saving everyone, and destroying him. I knew Roehl was waiting and ready. I had no doubt he'd been gathering power, threatening us with innocent lives so we would enter Morbeth on his terms.

Who knew what kinds of magic he would throw at us? I just prayed that the gods and goddesses would help us.

After hours of listening to Trystan's steady breathing, my eyes became heavy.

I was standing in darkness. Before me, a monstrous wall illuminated, as far as the eye could see. My insides trembled, knowing exactly where I was. I was back in Morbeth, and before me was the Red Wall.

"My pet." The deep, dark voice made my skin crawl.

I started to run, following the wall, but there was no exit. No way of escape.

I tried to call my power, but there was no warmth, not even a prick of magic was felt.

"My pet," the devil spoke again. "You have no power here."

Suddenly, there was light to the side of me, opposite the wall. I turned my head and stopped dead in my tracks. There were people lined up, with masks over their faces. They were standing at attention, not moving. Were they real?

Out from the shadows stepped a man wearing the mask of a horned demon. I knew it was Roehl. He wore the same mask at the Shadow Fest.

"You think you can defeat me, my pet?" His voice was filled with poison.

"Why am I here? Get the fuck out of my head."

"Such a foul mouth," he hissed. "My mages are powerful. Even from afar, they can cause you to dream of me."

I fisted my hands at my sides, my nails digging into my flesh. I didn't want to get into any unwanted conversation with him. He was trying to bait me.

"Wake me up," *I begged my power. But it didn't listen.*

"I have seen the armies gathering. I know they are waiting in Baelfast as we speak." He walked to the center of the line of people and paused, turning toward me. "I hope you know that tomorrow, you will not win. You will witness death and devastation. Not only will those who served under my father die, but everyone gathered outside of the Red Wall will die as well. Including your prince." He snarled. "I know you broke the curse. I know you have sealed the mating bond with him. But that won't stop me." He turned and pulled the masks from the two figures in front of him.

Sabine and Brynna looked at me, blood-red eyes, and tears-stained faces. They were gagged, their hands tied behind their backs.

I started running toward them, but Roehl screamed, "Stop!"

He held out a hand and my body froze. I could feel his power gripping me tightly as he turned and faced me. "Feel my power, Calla. You cannot defeat me." His eyes moved up, to the top of the wall behind me, and then he raised his hand.

I glanced to the side, and saw men on the top of the wall, arrows nocked, aimed at those innocent people.

Brynna and Sabine wailed. I begged and pleaded with my power to come to me. Commanded it. But it was bound so tightly, there was nothing I could do.

"This is what you will witness tomorrow, my pet."

Roehl let his hand drop. Arrows whizzed past me, their sharp metal tips landing with resounding thuds into my best friends. Into those who served my great-grandfather.

Screaming, I woke up in Trystan's arms.

"Calla, what's wrong?" His face was riddled with worry.

I fell into his arms, sobbing against his chest. "He was in my dream. That bastard," I wailed. "He had them lined up. All of them, including Sabine and Brynna. They were terrified, and I couldn't save them. I wasn't strong enough to break his hold on me."

Trystan stood from the bed and pulled me up, gathering me in his arms. "Hey, this is exactly why he came to you in your dream. He is planting seeds of doubt because he knows how powerful you are. If he can get you to doubt yourself and your abilities, he knows he'll win." Trystan raised my face. "My flame. Don't you know by now? He has no power over you."

I closed my eyes and fell back into his arms. "He said he was going to kill everyone standing against him. Every man on the other side of the Red Wall."

Trystan exhaled and shook his head. "He has Morbeth's army, as well as Incendia's. That is no more than ten thousand men. The armies gathering tomorrow will total nearly twenty thousand. He's terrified, and knows the only way he can win, is by planting a seed of fear inside you. You are the key to winning this war, Calla. And he knows that."

"Nicolae can't get in touch with Erro. If he or another Wanderer don't show up tomorrow, there will be no way for you to come to me."

Trystan gave me a look. A dead-serious look. "Who said I had to come to you?"

That one question changed everything.

CHAPTER THIRTY-ONE

WE DIDN'T SLEEP AFTER that. I stayed curled in Trystan's arms, savoring the feeling of his scent and his strength. In his arms, I felt invincible. But tomorrow, we would be separated. I had to find my way back to him.

Before we got out of bed, he bit his wrist and made me feed from him. His blood seemed to ground me and dulled the trembling inside.

"Come, I have something for you," Trystan said, slipping from the sheets. He stood and walked over to his closet and pulled it open, then came out a few seconds later carrying fighting leathers, only suitable for a woman.

He carried it over and placed it in my hands. "I had this made for you."

It looked just like theirs, black and trimmed with silver. However, the crest in the center of the chest was different. It was the crest of Incendia—the tattoo I had on my right palm, representing fire. And around it, guarding and protecting it, was a dragon.

"It's perfect," I breathed, my finger tracing the details. Tears welled and slipped from my eyes, seeing how perfect this was. Trystan was my dragon prince. Always guarding. Always protecting.

I slid from the sheets, stood from the bed, and hurried to the bathroom.

The fighting leathers were a perfect fit, tightly hugging my curves. I made a fist and hit the chest with my knuckles. It was solid, hopefully strong enough to block an arrow, or maybe even a spear, but not strong enough to withstand dark magic.

"You look like the goddess of war," Trystan said from the doorway.

Glancing at him, I smiled. He was shirtless, muscular arms crossed over his sculpted chest. "And you, my prince, are my god of war."

He purred, sliding over and wrapping his arms around me. "The Winter Festival is in a week's time. When we return, you will dance with only me."

"Your cadre are very agile dancers."

"Yes, I know. And so is Kai," he sighed. "They've all danced with you, and I have not had the privilege of one dance."

I ran a finger down his chest. "Are you jealous?"

"I am." He snatched my finger.

I pressed my head against his chest. "Then at the festival, I shall dance the entire night with you."

"Is that a promise?"

I pressed my lips against his. "Sealed with a kiss."

"I wish we had more time." He pressed his forehead against mine. "I need to get ready, and we must meet the others downstairs."

Suddenly, I was slammed with reality. And the sheer magnitude of it nearly dropped me to my knees.

"Are you okay?"

"I am. I'm going to the veranda to meditate while you get ready. I need to center myself."

He nodded, then strode to the closet to retrieve his fighting leathers, while I took a pillow and strode out through the gossamer curtains.

The sun hadn't risen, but its rays were peeking over the horizon, slowly stretching across the sky. I placed my pillow on the ground and sat on top of it, crossing my legs. Closing my eyes, I relaxed, inhaling and exhaling, finding my breath. Feeling it. Anchoring myself to the moment.

I focused on my body, relaxing every part of me, from my feet, all the way up to the top of my head. I let my thoughts, my concerns, float away for a moment, savoring the calm and serenity.

I needed to stay grounded. I needed to believe that my powers were stronger than any dark magic. Leora and Helia assured me they were. I just had to hold on to that and believe that no matter how dark and dangerous it would get, my power would rise.

Warmth and light caressed my face. The sun was rising, filling me with a renewed strength. With my eyes shut, I absorbed its wonderful gift for as long as I could.

"My flame," Trystan's voice said softly. "It's time."

I inhaled one last breath and slowly exhaled, opening my eyes to a beautiful morning. I soaked it all in—the sprawling trees across snow-covered hills, birds singing, the crisp bite of the air against my skin. Carpathia was magical.

I turned and took Trystan's outstretched hand. He nodded and smiled, then led me down to the others.

All the men were dressed in their fighting leathers, including Nicolae. His was similar to the cadre, but there was no crest on his chest. Markus was wearing the leathers and crest of Morbeth.

As soon as he saw my face, he spoke. "I am wearing this because I believe that after today, Morbeth will be renewed. I will help bring it back to greatness."

Markus was loyal to Morbeth. He had been loyal to the crown, protecting it with his life. I had no doubt he would carry that loyalty to whomever would rule.

I had hoped it would be Nicolae. There was no one better suited to rule Morbeth than him, and I knew if Markus was at his side, Morbeth could become a great and powerful country and ally.

"Any word from Erro?" I asked.

Nicolae shook his head, but I didn't let it phase me.

"This is what we are going to do," Nicolae said. "We will transport to where the armies are, and from there, Calla and I will ride to the Red Wall. Once inside, Calla will communicate with Trystan and keep him updated."

"I am coming with you," Markus said, stepping in front of us. "Roehl wants me just as badly as you. I directly defied him, helping Calla to escape. He will let me inside."

"Markus, no," I breathed. "He will kill you."

"Princess, he could also easily kill you or Nicolae. But I have decided. I want to be there just in case there is something I can do to save you." He closed his eyes and slammed a fist over his chest. "I swore an oath to the king. Dead or not, I will fulfill that oath. I will walk into Morbeth, and even if it means I forfeit my life, at least it will be trying to protect you."

My heart shattered. There was nothing I could say to stop him. He had already made up his mind. I knew Sabine was a huge factor in that decision, so I reached out and took his hand.

"If that is what you decide, I will not stop you."

Markus's eyes brightened. He dropped to a knee and bowed his head. "Thank you, princess."

I grabbed his arm and tugged him back up. "You don't have to bow in front of me. We're friends."

"Calla." I knew Kylan was concerned, but I shook my head.

"Markus has been Morbeth's Captain of the Guard for countless years. He can make his own decisions."

Kylan sighed and stepped back.

"Let's go," Nicolae said.

We all gathered in a circle, me, Trystan, Nicolae, Markus, Kylan, Brone, Feng, and Andrés. I sucked in a deep breath as we transported.

I gasped as we landed amid thousands of men dressed in black fighting leathers with crests that bore the insignia of Carpathia. The sky was filled with dark clouds covering the sun, and I wondered if anyone used magic, or if it was luck.

As soon as the men saw us — saw Trystan and his cadre — they slapped fists to their chests and bowed. Trystan gave me his arm and led me through the men. His cadre, Nicolae, and Markus followed us to the front line.

I looked to my left and right and saw a sea of men in fighting leathers from Sartha, Aquaria, Aquaris, Hale, Baelfast, and Carpathia. Ready to fight for their kings and countries.

A trumpet sounded and men from each country rode toward us. My heart was hammering against my chest.

Adrenaline rushing through my veins. I had to breathe. I had to steady myself.

"Is my father here?" Trystan asked one of his men.

The man bowed his head. "I haven't seen the king yet, Your Highness," he replied.

"What about Everett and Callum? The two Incendian guards?"

"They left," a man said in the crowd. "The Incendians left when we arrived and headed toward Crimson Cove."

Goddess above. I hoped they hadn't been captured.

I noticed deep creases embedded in Trystan's brow, so I stepped up to him and pressed my finger against the lines, gently massaging them. "Are you worried, my prince?"

His arms enclosed around me. "I am only worried about you, my flame."

"Have faith in me." I pressed a gentle kiss to his lips. "I feel much more powerful when you believe in me."

He sighed, pulling my head against his chest. "You are the one person I believe in most."

Horse's hooves stopped behind me. "We have your horses."

"We will need one more," Nicolae said. I turned to see the man hop off his horse, giving Nicolae the reins.

"We are here for you," Kai said, sitting atop a white stallion. He also looked handsome, dressed in his Aquarian fighting leathers, his silvery hair tied behind his neck.

"Thank you." I grinned at him.

Trystan took my hand and walked me over to a dappled mare, then helped me mount her. Feeling anxious, I held out my hand, and a flame danced in my palm. My magic was still working for now. But I knew that once we got inside, they would use a binding spell.

Trystan placed his hand over my flame, quenching it.

"Your flame — your power — is part of you. It cannot be bound unless you allow it. Remember that and return to me."

He had read my mind. "I will."

I gazed up into the darkened sky. *Flint. Wherever you are, I'll need you soon. Stay close.*

In the distance, over a mile away, the Red Wall stood, taunting me. Nicolae and Markus mounted their horses and flanked me.

"When you are ready, our armies will march halfway. We cannot go closer than that."

"We are ready," Nicolae said.

The men on horseback bowed their heads. "Gods be with you," one said, and the rest echoed.

Then, they took off toward their own armies, sounding trumpets.

Trystan also mounted a horse, ready to lead his army. The sight of him stole my breath away.

"Let's go," Nicolae said, clicking his tongue. His horse moved forward. Markus and I were right next to him.

"Slow your breathing, Calla," Markus said. "I can hear your heart from here."

I slowed my breath, focusing on the sound of the horse's hooves, and the men marching behind us.

War was upon us. But this war wasn't about who had the better archers or swordsmen. It was all about power and who had the stronger magic.

Every hundred feet, I called my power. And every time it answered, I exhaled in relief.

As we neared the Red Wall, I saw hundreds of men spread out across the battlement. Archers, just like in my nightmare.

I called my flame and nodded as it danced across my fingers.

Arriving at the halfway point, horns blared. The sea of men behind us stopped marching.

Nicolae glanced at me and gave me a smile.

"I will be right here," Trystan said. *"If you need me, I will find a way to come to you. No matter what."*

I nodded, then the only two massive doors that led into Morbeth opened. Two riders galloped toward us, stopping a hundred yards ahead.

"Be brave," Nicolae whispered.

"You, too."

We rode forward, meeting the men, and one of them spotted Markus.

"Traitor," he spat. "How dare you wear the insignia of Morbeth!"

"I look forward to seeing your punishment," the other cackled.

I wanted to say something, but kept my mouth shut. This was the first of what was to come. Even Markus kept quiet, but I knew he was seething. I saw the muscles in his arms and jaw tense. Watched his hands furiously twist around the reins.

I wished I had a connection to him, to reassure him and let him know Nicolae and I were here for him as well.

My heart and pulse raced as we neared the doors. Breathe. Breathe. Breathe.

They cracked open, slowly widening to let us in.

This was it. Once we passed through, we would be walking straight into Roehl's trap. We knew it, but it had to be done. Innocent lives were counting on us.

"Flint, stay close."

Glancing up, I saw a shimmer in the clouds above. I knew he was near. I could feel him, and that afforded me peace.

Straightening my back, I rode through the massive doors. As soon as my horse passed the threshold, I felt a tingle in my palms and a coldness sweep through my blood and settled into my bones.

I knew, at that moment, our powers had been sealed.

Behind us, the heavy doors creaked and bolted shut, sealing us into Morbeth.

CHAPTER THIRTY-TWO

MY POWER IS GREATER than any dark magic. I repeated the mantra over and over in my mind.

Ahead of us, an army of at least ten thousand men stood, all bearing Morbeth's crest. What worried me was that I didn't catch sight of anyone bearing Incendia's.

Where was Roehl?

Where were Sabine and Brynna?

Where were those who served under Romulus?

"Come, my pet. Your friends and I are waiting in the castle."

How the hell could I hear him? There was no connection between us. Fear started to seep into my mind, but I immediately shut it out. I would not give in. He had no power over me.

The two riders led us through the center of Morbeth's army. The men glared, hatred twisting on their faces. Some growled at Markus, calling him terrible names, spitting on him as we rode by.

As we neared the front of the castle, we dismounted our horses and continued following the men. Nicolae and Markus stayed close.

"We're in, making our way into the castle," I said separately to Trystan and Kai.

"Trust your powers," Trystan replied.

"You've got this, Sea Star."

A low murmur floated on the surrounding breeze. Straining my ears, I heard the soft muttering of a spell.

The bond of elements we condemn.
Silence the voices deep within.
Cleave the ties, whence they stem.
Severing connections that bind them.

Goddess, no.

"Trystan? Can you hear me?" I paused, but there was no response. *"Trystan?"* I shouted through our bond. *"Kai?"*

My heart fractured. "They severed our connections," I whispered to Nicolae and Markus. "There is no way to contact anyone outside."

Markus cursed, but Nicolae remained calm.

Walking through the castle doors, I felt a sense of dread. This place had drained me, had broken me down, leaving me as nothing more than an empty shell. And yet, after escaping, vowing never to return, here I was walking straight back into it.

The men led us into the throne room, and as soon as we entered, my body began trembling.

Nicolae grabbed hold of my hand and looked me in the eye, giving me a reassuring smile.

The room was almost empty, aside from ten guards standing against the walls who surrounded us as we made our way to the throne. The hair on my body stood erect as I spotted them.

Up on the dais, sitting on his throne, was the devil himself. Roehl's dark, crimson-rimmed eyes pinned on me, a wicked grin curling on his lips. Next to him sat Garinda. But it wasn't either of them that turned my insides to ice.

Two guards stood on either side of the thrones. Sabine was tightly gripped in one guard's arms, and Brynna in the others. Their mouths were bound, and so were their arms and legs.

I wanted to charge forward, stick my hand through Roehl's chest, rip out his heart, and then save them, but I couldn't. We were in hell and had to play the devil's game. We had to make sure there were no reckless reactions that wouldn't get them injured. Or worse. Roehl knew my weakness. He knew seeing them in this condition, watching them struggle, would break me.

Their red, swollen eyes widened as they watched us enter.

As soon as Sabine's eyes found Markus, she shook her head. I could feel the pain rolling in the tears down her cheeks. She knew he was risking his life coming into Morbeth. And I could see her eyes asking... *why?*

Roehl immediately took notice, and a sickening grin crept on his lips as we walked forward until we stood in front of him. His dark eyes glaring at Nicolae.

"There you are brother. Or should I call you murderer?" He was referring to his younger brother.

"If you call saving myself murder. So be it," Nicolae said calmly.

Roehl's eyes traveled down to our connected hands. "I see you have been reunited with your granddaughter. And you're holding hands. How sweet is that?" Roehl taunted. "And I must say, my pet. You are looking well these days. Mating looks good on you."

Disgusting prick. I held my head up, not giving him any satisfaction of showing fear.

"Tell me how I can assure the safety of my friends."

Roehl looked at me with disdain. "*You* cannot assure anything, Calla." He spat my name like it was poison. "I am king here. I call all the shots."

Garinda, who had been quiet, finally stood. She walked over to me and slapped my face. My cheek stung, but I didn't react.

"You little bitch. How dare you try to overthrow me?"

"You are not worthy of the throne. You are a fraud," I said through gritted teeth.

Garinda went to slap me again, but Markus stepped in front of me, her hand hitting his chest.

"Enough," Roehl growled. "Garinda, leave us."

She huffed, then brought her crimson lips to my ear. "You have yet to feel my wrath."

I smirked and leaned forward, a breath from her face. "Before this day is over, you *will* feel mine."

Her hardened expression faltered, and I saw it. Saw that moment of fear in her eyes before she growled and stomped out of the room.

"Where are the others?" I questioned.

Roehl lazily twirled his finger in front of him. "They are around." He shook his head, his eyes darkening, snapping at Markus. "I haven't forgotten about you, Markus the Betrayer."

Markus's head dropped. "I was only following the orders of my king."

"*Your* king?" Roehl let out a wicked laugh, then tapped a finger against his chin. "You mean the one that is lying in a shallow grave out back?"

"You bastard!" I screamed. "How could you kill your own father?"

"Very easily, actually." His eyes went distant. "Call off the armies outside, and I will let your friends go."

It was confirmed. Seeing the armies gathered outside did have an effect on him.

"What about the others?" I questioned.

"The others will die. As will Nicolae and Markus."

"You said if we came, you would—"

Roehl stood from his throne. "I said nothing!" he roared. "Your coming here never assured anyone's life."

Lying bastard. Manipulating words to suit his own agenda.

We came here to save the lives of my friends and Romulus's people. But he lied. And now, everything had changed. My sole mission was now to kill Roehl. He had to die.

I allowed his deceit to fuel the hatred inside. Let it burn until all fear abandoned me.

He thought bringing my friends here would weaken me, but all he was doing was making me stronger.

I would continue to play the role of an innocent victim. I would let him think he was breaking me down. But he wouldn't break me. I was stronger than him. And my magic was stronger than his.

"Just to be clear," he glowered. "Before we go any further, if you decide to make any moves against me, my guards are ordered to kill your friends." He raised his hand, and the guards withdrew daggers from their sides. "Their lives are literally in your hands."

Brynna wailed as her guard pressed a dagger against her chest. She was sobbing, tears streaming down her face.

Sabine stood still as her guard held a dagger to her neck. Her face was hardened and resolved. She'd grown up in Morbeth. She knew the dangers, and it toughened her.

Trystan and Kai must have known by now that our connections were severed. I just hoped they wouldn't move rashly. They just needed to give us some time.

"Take them," Roehl ordered his guards.

The men grabbed hold of me, Nicolae, and Markus, binding our arms behind our backs.

Roehl strode off the dais and came to stand in front of me. I flinched as he ran a finger down my cheek, over my lips. "Mating bond or not, you will never see the prince again."

"I hate you," I seethed.

A smirk. "You will hate me even more by the end of this day."

Roehl walked out of the room, and we were forced to follow him.

As we stepped out of the throne room, I saw his mages, at least twenty of them, cloaked in black with large cowls covering their faces.

My magic is stronger than any dark magic, I chanted in my mind.

Back outside, on the large open lawn, Roehl headed toward his army. As we reached the front, I saw a line of people on their knees dressed in long white linen robes, with their hands bound behind their backs.

They were those who served Romulus — his guards, servants, and witches. There were at least one hundred of them.

My eyes searched down the line, and my breath caught as they landed on Aurelia — Summer's mother and Spring's grandmother. She was one of the most powerful white witches in Morbeth, but now, she looked old and worn, like years had been drained from her.

Her tired eyes found mine, and she didn't look happy to see me. She looked devastated.

Roehl turned to face me, Nicolae, and Markus.

"Did you think I would let them live when their hearts and loyalties have been against me?" His expression was hard like stone, his voice cold as death.

With his wicked eyes locked on me, he raised his arm in the air. Above us, on the Red Wall, archers stood, arrows nocked and aimed at these innocent people.

"No!" I screamed, dropping to my knees. These people were loyal to their true king. Aurelia risked her life for me. "What will you have me do?" I cried, pleading. "Please tell me."

There was not one ounce of compassion in those cruel eyes. Not one bit.

"You will watch them die."

I wailed as his hand dropped. Pure agony rattled through my bones. I called to my power. Begged. Demanded for it to come. But it remained locked tightly inside.

Hundreds of arrows were released, and I couldn't do a thing. I couldn't save them.

I could only watch helplessly as the arrows sunk deep into the backs of these innocent people.

I couldn't breathe.

I couldn't move.

I watched in horror as the white linen gowns turned to crimson.

One by one, those who served my great-grandfather, fell forward, their bodies limp. Eyes wide open, but unseeing.

My heart was shattered.

I had come here to save them. These men and women were depending on me. On Nicolae.

And now . . .

They were dead. They were all dead.

I was trembling from the inside out. Tears burned and rushed down my face.

But I wouldn't let it paralyze me. I couldn't let it weaken me.

Turning my face upward, I gazed into those dark clouds above.

"Flint!" I bellowed into the heavens.

A loud screech revealed Flint, still in his crow form.

"Kill it!" Roehl ordered, his finger aimed at my bird.

Hundreds more arrows filled the sky. My breath froze as I saw Flint plummet toward the earth, spiraling out of control. An arrow had been shot through his chest and another through his wing.

Roehl laughed, but I didn't react.

I held my breath, knowing Flint couldn't be dead. He was a gift from the Fire Goddess. He was a phoenix. He couldn't die.

As Flint fell, his black feathers disintegrated to ash, and out of the ash, the firebird emerged. My chest heaved with hope and promise.

"Fire!" Roehl shouted to his archers.

Again, arrows shot into the sky, but they couldn't touch Flint in his true form.

Flint spread his fiery wings, his molten eyes meeting mine. Screeching, he folded his wings and shot toward me.

Roehl punched a ball of power at him, but Flint spun and dodged it.

"Can you call your power?" I asked Nicolae.

"I cannot. Our power is dead here. Only you will be able to break its hold."

I stood to my feet, hands still bound behind my back.

This was it. The moment for which I had waited.

Roehl continued to throw his power, while his mages began muttering spells directed at Flint. But Flint was nothing they had ever come across before. He was pure and refined. A vessel containing the raw power of the Fire Goddess who had created him.

As Flint flew closer to me, Roehl realized he couldn't hurt him.

His eyes, black as night, fixed directly on me. I was his new target.

He threw his power, the red ball sailing toward my chest. Before it hit, Nicolae shoved me out of the way. I hit the ground and rolled onto my back.

"Nicolae! No," I wailed.

Above me, Flint had arrived. On my back, his fiery figure slammed into my chest, expelling the air from my lungs. My vision suddenly turned red, my power instantly released, surging through my entire body.

The binds around my hands dissolved, so I quickly crawled to my grandfather.

"Nicolae!" I wailed, shaking his arm. "Nicolae."

His body lay prone, face down and motionless. Blood poured from his mouth and nose. On his back, where Roehl's power had hit, was a wide-open wound. Blood was gushing from that wound, creating a puddle around him, so I threw my trembling hands over it and pressed down, using my fire to cauterize the injury and slow the bleeding.

The guards behind me swung their swords, but with a fist, I punched forward. My power slammed into them, sending them flying backward. Turning to Markus, I touched his binds, and they fell away. He grabbed a sword from the hand of a dead soldier, then charged forward, clashing blades with the men coming toward us.

I quickly unbound Nicolae's wrists, and they fell to his sides.

He couldn't be dead. He couldn't.

"Kill the armies outside," Roehl shouted.

No.

The mages were gathered around a large set of runes filled with candles and dead animals. Above us, I saw the same black cloud that had come after me and Melaina in Dead Man's Land. The shadow of death.

They were going to kill the men. Where the armies stood, I knew the powers of all purebloods had been locked and Trystan and Kai were powerless.

Hundreds of balls of fire sailed toward me. I threw a shield around us, protecting me and Nicolae, just in time. The flames slammed against my shield. Battering it, one after the other.

Focusing on the unrelenting attacks, I realized their source. Hundreds of Incendians charged forward, palms aimed at me.

I wanted to end this war without help, but I couldn't do it alone.

"Nicolae," I sobbed, my head pressing against his back. I couldn't breathe. My heart was shattering. "You can't leave me," I begged. "Don't leave me. Not now."

The cloud of death was sent, moving toward the Red Wall.

I had to pull myself together. I had to stop it.

"Markus!" I shouted.

He ran toward me, pushing his blade through a man's chest, through his armor.

As he neared me, I released my shield, grabbing his arm, transporting the three of us directly in front of the armies.

"Calla!" Trystan yelled, galloping toward me. His cadre was right behind him. Trystan slid off his horse and fell at my side, wrapping me in his arms.

"Help him," I sobbed, falling onto Nicolae's back. "Take him to a healer."

I wasn't going to believe he was dead. He was Nicolae Corvus. He had survived all this time, evading Roehl. Evading death. He couldn't be dead.

Men picked up Nicolae's limp body and carried him away.

Tears streamed down my face as I turned to Trystan, desperate. My finger aimed behind me. "The mages sent the shadow of death to the armies. Everything it touches will die."

"My father is here. He brought every witch from Neverton. One hundred strong."

The cloud was growing, spreading across the sky. I could feel its power humming through the atmosphere. The witches of Neverton moved ahead of the army, wands raised. Melaina was with them, near the front, her eyes focused, muttering a spell with the rest of them.

I watched in wonder as the black cloud of death paused, pulsing with rage and malice. The Neverton Witches' spell was working, keeping it at bay.

"Do you have powers?"

Trystan shook his head.

I had to find a way to unlock his powers.

"We have to go back," Markus urged. "Sabine is still inside."

"Take us," Kylan said. Trystan's cadre stood in front of me, ready and waiting.

I nodded. "When we get inside, be prepared. The Incendians are using their powers. I'll need time to open the doors."

"I'm coming, too," Kai said.

Thalia ran up with a bow in her hand and arrows strapped to her back. "Me, three!"

"Thalia, no. It's too risky without your powers."

"You have no idea what I can do with a bow," she scoffed.

I nodded, but worried. Not only for her, but for all of them.

Trystan spoke to the leaders of his army. "Be ready when the doors open." They bowed and took off, letting the leaders of the other armies know.

Gathering in a circle, I'd never transported seven people on my own. But I'd never had Flint with me.

Closing my eyes, I transported us right back into Morbeth, directly behind the army.

CHAPTER
THIRTY-THREE

Trystan's men ran in, clanging swords with the enemy. Thalia nocked and shot her bow, and in seconds, had taken out three men.

"Markus, find Sabine and Brynna," I urged. He nodded and left the fight, heading back toward the castle.

Roehl's dark eyes spotted me. He immediately threw his power.

Bending backward, the ball of power whizzed right over my face, slamming into a nearby statue. Shards of stone blasted in the air.

The mages were still in a circle, holding hands, chanting. I heard a cry of pain behind me and turned to see Feng drop to the ground, writhing in pain. He was grabbing at his chest, but there was no injury.

Suddenly, Andrés dropped to his knees. Pain wracked his face as he cried out, also grabbing his chest.

It was the mages.

Rage filled me. I let it rip through my blood, burning and strengthening me.

I transported behind the mages, dropping, and digging my fingers into the cold ground. I sent fire and earth toward them, turning their wicked magic circle to molten lava. It devoured everything inside.

Before they could turn on me, I stood and called my wings.

Wings of fire extended from my sides, my body encompassed in flame.

I immediately flew above the mages and sent a blast of fire and wind into the center of their circle, but it never reached them. There was a shield around them.

Frustration and rage built inside as I sent a battery of wind and fire on top of them.

They remained untouched.

Glancing over to Feng and Andrés, whatever I did worked. Temporarily.

Kylan helped Feng back to his feet, and then Andrés. They took up their weapons and were right back in the battle.

Searching the field, I watched Roehl's eyes lock onto Trystan. A look of death narrowing within them.

Hell no.

Moving like the wind, I ended up in front of Roehl. He cursed as I grabbed his arm, transporting us into the forest nearby. His fist, encased in a red ball of power, slammed into the side of my chest.

I felt a crack, and it was suddenly hard to breathe.

Dropping to my knees, my fingers melted the frozen earth, digging into it. Focusing through the pain, branches shot forward, wrapping around Roehl's wrists and legs, holding him in place. I tried, over and over to impale him with the roots and branches, but he was also shielded.

"This won't hold me," he growled.

I glared at him. "It will hold you long enough."

I transported back to Trystan, who was now flanked with his cadre and Kai.

Thalia had her back to the wall, and was still picking off men, one by one with her bow. As soon as they dropped, she ran forward, extracting arrows from their bodies and reusing them.

Quickly pressing my palm to my chest, I redirected my power, focusing on my injury. Nicolae said he could heal. I couldn't fight if I was injured. I felt my chest heat. There was a pop and I could finally breathe freely.

Glancing at Trystan, I noticed that even without his power he was deadly, slaying man after man. They were all beautiful and deadly warriors. Blocking, striking, and moving as one.

I dropped to my knees, in front of the Red Wall, digging my fingers into the cold earth.

"Bring down the wall." I demanded.

The ground shook violently beneath me. Men fell from the battlement above, and then . . . there was a loud crack. The ground opened up and swallowed an entire section of the Red Wall. Quickly pushing my power toward the huge crevasse, I sealed the ground, creating a way of entry.

Trumpets blared on the other side of the Red Wall, and I heard the armies advance.

I'd done it.

But the war was far from over.

Morbeth's army rushed toward the opening to keep the advancing army out.

Five hundred Incendians also rushed forward. Many began using their powers against me.

I threw a fire shield around me, but I had to take them out of the equation. They were still my people, Incendia's only army, and they didn't know better. They were under the dark mages spell.

My power wavered. The fire shield dimmed.

No. The mages must have been casting another spell.

I quickly dug my fingers into the ground and called the earth. Hundreds of branches and roots shot out from the nearby forest, wrapping around the Incendian men. I heard their screams as they were being dragged away, into the deep woods.

"Keep them bound. Don't kill them," I ordered the earth.

The Incendians were safe for now, but the use of my power was draining me. I could feel the throbbing ache in my fingertips and in my palms.

The battle outside began. War cries resounded as thousands of swords clashed and clanged. My eyes shot to the cloud of death, but it hadn't moved. It was still bound by the Neverton Witches.

A thundering growl ripped through the air, catching my attention.

Ahead of me, Roehl stood at the entrance of the castle. Two guards stood at his sides, holding Brynna and Sabine.

Markus was on their left, fighting his way through men, desperately trying to reach them.

And then, a fatal smile rose on the devil's lips. I watched in complete panic and terror as he spoke two words.

"Kill them."

I transported to them, but as soon as I appeared, Roehl's fingers wrapped tightly around my throat. I slammed my power down on his arm, making him release, but I was too late.

Sabine's guard ran his blade across her throat.

Brynna's guard pushed his dagger into her chest.

"Nooo!" A heart wrenching wail burst from my chest as I watched my best friends fall to the ground.

Thalia paused, her eyes widened in horror. Kai grabbed her arm, yanking her out of the way of a sword. She quickly snapped out of it, nocking and shooting arrows, killing men with vengeance and rage filled in her tear-filled eyes.

My power was flickering, but I slammed my fist into Roehl's face.

He was thrust backward, as Markus continued to fight, his rage pushing him toward me, swinging his sword and beheading the two guards easily.

Markus fell to Sabine's side, pressing his hand over the wound on her neck. Her eyes were wide, tears trailing down the sides of her face, blood gushing from her injury.

I quickly threw a fire shield around the four of us.

"Change her, Markus," I cried.

My heart was fracturing into tiny splinters. Sabine was dying.

Markus looked at me. His dark, tear-filled eyes were laden with confusion as Sabine choked on her blood. "She told me she doesn't want to become a tick like us."

Grabbing hold of Markus's bloodied hand, Sabine smiled up at him and gave him a nod. "I don't want to die, Markus. I want to be with you. Forever."

"Change her now!" I ordered.

Tears flowed from Markus's eyes at Sabine's words. His incisors lengthened as he leaned over and sunk his teeth into her shoulder.

Blood gurgled in her throat and mouth, coating her teeth, running down the sides of her lips.

Markus finally pulled back, his lips coated with Sabine's blood.

And then . . .

Sabine's eyes glassed over. Her body went limp in Markus's arms.

"No, no, no, no, no."

My chest heaved as I leaned over and grabbed her hand.

"Markus?" I couldn't breathe. My chest throbbed with agony. "Why?"

His own eyes were filled with dread and despair. "I—I was too slow."

Markus slouched forward, hugging Sabine in his arms, rocking back and forth. Tears streamed down his face, and for the first time I heard him sob.

My heart couldn't take any more pain. I couldn't bear it.

"Calla," Brynna reached for my hand.

I quickly moved to her side, my hand hovering above the blade stuck in her chest. Blood oozing from the wound.

I wiped my tear-stained face. "Brynna, I'm going to get someone to turn you."

I went to stand, but she grabbed hold of my wrist. "No."

"Why?" I shook my head. "Bryn, I can heal you. You can live a long, immortal life."

"And then what?" she breathed, her eyes full of sadness. "I don't fit into this world anymore, Cal. Honestly, I don't want to. Not after what I've seen and been through."

"But you'll have me. I'll be with you. I'll help you through it."

Brynna shook her head, then sucked in a sharp breath, wincing in pain. "I don't want to be immortal. I want to fall asleep and wake up in the next realm with my parents."

"No. You're supposed to be my maid of honor."

Brynna paused, a sad smile rose on her lips. "I know about the secret wedding, Cal."

"What?" I gasped.

"Trystan came to me, knowing you were my best friend. He asked my permission and begged me to keep it a secret. Even from you."

I shook my head, tears pouring down my face. "Oh, Bryn."

She winced again, her breath rasped. "Do you have the ring?"

I nodded, holding my hand up in front of her.

"It's beautiful." She smiled, gently stroking it. "I'll be around to watch the formal wedding. I wouldn't miss it."

Her eyes were getting heavy, her breath was short and slow.

"Bryn," I sobbed, squeezing her hand. "Please, Bryn. Please let me turn you."

"Don't you dare." Tears fell from her eyes and ran down the sides of her face. "If you do, I will hate you for the rest of my immortal life."

"You're my best friend. My sister. I've already lost my parents. I can't lose you too. I can't."

"Look at me." Brynna grabbed my hands. "You were born for this world. You were created for it and are thriving in it. All I ask is that you remember me."

Deep sobs ripped from my chest. "How could I ever forget you? You have been with me throughout my entire life."

She gave me a sad smile, lips trembling, tears still streaming down her face. "I'm proud of you. I will die happy, knowing you found your prince." She winced again, her eyes pinching shut. When they opened, she pulled me close. "Finish this, Cal. Kill that bastard and live happily ever after."

I nodded.

Her hands gripped me tighter. "Promise me."

"I promise."

Brynna's head fell back, her body relaxed, and her eyes focused on the sky above.

"Don't cry for me. This is what I want. I'll finally be at peace."

I shook my head, tears coursing down my face.

"I love you, Cal."

"I love you, Bryn."

Brynna closed her eyes, and then I watched her chest fall, knowing it would never rise again.

CHAPTER THIRTY-FOUR

Everyone we had come to save was dead.

Fisting my hands at my sides, I closed my eyes. I had to end this. I had to find a way to break through their shields.

"Please speak to me." I whispered to the air. *"Tell me what I need to do."*

"I believe in you, Calla." Leora's voice sent a wave of calmness through me. *"You are my heir and have been bestowed these gifts for a purpose. I have no doubt your light will triumph over any darkness."*

Heat punched through my chest. It radiated outward, through my limbs and I watched as the veins in my arms glowed gold.

"Everything you need is inside of you, Chosen One. The power of the twin flames can crack through any shield and break any curse."

Helia. The Fire Goddess had also answered my call.

I grabbed hold of Markus and Brynna, transporting us to the tents used by the healers, far behind the battlefield.

A man rushed toward us, stopping as he came near.

"Markus." I touched his arm that was still cradling Sabine. "I have to go."

He looked at me, and I had never seen such pain in one's eyes. They slid back to Sabine, then closed. Gently lying her down he leaned forward, pressing his lips to her forehead.

"I'm coming," he said, wiping the tears from his face.

"You don't have to come."

He stood to his feet and held out his bloodied hands to me. "Yes, I do. I want to be there when you finish this."

"We will finish this, Markus. I promise."

I turned to the healer. "Please take my best friends inside and clean them up."

He bowed his head. "I will."

Turning my eyes toward the battlefield, thousands of men were still fighting. But there were hundreds sprawled out across the ground.

Dead Man's Land was claiming even more lives.

I took hold of Markus's hands.

Take me to Trystan.

We appeared feet away, watching my prince dodge a blade, then spin and shove his blade into the man's neck. Another came at him, but I threw out my hands. A ball of fire slammed into his chest, thrusting him and three others away.

To my right, Kai and Thalia fought bravely, side by side, moving in unison.

Markus charged toward the cadre and fought alongside them, swinging his sword with power and efficiency.

"Calla!" Trystan turned, his breath heavy.

"I need you."

He stepped toward me, and I wrapped us in a cocoon of flame.

I held up my palms facing him. "We have to end this."

He sheathed his sword, his eyes narrowing. "I have no power."

I shook my head. "The gift of the Fire Goddess was a connection of our power. We are one."

Trystan gazed into my eyes and smiled, placing his palms against mine. Power surged through our connected hands. I stumbled back, but he laced our fingers, keeping me close. Heat shifted in my chest. Flames encircled our joined hands and coiled up our arms and around our bodies.

A grin rose on Trystan's lips. Our power had connected, and it was stronger than ever.

"Kylan!" Markus shouted.

Roehl was behind them. A sword was in his right hand, and a ball of power in his left.

Everything from that moment happened so fast, but it played out as if it were in slow motion.

Kylan spun, but Feng used his staff to push him out of the way. As he did, Roehl thrust his sword forward, sinking his blade into the middle of Feng's chest.

Feng's eyes widened. His staff dropped from his grasp.

Extracting his blade, Roehl spun and pushed his power toward Brone, who was charging toward him. The red ball of power hit him in the chest. He flew twenty feet back, slamming into the ground.

I instantly dissolved our shield and ran toward Feng.

This couldn't be happening. We couldn't lose anyone else.

Suddenly, my arm was grabbed and twisted behind my back, a blade pressed to my throat.

A vicious growl ripped through the air. "Get your fucking hands off my mate!" Before Trystan could move—

Rage filled me. It tore through my veins.

This bastard had killed my parents. He killed Brynna's parents. He killed Nicolae, and Brynna, and Sabine.

Anger overpowered me. It ripped through me like a tidal wave.

I grabbed Roehl's hand and twisted out of his hold, slamming a flame into his face.

His shield kept him from burning, but the power, sent him to his back.

I dropped, straddling his waist, pounding my power into his chest. Into his face. But it wasn't penetrating his shield.

"You bastard! You killed my entire family!" I roared, as rage seized me.

My fists slammed against his shield, over and over again. My power obliterating everything around him.

But not him.

"I hate you!" I screamed. "I hate you!"

I kept pounding my power down on him. Rage pulsed through my veins and ran down my face. I'd never wanted to kill anyone in my life. But I wanted him to die. I wanted him to suffer.

Then, I saw blood running from his nose. I was hurting him.

I quickly called the earth.

I slid to the side as roots from the nearby forest shot toward us, wrapping around him. Raising my hand, the roots followed, carrying his body skyward.

Dropping my hand, they slammed his body into the ground. The force enough to break any man's bones.

Roehl let out a wicked laugh. His eyes glared at me, merciless and savage.

"You will all die today. Every single one of you."

Screaming, I unleashed my power at him.

But he disappeared.

Trystan pulled me into his arms. I was trembling with rage, my eyes swollen with tears.

Trystan let out a loud whistle, and Nyx flew out of the woods and circled overhead. He closed his eyes as I slid to Feng's side, throwing a shield around the three of us, while the others fought bravely outside.

I had to find a way to end this. He had to die.

Trystan's eyes slid open. "He's in the courtyard with the mages."

I placed a hand on Feng. "Please don't die," I sobbed. "I can't bear to lose you, too."

He nodded and grabbed my hand. "I'll try," he exhaled. "You can end this, princess. I believe in you."

I nodded and held out my hand to Trystan. "Let's end this."

Trystan took my hand, and we transported to the courtyard. I laced my fingers back through his, making sure I wouldn't lose his grip.

The dark witch bitches were facing us, their hands outstretched, muttering another spell. Black tendrils of smoke shot toward us, wrapping around our legs. This time, I had no fear.

Roehl laughed, standing behind them, and at his side was Garinda with a wicked sneer. The dark mages poisonous spell was crawling up our legs, burning my skin. I hissed, glancing down.

"Cowards!" I shouted. "Why are you hiding?"

"We're not hiding," Roehl snapped. "We're going to enjoy watching your end."

I turned to Trystan and laughed. "My prince, do you think this is our end?"

A grin tugged on his sinful lips. He leaned over and pressed those lips against mine. "No, my flame. This is our beginning."

Facing each other, we placed our palms together. Flames encompassed our bodies, instantly and easily shredding through and incinerating the dark mages wicked spell.

I held out my hand and a large ball of fire grew in my palm, pulsing with blue, red, and gold. Trystan did the same, and a twin flame pulsed in his palm. Bringing our hands together, the two orbs became a massive ball of pure energy.

The overwhelming power coursing between us made my legs weak and left me breathless.

Thunder rumbled and lightning cracked overhead. The ground shook beneath our feet and the branches in nearby trees rustled. Air, flames, and water from the melted snow spun around us. Fire, water, earth, and air were in our grasp. Our gift from the Fire Goddess.

My fingers, palms, and body hummed with the unmitigated power held in our hands, superior to any other.

I slid my eyes to the mages, who appeared rattled. Then, I turned my attention to Roehl.

A wicked grin rose on my lips.

"This kingdom was never yours, you selfish prick," I seethed. I let out a wicked laugh and glared at Garinda. "And you. You bitch. You're nothing but a wannabe queen who doesn't have one drop of royal blood. You've held the Incendian people in oppression for too long. That ends today."

Roehl and Garinda laughed as Trystan and I took a step forward. My prince stayed silent, letting me lead, a smirk frozen on his lips.

The mages quickly gathered together, holding hands, muttering another spell.

Roehl called his power and thrust it at us, but before it hit, it dissolved as if it were nothing. For the first time, I saw frustration in his eyes. And a hint of fear.

Roehl withdrew his sword. Rage burned in those crimson-rimmed onyx eyes. "Your power is not greater than mine!" he roared.

I gave him a death stare. "You. Know. Nothing."

Roehl was wicked to the core. He tortured and killed countless people without remorse. His greatest flaw was his overwhelming desire for power. Whether it was magic, or the throne, he didn't care how he achieved it. He was a ruthless murderer who deserved nothing more than death.

A dark shadow grew above the mages. They had conjured another death cloud. Seeing the shadow of death, Roehl's lips curled into a wicked grin. "I will finally watch you suffer and die."

I shook my head, a vicious grin rising on my own lips. "*You* will suffer and die today, along with those who serve you. And we will rule your kingdom."

I glanced over to my prince, and he gave me a nod.

The mages released their death cloud, but Trystan and I raised our hands, raised the pure, pulsing power between us.

Thrusting it forward, the ball hovered and spun above the mages, emitting a light so bright they fell to the ground, shielding their eyes.

The shadow of death screamed as it disintegrated, unable to withstand the raw power of the orb.

Roehl's smile was wiped from his lips. His eyes widened, realizing he no longer had power over us. That our power was so much greater than his. Fear swam in his eyes for a moment, but then . . . they went hard. He wasn't going to surrender.

He raised his sword over his head and charged toward us, but vines of light shot from the orb and wrapped tightly around Roehl. He gasped, his eyes widening as it yanked him back, pulling him up into its center.

Roehl let out a blood-curdling scream as the light touched him. Instantly immobilized, the power of the orb suspended him in the air, facing me and Trystan. We watched as his skin blistered and burned, and slowly started to melt off his bones as if he were a normal vampire out in the sunlight. But hatred remained racked in those wicked eyes.

I glared at him, a smile rising on my lips, watching him suffer for all that he'd done.

The mages and Garinda turned to run. More vines of light shot out from the sphere, ensnaring them, squeezing them with its energy.

Garinda clawed at her neck as the light coiled tightly around it. I watched her eyes expand, bulging from their sockets, turning blood red. Her mouth was agape, but there was no sound. No screams. The vines had stopped her airway.

She kicked and clawed violently as the vines of light continued compressing, moving through flesh, ligaments, and bone. Blood ran from her eyes and from her nose and mouth. And then, those vines of light severed Garinda's head.

Her head fell from her shoulders and tumbled to the ground, rolling into the molten circle. I watched as it caught fire, flesh melting from bone before the magma devoured her skull.

Roehl watched in horror as the vines of light tightened around his dark mages, snapping their bones and compressing the life out of them. I pushed my hands over my ears to dull their agonizing screams.

It was his turn to watch helplessly and powerlessly as those who served him suffered and died.

Roehl's eyes grew wide, racked with agony and fear as the vines of light began to coil around his wrists and ankles. He fought hard against them, his excruciating screams continued as those vines began to pull. I heard it first, those low hollow pops of his joints being dislocated. Then snapping of bones as they stretched further.

Roehl's tortured screams resounded through the courtyard as the vines continued pulling. Stretching until the sickening, squelch of tearing flesh was heard. He wailed in agony, as his limbs were severed from his body. And then, I watched, in victory, as the life in his eyes extinguished, and his screams finally stopped.

There was a hint of redemption, but it wasn't enough. Not nearly enough for those he'd tortured and maliciously murdered.

With Roehl, Garinda, and the mages gone, the sphere of light began to spin faster and faster, growing bigger and brighter, rising into the sky.

I wasn't sure what we had unleashed, or if we could stop it.

Transporting us to Trystan's cadre, I realized they had all surrounded Feng. I called to them, and they all came — Thalia, Kai, Markus, Brone, Feng, and Andrés. As soon as they were near, I threw a fire shield around us.

"What the hell is that?" Kai panted, his finger aimed at the orb, his face smeared with dirt and blood.

"Pure power," Trystan exhaled.

Suddenly, the sphere of light detonated. The explosion was deafening. The energy from that blast radiated outward. The pressure of it leveled every single man on the battlefield.

There was dead silence.

Men began to moan as they returned to consciousness.

The Incendian army stumbled out of the forest, many holding their heads. I could hear their confused murmurs. They were clueless as to what had happened and wondered where they were.

The spell over them had been broken.

My eyes turned skyward. The larger shadow of death had vanished, obliterated by the power of the orb.

As men began to rise from the ground, I grabbed hold of Trystan's hand. He gave me a knowing smile and a nod before I called my wings and flew to the top of the Red Wall, to the portion that remained, and stood on the battlement.

Every eye on the battlefield below followed me, watching. I could hear their gasps and murmurs as my body enveloped in flame, my fiery wings spread out to my sides. I called to the air, using it to project my voice so every man below could hear me.

"Soldiers of Morbeth," I bellowed. "Your prince is dead. As well as his mages. As Romulus's great-granddaughter, and heir to the throne of Morbeth, I order you to drop your weapons and surrender."

The battlefield stayed silent.

I turned my eyes to the five hundred men who had emerged from the forest. "Soldiers of Incendia, the spell placed upon you by Morbeth's mages has been broken. Your false queen is dead. *I* am your queen, the true heir to the Incendian throne, chosen by the Fire Goddess."

I looked out over the sea of men. "I declare to you now . . . this war is over!"

One by one, Morbeth's army released their weapons. They faced me, dropping to their knees, slapping their fists against their chest, and bowing their heads.

"Hail to our Queen!" one of the Incendians bellowed. The men around him echoed his cry.

I watched the Incendian army fall to their knees. One by one, they placed their foreheads to the ground, then rising, they rested their palms over their chests.

Their eyes no longer held the hatred I'd once seen in them. In their eyes, I now saw allegiance and loyalty.

Glancing down, my eyes met Trystan's. A wide smile adorned his lips, his expression filled with pride. *"You are glorious, my flame."*

Kai was smiling with Thalia at his side, their hands laced together. *"You're a total badass, Sea Star."*

Trystan's cadre and Markus also had broad smiles on their faces. They slapped their fists over their chests and bowed their heads.

The Neverton Witches raised their wands toward me. I spotted Melaina's red hair and her bright smile. I was so happy to see her well.

The rest of the countries raised their swords in the air, their cheers rang out loud and clear.

My eyes swept the battlefield, taking in the thousands of men and women below. Emotions brimmed inside, threatening to fill my eyes and spill down my cheeks. It was overwhelming.

These people. These tens of thousands, had joined and fought for this moment. Fought for Morbeth and Incendia's freedom.

And while we lost many good men and women, those that survived would now have a future they looked forward to. A future that would finally be filled with hope and peace.

I transported us back to the healer's tents.

Brone and Kylan carried Feng into one of them, demanding help.

One of the healer's came up to me and bowed. "You were the one who brought the bodies here for us to clean?"

I nodded. "Yes."

"Please come with me."

"I'll be right back," I whispered to Trystan, then followed the man into one of the tents. He led me over to Sabine's still body.

Her eyes were closed. She looked so peaceful.

"Do you notice something?" he asked.

I wasn't exactly sure what he was asking. She wasn't breathing or moving. What was I supposed to notice?

My eyes focused on her face and moved down to her neck.

Her neck.

I ran my fingers over smooth skin that earlier had a wound. My eyes snapped to the healer. "Is she—?"

"She's alive," he confirmed. "Asleep for now, but I'm afraid she still must endure the transformation."

Sobs ripped from my chest as I dashed out of the tent.

"Calla, what's wrong?" Trystan asked, immediately at my side.

"Sabine is alive."

Markus spun around, his eyes wide. I nodded as tears poured down my face. "It worked."

Thalia's face also lit up at the news. She followed Markus as he ran through the tent, but she stopped near the entrance, giving him some space.

Markus stilled as he neared Sabine's body, his eyes sweeping over her.

"She still has to go through the transformation," I said. "She'll need you."

He nodded and took her hand, then turned to me with a smile.

"Thank you, princess. She is alive because of you."

"And you." I backed out with Thalia, allowing him to be with her alone. "Take care of her, Markus."

A tear rolled down his cheek. "I will."

Walking out of the tent, the men were lined up in a row, their faces solemn. I narrowed my eyes on them. "What are you guys doing?"

They stepped aside and my heart stopped beating.

Nicolae stood behind them with a broad smile on his face.

"Granddaughter," he breathed, his arms opening wide.

Running into his arms, they enclosed around me. He pressed his lips to the top of my head.

"You're alive," I sobbed into his chest.

"Of course, I am," he chuckled, running a hand down my hair. "I'm so proud of you, Calla." Nicolae hugged me tightly.

"I couldn't die, because I knew how much you needed me. Someone needs to rule Morbeth."

I gasped and pulled away from him, peering into his golden eyes. "You will become king?"

He nodded and smiled. "I will."

My heart felt as if it were going to explode. I fell back into his arms and cried tears of joy.

The day was filled with too much emotion. I was physically and emotionally drained and knew it would take time to heal from it all.

In the meantime, I just had to remember to breathe.

CHAPTER THIRTY-FIVE

THE WINTER FESTIVAL

A WEEK HAD PASSED by extremely fast, and I spent most of it recovering in bed with Trystan. Especially after the funeral. We had finally made contact with Erro, who had brought my Parents' bodies to Carpathia. The king laid each of them in quartz coffins and had another specially created for Brynna.

The service was held in the royal cemetery where they would rest forever. Trystan assured me it was one of the most magnificent places in Carpathia during the spring and summer months, hemmed in with lofty flowering trees, wildflowers, and lush green shrubbery.

My prince held me tight during the ceremony as I mourned them. Deep inside I knew they were all together, happy, and in no pain. I knew they were there, still watching over us, smiling down on us.

Realizing this — along with having Trystan by my side — gave me the strength I required to move on. They would all want me to move on.

Feng had survived his injury. Roehl's sword had missed his heart by millimeters, and after a few days of rest, he was good as new and out practicing again with the rest of the cadre.

In a few hours, a significant celebration would be held in Carpathia. Their Winter Festival was claimed to be one of the finest on Talbrinth, and I was genuinely looking forward to it.

After so much death, I thought some music and dancing might help to drag me out of the dark slump I had been wallowing in.

Trystan left the room as Jewel and Maia strolled in with a silver gown and a basket full of essentials for my hair and face. And an hour later, after working their magic, I was ready for the festival.

"You look beautiful, princess," Jewel said with a bow.

Maia beamed at her side, appreciating her workmanship.

"Thank you. I would never look this put together if it weren't for you two."

They giggled and left the room, while I slipped on my silvery heels. My hair was pinned up in loose curls, some falling down the sides of my face. And affixed to the top of my head was a silver tiara affixed with azure stones. The silvery gown sparkled like fresh snow on a moonlit night. It was sleeveless, hugging my breasts and waist, then gently swept down to the floor.

Peering down at my finger, I smiled at my wedding ring, then touched the amulet around my neck. So many incredible memories. But there were dreadful ones too.

I was relieved that Roehl and his mages were gone for good, but the death of Brynna had hit me hard. Given time, I knew I would be able to breathe fully and be at peace again.

I hadn't heard the door but grinned as Trystan's arms coiled around me from behind. I let my head drop back into his chest. I inhaled his enchanting scent and let it fill me.

In true Trystan fashion, he wore a black suit, with gray trim. His hair was combed back, a few strands falling askew, just like I loved it. He was gorgeous. He was mine.

"You look radiant, my flame. You will be the envy of every female at the ball."

"All I want is to be in your arms, dancing the night away."

His chuckle tickled my ear. "Your wish is my command. And my duty"

The ballroom was magnificent, decorated to look like a regal winter paradise. Long tables were set with fine white linens, wide metallic silver goblets, and glass vases filled with fresh winter blossoms and lush greenery. A delicate balance of candles, and sconces in wintry hues set the scene toward a more romantic mood.

Musicians stood on a raised platform, attired in silver. Behind them, naked trees sprayed in white, along with hundreds of glittering lights, and a mist at their feet, created a magical scene. Pleasing, soothing melodies of lutes, citterns, violas, and drums filled the air.

Guests, dressed in their finery, were intermingling around the room. Some were already being whisked around the dance floor.

Kylan, Brone, Feng, and Andrés arrived, and looked dashing wearing all-white suits.

When they joined us, they bowed at their waists.

"You look exquisite, princess," Kylan said.

"And of course, our prince would wear black to a winter festival," Brone snickered.

Trystan beamed and tugged at his collar. "Black suits me."

"Calla, will you save a dance for me?" Andrés asked.

Trystan shook his head. "You've all had a chance to dance with her. Tonight, she is mine."

Andrés sighed. "Fine. But I am claiming a dance at the next ball."

Trystan slapped a hand on his back. "Only if she agrees."

He looked at me through wide puppy dog eyes.

I giggled and crossed my arms over my chest. "Of course."

"You know, that counts for all of us," Brone said, his finger sliding from him, to Kylan, to Feng.

I bowed my head to them. "I will be honored to dance with Carpathia's finest champions."

They laughed and slapped each other on the back.

Heads turned as Markus and Sabine strode in with Kai and Thalia.

They were beautiful. All of them.

Kai and Markus were donning white suits, like the cadre.

Sabine was dressed in a light blue gown that sparkled and flowed from top to bottom. Her hair was half up, half down, with white flowers in her hair.

Thalia was dressed in a deeper blue gown that hugged her entire frame. Her golden hair was curled, spilling over her exposed shoulders.

I flung my arms around Sabine. "You look stunning."

She rolled her eyes. "I'm shocked I look this decent, especially after enduring days of that hellish transformation." She grabbed my wrist and squeezed. "Girl, I thought I was going to die. My body felt like it was on fire, and I couldn't put it out. I cursed at Markus so many times. I screamed that I regretted he turned me. But he stayed with me, right by my side, until it was over."

"And what about now?" I questioned. "How do you feel?"

"I feel amazing." She turned to Markus and smiled, gently patting her gloved hand against his cheek. "I apologized to him. And made it up to him in more ways than one." She gave me a wink and a sly grin.

Markus cleared his throat, his face blushing bright red. Trystan reached over and gave him a firm pat on the back, while his cadre smiled and nodded.

I walked over to Thalia and wrapped her in a hug. "You look beautiful, cousin."

"So do you," she said, bowing her head.

Kai took my hand and pressed his lips to my fingers. "You look beautiful, Sea Star."

"Thank you." I curtseyed. "And you are quite dashing, Your Highness."

He exhaled loudly, tugging on his collar. "I hate these stuffy suits." Thalia nudged him in the side. "But I will bear it for the night." He gave her a toothy smile.

I laughed and shook my head.

"Kai, what have you been up to?" Trystan stepped beside me, sliding his arm around my waist.

His eyes slid to Thalia. "We've been busy. I took her to Aquaria to spend time with my family. Hali loves her company."

My eyes narrowed on my cousin, and she shook her head. "He knows full well what my plans are. Bringing Incendia back to its former glory will be my highest priority. For now, Kai and I are friends. But who knows what the future holds for us?"

"Yes," Kai said, slipping his hand into hers. "But no matter what, I will be there for her."

I grabbed Thalia's other hand and swung it. "That makes my heart happy."

Nicolae stalked into the ballroom, his hands tucked into the pockets of a dark blue suit. His mahogany hair was combed back neatly, and his beard was trimmed. He looked handsome and very regal.

"Grandfather," I said, striding up to him. He folded me in his arms and squeezed, giving me a kiss on the cheek. "You look so handsome."

He let out a laugh. "I guess I cleaned up pretty well." He raised my hand and spun me in a circle. "You are breathtaking."

My cheeks flushed with heat.

"I'm starving," Kai said. "I see real food on the far table." His eyes slid to Sabine. "I'm sad you won't be able to join us."

Sabine shooed him away with her hand. "Don't tempt me, Kai. If I give in, I will find you and vomit all over you."

Kai's face twisted. "Have you fed? You are in a foul mood."

Sabine growled at him, so he held out his arm to Thalia. "Let's get out of here." Thalia giggled and took his arm.

Markus led Sabine over to the tables while Nicolae followed. Trystan's cadre followed after them.

I exhaled, observing.

In a weeks' time, Nicolae would be leaving for Morbeth where he would assume the throne as King. Markus and Sabine would follow him.

Markus had pledged his service to Nicolae, agreeing to be his Captain of the Guard. He vowed to clean up the guard, train new ones, and would be putting together a trusted core to protect Nicolae during his reign as king.

I was thrilled they would be working together to lead Morbeth into a glorious future. Sabine was also eager and anxious to get back to the castle to help with the cleanup. I knew she would be a great and necessary asset, while keeping Markus in line.

Thalia had also accepted her position, to act as my regent and rule in my place. In three days, we would be traveling to Incendia where I would crown her.

Everett and Callum had been found. They were bound and thrown into Morbeth's cells and had avoided the entire war. They vowed their service to Thalia and would help rebuild the guard.

Thalia had big plans and revolutions in mind for Incendia, and I was eager to give her my full assistance and backing.

Trystan drew me into his arms, forcing me back into the moment. "Dance with me, wife."

Leading me out to the center of the room, the musicians started to play. The music ebbed and flowed as I gave Trystan my hand, and he swept me around the dance floor.

Gazing into his eyes, I saw so much love swirling within them. I saw want and need.

I saw my future.

Every other couple stopped dancing and withdrew, watching us glide across the floor.

"My prince, you are an incredible dancer," I breathed.

His hand tightened around the small of my back, pressing me closer. "I've had countless lessons, all leading up to this moment. I hated them all, but hearing your words makes it all worth it."

I laughed and pressed my cheek onto his chest. "I look forward to many more dances with you in the future."

"Our wedding is in a few months, and then my coronation. You will become my wife and Queen of Carpathia. Are you ready, my flame?"

My heart swelled.

Never, in my wildest dreams would I believe this would be the outcome of my life. In a years' time, I had changed from mortal to immortal. I had been hunted, kidnapped, tortured, and thrown into a cell. I was rescued by a prince who became my lover. My blood bonded. My mate. My husband. And soon to be . . . my king.

I lost my parents, but I also found Nicolae and gained many friends who became a part of my new family.

Although it was filled with heartbreak, loss, and sorrow, I embraced my past. It tested my grit, pushed me past my limits, and drove me to my knees. It battered me, bruised me, and burned me. But from the ash, I emerged a different girl. I was stronger. Confident. Brave.

I liked the new version of myself, and I looked forward to creating a bright and beautiful future with Trystan.

So . . .

Was I ready?

The answer was resounding.

I kept my eyes on Trystan, on those gorgeous azure eyes that had captured me, heart and soul and had never let go, and replied . . .

"Yes, my prince. I *am* ready."

FROM THE AUTHOR

Dear Reader,

Thank you so much for making it this far. I really hope you enjoyed this series and have fallen in love with the characters as much as I have. Just FYI — I will be revisiting this world again in the future (not sure when), creating a spinoff series for these characters. I hope you're up for taking another wild adventure with me. Thank you again for reading my stories and breathing life into the pages. Until we meet again in another adventure . . . I wish you well.

Happy Reading,

ACKNOWLEDGMENTS

This book would not have been possible without the help and advice of my kickass – BETA TEAM
Halee Harris, Ewelina Rutyna, Karla Bostic, Kimberly Belden, Amber Garcia, Cheree Castellanos, Jaci Chaney, and Emily Piland.

—

I have to thank my amazing PA – Amber Garcia – who has been with me for almost 10 years.
Thank you for loving my books and spreading the word, because we both know I suck at social media.

—

And as always, I have to thank my husband.
My twin flame, my rock, and my greatest support. I love you!

ABOUT THE AUTHOR

Cameo was born in San Francisco, raised in Maui, Hawaii, and now resides with her husband in Las Vegas. She is a dreamer and caffeine addict who loves to laugh and loves to read to escape reality.

One of her greatest satisfactions is creating fantasy worlds filled with adventure and romance. It is the love and incredible support of her family and readers that keeps her going. One day she hopes to uncover a magic wardrobe and ride away on a unicorn. Until then . . . she'll keep writing!

Made in the USA
Middletown, DE
05 April 2023

27759191R00262